Disney

VILLAINS

HAPPILY NEVER AFTER

VANESSA

FOR KELLY,
WHO ENCOURAGES ME TO
BELIEVE IN THE IMPOSSIBLE

Published by Scholastic Australia in 2022.

Scholastic Australia Pty Limited
PO Box 579 Gosford NSW 2250
ABN 11 000 614 577
www.scholastic.com.au

Part of the Scholastic Group
Sydney • Auckland • New York • Toronto • London • Mexico City • New Delhi
Hong Kong • Buenos Aires • Puerto Rico

ISBN 978-1-76120-528-6

A catalogue record for this book is available from the National Library of Australia

Printed by McPherson's Printing Group, Maryborough, VIC.

Scholastic Australia's policy, in association with McPherson's Printing Group, is to use papers that are renewable and made efficiently with wood from responsibly managed sources, so as to minimise its environmental footprint.

The paper in this book is FSC® certified.
FSC® promotes environmentally responsible, socially beneficial and economically viable management of the world's forests.

10 9 8 7 6 5 4 3 2 1 22 23 24 25 26 / 2

Disney

VILLAINS

HAPPILY NEVER AFTER

VANESSA

BY LORIE LANGDON

SCHOLASTIC
SYDNEY AUCKLAND NEW YORK TORONTO LONDON MEXICO CITY
NEW DELHI HONG KONG BUENOS AIRES PUERTO RICO

PROLOGUE
URSULA

THE CAVERN trembled, rolling with waves of power. Ursula threw back her head and let the currents fill her veins. The nautilus at her throat—a gift from her long-dead father—throbbed against flesh.

The shell pulsed, ravenous. Wanting.

Never before had one of the merfolk transformed into a human. She would be the first.

With meticulousness and pleasure, Ursula had gathered all the necessary fuel for the spell. She'd harvested the eye of a telescope fish, plucked a bioluminescent light from the stem of a regal angler, and ripped out the heart of a seven-gilled beast that had nearly bitten off one of her magnificent tentacles. She'd even chanced detection on land by collecting the ebony-and-copper wing from a butterfly perched on a seaside hyacinth. Her prey had fought—in some cases valiantly—but in the end, they had all fallen to her whim.

Now Ursula dropped the treasures, one by one, into a fizzling cauldron. She was giddy with excitement as the brew devoured bits of flesh and scales. Sparks illuminated a crescent curve of teeth: Ursula's smile was a wonder and a terror to behold.

All of Atlantica would learn one day that they could not force her magic into the shadows like a shameful child. Those single-finned merfolk would regret ridiculing her extraordinary abilities and making her feel like an outcast. They would boil with envy at what she could do that they could not.

One day they would *all* bow and scrape and submit to her glory.

But not yet.

She would go to the human world and find a power that would make her unparalleled in greatness beneath the water, in Atlantica. Something mysterious and sensational called to her from the land, and she knew she had to follow. It was the only way to get what she deserved, what had been stripped from her unjustly and denied her for far too long.

Respect. Wonder. Adoration.

All at once, the potion exploded, glittering tendrils flooding inside the arc of the nautilus, spiraling deep. The call of a humpback whale hummed in her blood. A shoal of scales and fins clicked into skeletal formation. Electric serpents slithered in circles and loops, firing synapses.

The spell kindled in her bones.

Back arched; arms wide; magic melded into beauty. A vision of ebony waves and glowing violet eyes. The Ionian tides pulsed through a heart that beat in double time—a human heart, warm-blooded and intended for the golden rays of the sun, the air of the open sky, the tides of the moon.

New legs kicked, once. Twice. Arms waved through silt. Sinking.

The sea that had housed, fed, and nurtured the woman-creature could not contain her.

Nothing would ever contain her again.

PART 1

THE CURSE

Come away, O human child!
To the waters and the wild
With a faery, hand in hand,
For the world's more full of weeping
than you can understand.

—William Butler Yeats

CHAPTER 1
ANDRE

SNAKE-OIL SALESMEN had nothing on Andre Baros and his Wagon of Wonders.

Known throughout the land for having the best elixirs and the most effective tonics money could buy, he never claimed them as medicine, exactly, but there was something unique to their benefits that other purveyors of similar goods couldn't claim. They were therapeutic in many a case if he selected just the right herbal combination for what ailed *and* if the customer followed his instructions. Restorative, even, if taken along with dietary changes and a refreshed routine.

But he was no doctor. The only physician who had serviced their isolated string of coastal villages had died years earlier, before Andre had traveled the route with his father and learned the trade of homeopathy. Before he'd learned that a warm compress of cypress, wintergreen, and rosemary oils could ease a whole slew of aches and pains. Or that a mixture of lemon, peppermint, clove, and eucalyptus was far more effective than leeches at curing a fever. In fact, in his almost twenty years on the earth, he'd never seen a leech do anyone a bit of good, although he kept a jar filled with the creatures in the corner of a topmost shelf for when he received the occasional request for the archaic treatment.

His sales wagon had two open sides—one filled with teas and tonics, the other stocked with odds and ends he'd amassed through his journeys along the coast. He loved collecting an eclectic array of items—books, toys, trinkets—from sea merchants. As Andre closed up the assorted-goods side of his display, he adjusted a tribal mask from southern Africa, tucked in a multihued sari from Mumbai, and secured a pair of strange telescopic goggles he'd been told by the seller had belonged to a giant-balloon-flying aeronaut from the South of France. Andre purposefully never asked how the rarefied items had come into the merchants' possession. Most times it was best not to know.

The sun sank toward the sea, washing the ring of village buildings in vermilion and gold. As the scents of woodsmoke and roasting meat wafted through the square, the other merchants scurried to close up shop, loading cartons of fruits and vegetables, racks of colorful fabrics, and tubs of icy spring water and fresh-caught fish back onto their own wagons.

That was Andre's signal that it was time to head home to the small cottage he shared with his sister, Sara, and their grandmother. He had close to an hour's drive ahead of him if the weather held. Hopefully Yia-Yia would have dinner waiting when he arrived. He hadn't eaten more than an apple all day, and in the Baros household, Wednesday was capellini night: delicate pasta covered in rich lemon butter sauce and fresh herbs. And, if the budget allowed, steamed clams or sautéed shrimp.

Andre moved to the back of the wagon, closed the tailgate, and secured the tarp flaps over a cozy den where he could seek shelter from the rain or the hot Mediterranean sun. Occasionally, he used the space to hold a private consultation with a client or to catch a quick nap during his travels. He rounded the side of the merchant cart and slammed the shutters closed over colorful bottles and jars, glass clinking and liquid sloshing, his muscles pulled taut with the effort. It was a good setup, his Wagon of Wonders, identified by the flourish of letters painted on the cart.

But truly, what good were the potions if none could help Sara?

Just the previous night, she had fainted while walking up the stairs to her bedroom. He'd swooped her up in his arms—her thin blond hair, so unlike his own thick dark locks, fanned out behind her—shocked that his twelve-year-old sister weighed little more than a bag of cockleshells. With all his knowledge of herbs and remedies, Andre had little idea how to mitigate her growing weakness, no more than he had two years earlier when the mysterious, unexplained symptoms had first started to affect his sister.

After Andre made her a tea of soothing lavender and orange, Sara had begged him to tell her a story. It had been many years since he had thought back to the tales his mother used to spin to induce his childhood sleep.

As he reclined on the bed beside her, he recalled the

old yarn of a king who wished for a child so desperately that he traded half his kingdom to a puck, a malicious fairy, who vowed if the king brought him the heart of a sea dragon, they would both have their greatest desires fulfilled: a child for the king and boundless power for the fairy. Sara fell fast asleep before Andre could finish the ending, about the power that had only brought the puck misery, and the true happiness the compromised king found through the love of a daughter.

The memory sparked urgency in his heart. What if Sara had taken a turn for the worse? When he'd left that morning, she'd still been asleep, her skin so pallid he'd checked to make sure she was breathing. What if she needed him? Taking a quick final look around the wagon, he patted his mare, Ella, and checked her rigging before feeding her his leftover apple. "We'll need to make double time getting home, girl," he said to her softly.

"Excuse me. Are you the legendary Mr. Baros?" The voice of an old woman shook along with the tap of her cane as she approached.

Andre put on his most charming smile and pivoted on his heel, never one to turn down a potential customer, even in his rushed state. "At your service, madam." As he bowed and rotated his hand in a charming flourish, he took in the woman's appearance: stooped shoulders, unkempt hair, yellowed teeth, and a gown from a century past. Her most likely complaint would be arthritic pain. A tincture of balsam fir and marjoram should do the trick. Of course, frankincense would have worked best, but it was a costly import he could not afford. "And what may I call you, miss?"

The old woman grinned, a coquettish twinkle in her pale eyes, her colorless hair curling wildly around her frilled cap. "My name is *Mrs.* FaniFani Nasside, and you, young man, are quite as charismatic as they say, but I hadn't heard about that bone structure or those arresting green eyes. . . . Oh my, if I were sixty years younger . . ." She let her insinuation trail off.

Andre gave her a bald wink. "If you were *thirty* years younger, I would whisk you away."

The woman's wrinkled cheeks pinkened, and Andre laughed, suspecting he could sell her a tonic for every day of the month.

It was far from the first time Andre's appearance had won him favor. His good looks had served him quite well as a traveling merchant. Most people trusted a symmetrical face and a quick flash of straight white teeth. He knew how to play the game, but he also genuinely enjoyed it.

CHAPTER 1

Every person he came across was unique and interesting in his or her own way. He had a feeling this woman had seen and experienced more than he could imagine, and normally he'd want to sit down and hear her stories. But that day he just wanted to make a sale and start for home.

With an arch of his brow, he motioned her closer. "Let's see what we can do for you, shall we?"

The lady hobbled forward, and Andre unlatched the shutters on the homeopathy side of the wagon and flung them wide. Then he leaned in and studied the woman's eyes. His father had trained him to look for signs of illness in the cornea. Andre guided her chin to face the sun and cocked his head to get a better look. The gray of her eyes looked faded, as though time and life had leeched the original vibrancy from them. But more relevant was the silvery ring around the edge of the iris.

Andre's stomach sank. Heart failure.

"I don't suppose you have anything in that cart of tricks for me, young man," the woman whispered, noticing the change in his expression.

He turned his back and began to search through his vials and jars. *Never leave them without hope.* His father had lived by that motto, and so did Andre. "On the contrary, I think I have just the thing, Mrs. Nasside."

The woman slumped to sit on a nearby crate. "I moved here to Aoannis last month, to live with my son." She shrugged. "I suppose he brought me here to die." Andre's heart squeezed a bit as he selected a custom mix of rosemary, chamomile, and vetiver. His grandmother was about the woman's age.

Mrs. Nasside stared into the distance and then glanced back toward him, her gaze feverish. "Have you heard of the Grimaldi Treasure, lad?"

Andre took a deep breath and pushed a swath of dark hair out of his eyes. The piazza had emptied out, all the merchants headed home for the evening. As much as he wished to ease the old lady's loneliness, at that moment he wished more for a warm dinner and a bit of fishing afterward.

But as he looked at her earnest face and hopeful eyes, he propped a shoulder against the wagon, resigned to listen. "The Grimaldi Treasure, you say? Can't say I've heard of it."

Mrs. Nasside leaned forward, her voice a low murmur. "It's a collection of potions touted to cure any malady, physical or otherwise. To bring joy to the downtrodden, strength to the weak, and true love to the lonely."

"I stopped believing in magic long ago, Mrs. Nasside."

Andre offered a grin to soften his words as he took his hat from the wagon seat, flipped it, and set it jauntily on his head. Fairy tales had died along with his parents, many years past.

Suddenly, Mrs. Nasside drew herself up to her full height, stooped shoulders pulled back, a mantle of authority transforming her features from soft and weathered to sure and strong, a glimpse of a soul beneath the withered flesh.

"Troubles are usually the brushes and shovels that smooth the road to a man's good treasure, of which he little dreams," she said. "Many a man curses the shower that falls upon his brow, and knows not that it ushers the abundance to drive away hunger." Intensity laced the lyrical, near-poetic speech with menace.

Andre blinked and jerked his arm away from her fingers, which had encircled his wrist. He realized that her words had caused him to push off the wagon and stand straight, yet even as he towered over the woman, her speech had seemed to cage him. "I—I don't understand."

"'Tis but an old folktale. Just a bit of wisdom." She took a step back, her shoulders stooping once again as she melted into the frail old woman she'd been but a moment before. "Everything you seek is within your grasp."

"There's nothing I seek except home and a warm supper." Andre's tone was short, and without meeting her probing gaze, he reached over, closed the shutters, and secured the latch once more. "If you'll excuse me, Mrs. Nasside, I must be off."

"But the treasure?"

"I have little time for children's games, ma'am." He tipped his hat in farewell and climbed into the driver's seat of the wagon. Ella pranced, ready to be off. If he took the cliff path, he might make it home before dark.

"Not even for Sara?"

The woman's whisper wrapped around Andre's throat and chilled his blood. How could she possibly know of his sister's suffering? Andre did not speak of her ailments except to ask around within his homeopathic circles for possible cures under the guise of building his knowledge of natural healing.

"Mágissa." Andre muttered the unholy word. There was no other way she could have known. Yet the practice of black magic had been outlawed long before. He narrowed his eyes at her, his every hair standing on end. "What do you know of my sister?"

To Mrs. Nasside's credit, she did not shrink back. "I am no witch, young man. I merely need someone to retrieve the treasure so I may live out my remaining years in relative comfort."

"If you want it so badly, why not find it for yourself?"

She scoffed. "It is hidden among the crags and cliffs of the coast. A frail woman such as myself would surely perish should she attempt it."

"Why not send your son or someone you trust? Why enlist the help of a complete stranger?"

"The treasure will only appear to the desperate—to one with a pure heart who does not seek gain for himself." Mrs. Nasside gripped her cane and stretched once again to her full height. "One, Andre Baros, who *sees* beyond what is known into that which is believed."

CHAPTER 2

VANESSA

ANOTHER CONVULSION ripped through Vanessa's chest, and her body seized. The sun-dried rocks were smooth against her hands. She gripped the stone as the tide sucked at her waist, her legs dangling uselessly in the current.

A lifetime underwater had not prepared her for this. Nothing in her world ever could have.

Air burned her skin, her eyes, her throat even as the distant presence of an unnamed power tugged at her senses.

CHAPTER 2

She fixed her eyes on the outline of a village perched far above on a hill. Energy, dark and writhing, hovered over the town like a cloud—a cloud pulsing with a new kind of magic. But the ocean's song beckoned her back, its seductive music enveloping her as she relaxed and let herself slip beneath the silky surface. With a sigh, she welcomed the living liquid into her mouth and lungs.

Fire burned her throat, and she scrabbled at her neck as darkness suffused her vision.

Air.

This new body desired air. Craved it. *Needed* it to survive.

She tried to push through the water, but her human limbs felt like limp seaweed. Sinking deeper, Vanessa stared up at the dwindling light of the sky. Uselessly, her hands clawed as her heart pounded in her ears. Red curtained her vision, and she reached out for help with the last bit of her consciousness.

A pod of dolphins swam too far beyond the reef to reach her in time. Crabs scuttled below. A miniature octopus scurried into a shell. Useless jellies rode the waves. And a sand shark stalked close. She didn't normally fraternize with sharks, since they tended to be unpredictable and snappy. But desperate times called for quick action.

At a single command, the large fish darted to her side. Focused on staying conscious, she grasped its slick fin and directed the animal up toward the light.

Up . . . Up . . . Up . . .

Her head broke the surface and she gasped, air burning a path to her lungs as it ignited her blood.

Great Neptune! Who knew breathing could hurt so terribly?

Vanessa released the shark from her thrall and gripped the rocks again, this time clawing her way onto the outcropping. Exhaustion flooded her muscles and tugged at her mind. As she reclined and sucked in ragged breaths, the sun crested the horizon, bathing the vast sky in shades of shell pink and vivid coral. Lovely, she had to admit. And even more fathomless than her beloved sea. She faced the cerulean waves crested in bloodred and sparks of gold. The unseen depths called to her, whispering her name with each crash of the surf.

Still gasping for breath, Vanessa paused to consider her next move. Perhaps the experiment should end there: she'd proven she could transform herself, something no creature in Atlantica had ever accomplished—not even the self-righteous king Triton. But her motivation had not been just to prove she could become human, Vanessa reminded herself, but to live as one with them. To gather experiences and knowledge of land magic. To grow her craft and expand her mind. And to show that pompous king that there was more to the world than his limited views accommodated.

She propped herself up on a shaky arm and lifted her chin with a victorious half laugh, half gasp. *I am Vanessa. Human. A new creation with a whole different world to explore.*

She could start over, become whoever she wished. More than those fin-flapping hagfish in Atlantica would ever dare. More than their narrow minds could even dream.

Still, she'd never felt more vulnerable as she ran a hand down one of her supple limbs—and stopped to correct herself. From her studies of the human world, she recalled that the proper terms were *legs* and *feet*. Vanessa stared at her thin appendages, the leg tapering all the way down to the ankle, from which the foot protruded, complete with its knobby—what was the word?—toes. How was one supposed to walk on such a narrow platform? In theory, it had seemed simple. But outside the water, her body felt clumsy, and every movement required immense effort. She pointed her toes and swiveled her delicate ankle.

Her new form had been designed for beauty and allure, her vision based on a bewitching lady she'd watched late one night dancing on the deck of a ship. Her dark hair had fallen in heavy waves from its pins as she'd spun and raised her arms to the sky. Carefree and seductive, and a bit wild, the woman had enraptured every single human in attendance with the curl of her finger or the sway of her hips. Each one had wanted her or wanted to be her.

As Ursula had hidden among the indigo waves, a name, engraved in golden script along the side of the ship, had set her quest in motion: the *Vanessa*.

Her studies of the human world—everything from anatomy to history to culture—had not prepared her for making her dreams a reality: being transformed into Vanessa, a goddess among women. The outcast would now become the envy of all who knew her. Every soul who met her would wish for her companionship, thirst for her laughter, long for a moment of her attention. They would worship this human creature.

She bent her legs and pulled her toes from the lap of the warm surf. The moment she no longer touched the sea, she couldn't breathe, couldn't think, her mind whirling like a wild vortex, threatening to suck her down to the dark depths. Quickly, she plunged her feet back into the water, her thoughts steadying. Legs immersed to the knee, she wiggled over to a boulder and rested her back against it as her fingers played along the surface of the sea, beckoning liquid tendrils to spin in her palm.

Perhaps finding the greater power that awaited her in the human world would need to wait a bit longer.

CHAPTER 3

ANDRE

ANDRE WAS STILL fuming as he arrived at the spot Mrs. Nasside had mapped out for him. He could not imagine how he had let himself get talked into the ludicrous scheme; perhaps it was desperation, like she had said.

He peered around dismally. The wind picked up, carrying heavy air from the sea. Ominous clouds rolled across the moon, the sky lowering to suffocating levels. Storms along the coast came on quickly and brutally.

CHAPTER 3

Perhaps it was not desperation but stupidity.

Andre hurried to tie Ella's lead to a tree and spoke softly to the loyal mare. "I'm sure this won't take long. You'll be tucked into your stall with fresh hay in no time." *I hope,* he added silently as he tugged on his coat and studied the loose sketch. He marked the rock formation to his left that rose above the trees in three ragged points, and recognized Stefanos Lagoon. It was a spot Andre knew from his travels, where the forest opened into a lovely glade. He'd stopped there many times over the years to eat lunch or to cool off with a quick swim.

As Andre made his way down the overgrown path, he continued to berate himself for acting a fool. What had the woman said that had convinced him to undertake the mad errand? Surely she'd employed *mageía* to make him bend to her will.

But even as Andre tried to justify his behavior to himself, he knew: it had been Sara. Andre would try just about anything to help his little sister. Even if it meant going on a wild-goose chase after a mythical magic treasure.

He ducked under a branch and paused. The forest was eerily silent save for the soft sound of falling water and a low, distant drone of thunder that seemed to carry the old woman's final instructions, the words that had dissolved the last vestiges of doubt he'd had in taking on her request.

As he'd plucked the map from her shaking fingers, she'd whispered, "Though we walk in flesh, we do not war according to the flesh."

His mother had spoken the same ancient verse to Andre many times before she had passed. A reminder that not all battles could be fixed with tonics and potions of humans' making. That there were other forces in the world beyond what people could see: supernatural beings that lurked in the shadows, lying in wait to prey upon fear, mystical occurrences unexplained by science.

Magic did exist. Few could wield it, and it was seldom seen, but that didn't make it any less real. And if this Grimaldi Treasure did indeed exist and was one such power that could cure Sara, Andre would find it.

He lifted his hat, scraped the sticky hair off his forehead, and then rearranged the bowler on his head with renewed purpose. He'd come that far. He would see it through.

Determination lengthened his strides as he traversed the path. Soon the trees opened onto a picturesque lagoon fed by a tinkling waterfall. During the day, sun filtered through the leaves to create lacy patterns. Thick arches of curved branches and emerald foliage curtained the water from the outside world, giving the glen an enchanted feel, as if pixies might at any moment appear to dance in the golden streams of light, or tiny men carrying sharp pickaxes might march in to mine jewels from the stones.

Now the shadows leaked vines into murky water, and the soft splash of the falls was drowned out by approaching thunder. Trees arched and knit overhead, their branches clacking like brittle bones. Andre quieted his movement, careful to avoid the rocks ringing the waterline. Wind swirled fallen leaves into a maelstrom that twirled up and up, nearly to his height. His heart skittering, Andre stumbled back until the unearthly vortex careered over the water and collapsed there, dead vegetation scattering over the surface of the pool.

He pushed out a slow breath and reminded himself that this was the same familiar alcove he'd visited many times. Nothing bewitched here.

Unless the old woman was right, the niggling voice in his head reminded him. He was torn between hoping to find the treasure and wondering if it was all a hoax.

For Sara's sake he would see it through. Andre clutched the Saint Raphael medal at his throat. It was a gift from his father that he never removed. He ran a thumb over the engraved patron saint of healing, reminding himself that more was at stake than his jittery nerves. Suddenly, a flash of lightning lit the clearing, and he spied near the smaller pool the large, flat rock Mrs. Nasside had claimed would hold the treasure. Ready to have this done and over, he raced to the outcropping, fell to his knees, and began to feel around the stone for a fissure in the rock.

The best Mrs. Nasside could do was tell him the treasure was hidden inside the largest rock at the edge of the lagoon. *Inside*. What did that mean?

Light split the sky, followed close by a crack of thunder. He would soon be caught in a deluge. After patting down all three sides of the rock as far as he could reach without any luck, he leaned back on his haunches and stared at the sky in frustration. Surely his parents were looking down from heaven, shaking their heads in disbelief at his folly. Had he really believed he would find a magical cure for Sara, for Mrs. Nasside . . . for them all? Every sick customer he couldn't help, every hurting person he came across in his daily travels chipped away a bit of his heart. He tried hard not to internalize their pain. His father had warned Andre that his sensitive spirit was both a blessing and a curse.

Another flash broke open the sky, rain pouring down

onto his upturned face. He swiped the water from his eyes and stood. It was time to head home to his dinner—now cold—and warm bed.

As he started to turn back to the path, a splash sounded in the pool, followed by a slap of flesh against rock. Andre looked just in time to see the tips of a tail submerge near the bottom of the huge boulder. His gut knotted. Was the fish showing him that there was one spot on the rock he hadn't yet searched? Andre had already ruined his evening; what was another few minutes?

Before he could change his mind, he shucked off his coat. Rain saturated his clothing as he toed off his boots, climbed onto the boulder, and slipped down its smooth edge into the water.

Cold black enveloped him as he submerged, the silky liquid closing over his head. He twisted toward the rock face, kicking until he broke the surface with a gasp. Lightning flashed in quick succession, highlighting his hands as they scrabbled for purchase. At last he gripped the slimy surface with one hand, searching for an opening with the other.

Rain continued to pour, relentless, plastering his hair over his eyes. He whipped it away, squinting in the growing darkness and treading water as he prayed for another streak of light to show him the way. The side of the rock facing him was coated in slick moss, and as he ran his fingers systematically over its surface, not even a crevice was apparent.

Three successive flashes lit the pool as Andre frantically searched the rock face. Nothing. Heat flooded his skin. An *anóitos* was what he was—a stupid, stupid person. Swimming around in a lightning storm, searching for a magic treasure. Laughter exploded from his chest. What a story he'd have to tell Sara when he got home.

The rain slowed to a drizzle, and he floated on his back, letting the gentler drops cool his heated face. Weightless and with his eyes closed, he was aware of the logical side of his brain overtaking the emotion. He'd lost nothing but time. And mayhap a bit of pride. Now it was time to face the long, cold journey home.

Pain ripped into his toe, and he let out a curse as he stiffened, sinking. He stilled beneath the surface, looking for his attacker. A soft bluish glow radiated from the underside of the boulder perched on the edge of the pool. Could that be it, the treasure he'd been searching for?

Andre swam toward it, his lungs beginning to burn. But he feared if he surfaced, the light would be gone when he went back down. He kicked closer, reaching out. His long fingers were immersed in unearthly radiance. Invisible bands tightened around his chest as he reached deeper. And deeper still.

He touched metal, slick and cool.

Andre's vision darkened at the edges, signaling his breath was beginning to run out, and he had no time for hesitation. He gripped the object and pulled it from the crevice. It was a box, weighing more than he had expected, and he sank, his feet landing in a tangle of underwater growth. He tucked the box under one arm, heart ready to explode, and kicked hard and clawed his way to the surface. A desperate gasp of air revived his flagging muscles as he swam to the shore. With a grunt, he tossed the box onto solid ground. Then he heaved himself out of the water, lay flat on his back, and wheezed in breath after blessed breath.

The rain had stopped. Andre took in the acrid scent of wet vegetation and pungent earthworms as a bird twittered nearby and sonorous insects hummed. Frogs belched a chorus. But underneath it all, a low drone vibrated the ground, jarring his bones.

Andre cracked open one eye to find the clearing bathed in moonlight. The box at his side purred like a cat craving attention. He sat up, rivulets of water streaming off his body. The box had not a spot of rust to mar its silvery surface. The glow dissipated as blue light seeped from the edges of the opening.

Magic.

Breathing hard, he stilled. Only the worst kind of coward would back down now.

He reached out. Fingers tingling, he yanked back his hand. Then, with deft movements, he tried again, flicking the latch and flinging open the lid. Inside were seven glass vials filled with glittering silver-blue liquid. Andre leaned in closer and read aloud the words the flasks were labeled with: "Friendship. Happiness. Love. Time. Hope. Dreams. Healing."

He tilted back the box to find words engraved inside the open lid.

WISHES THAT MONEY CANNOT BUY

Chills skittered over Andre's wet skin. In his wildest imaginings, he hadn't conceived of such miracles existing. Potions that granted wishes. Could it be real? Had old Mrs. Nasside been correct that only someone who did not wish to use the treasure for themselves could find it? Because in truth, all Andre wished for was a cure for his sister.

CHAPTER 3

Health and strength. Growth and energy. Life without pain.

There was no time like the present to try.

He sprang to his feet and snatched up the box. Then he grabbed his coat and boots and raced along the path back to his wagon. Ella should be rested. If he pushed her hard, they could make it home before Sara's bedtime.

***

The lagoon hadn't been too far out of his way, but the hour had grown late. Light flickered through the trees as Andre guided Ella the last few paces off the main road and onto the winding drive that led to his home. The Baros family's home, perched on the edge of a sparkling inlet and made of strong timber, thick stucco, and stones, had stood for generations. It wasn't large, more of a cottage than a villa, but as Andre pulled the wagon to a stop in front of the barn, he felt the tightness melt away from his shoulders and he let out a sigh. Bless Yia-Yia for keeping the lamps burning for him.

He leapt from the driver's perch and unhooked Ella, then rubbed her down and gave her fresh water and feed in record time. Once the horse was tucked into her stall, he grabbed the metal box and ran into the house, shouting for his sister as he flung open the door.

"Sara!"

"I'm up here, Andre."

Andre raced up the stairs to the second floor and into his sister's cozy, neat-as-a-pin room. A lamp beside her bed illuminated her pale form, propped up on a pile of pillows as she read a book. A fire crackled in the hearth despite the warm night. Small for her twelve years and painfully thin, Sara resembled a tiny angel. The golden hair tumbling around her shoulders used to be thick and lustrous but had grown thinner and dull; her eyes, however, were still a luminous blue. Love and protectiveness constricted Andre's heart as he perched on the edge of her mattress.

"You missed dinner," Sara admonished as she placed a scrap of paper inside her book and set it on the bedside table. When she faced him, her forehead crinkled in confusion as she took in his damp clothing. "Did Ella dump you off the Sorrento Bridge again?"

"Again? When did . . . Oh, yeah, I deserved it that time. But no." Andre took off his hat and raked his clumped hair off his forehead, remembering the time he'd pushed his horse to tow the wagon all the way home from Atrani Marina at a full gallop after a particularly dubious meeting with a seafaring merchant. And by *merchant*, he meant a pirate with a knife-wielding crew who didn't appreciate that Andre had negotiated with their captain to obtain a crate full of silks for a fraction of their worth.

"So why are you late and soaked to the skin?"

Andre glanced over his shoulder into the hallway. "Where's Yia-Yia?" Something in his spirit told him to keep news of the treasure from his grandmother. At least for now. Her superstitions had reached delusional levels in recent years. She still insisted kelpies had caused the boating accident that had killed his parents.

"She went right to bed after dinner. Said she had one of her headaches." Sara pushed herself up straighter in bed. "Andre, what is going on? You're acting strange."

In a rush, Andre summarized what had happened with Mrs. Nasside and how he'd followed her map to Stefanos Lagoon. "You should've seen it, Sara. It felt different from any time I'd been there before. Like a haunted forest."

She wrapped her arms, thin and white as birch twigs, around her bent knees. "What happened?"

Sara's eyes eclipsed her face as Andre filled her in on the storm and the black waters. He at last pulled the small box from beneath his coat and opened it to reveal the shimmering silver-blue tubes. Sara read the engraving and ran her fingers along the vials, the liquid inside shifting colors beneath her touch. "It's real, isn't it?" she whispered.

Andre shot her a dimpled grin. "I believe it is. Do you want to try it?"

Sara picked up the vial marked *Healing*, and the contents shifted to an iridescent yellow. "Just a bit?"

"Yes, I thought a few drops in a cup of tea to start. And then see how you fare."

She stared at the flask for several long moments. "Mother always did say that we should believe in things we can't see."

Andre swallowed hard. Their mother had been the strongest woman he'd ever known, and no matter how many times her efforts went unrewarded, she had never allowed failure to make her bitter. She loved with a fierce devotion and gave to all of them with her entire heart. Andre stared at Sara and saw the convictions of their mother in the depths of her azure eyes.

Sara threw back the covers and set her tiny feet on the wood floor. "Let's do it."

CHAPTER 4

ANDRE

EARLY THE following morning, sunlight rippled and undulated on the ceiling from the reflection of the saltwater cove outside Andre's window. At certain times of year, the aquatic echo appeared to envelop his entire room. As a child, he'd pretended to breathe underwater and swim from his bed, his voice a gurgle of bubbles as his mother called up to ask what he would like for breakfast. His best friend had been an imaginary puffer fish named Quill, whose broken spines Andre claimed to use as writing implements.

When had he lost that childlike wonder? That anticipation, the feeling that when he woke up, anything could happen?

Responsibilities . . . fears . . . disappointments . . . loss—all those things had stripped the possibilities from life.

He saw it on the faces of the people he sold to each day. Their very lives an indelible weight on their shoulders. When he offered them a trinket from a faraway land with a smile and a perhaps slightly embellished story about the item's origin, he spied a secret spark in their eyes. Or when he proposed a remedy that promised relief, he watched a tiny bit of that heaviness release in the slight upward curving of their lips or a heartfelt thank-you.

The impact Andre made on others, however temporary, fueled his joy. That little high that showed him hope was possible. But inevitably, that lightness was always replaced by the looming drudgery of another day just like the day before, working to survive, to support the ones he loved, and to maintain a certain level of comfort and fleeting happiness.

This day, however, seemed different. Something big and bright filled his chest. His limbs felt light, as if he might float from beneath his covers. A broad smile stretched itself effortlessly across his face. The high notes of a piano tinkled a tune across his brain. Everything was about to change. He could feel it.

Andre's gaze focused on the box sitting on his dresser. A bit of watery sunshine ignited the metal surface. The Grimaldi Treasure. Had he found a solution? Not a temporary fix but a cure for what was broken?

As if in answer, his frail sister ran into his room.

Ran.

"Andre. It worked! It worked!" Sara rose onto her toes and performed a graceful pirouette.

The musical notes in Andre's soul soared to a crescendo as he leapt up and threw his arms around his sister, lifting her off her feet. "I can't believe it!"

She giggled as he twirled her in a circle. When he set her down, he looked closely at her face—rosy cheeks, bright eyes, and a smile so wide it cracked his heart. The grayish pallor was gone, and so was the strain that normally showed on her pretty face from constant headache, pain, and fatigue. He rushed to the box and lifted the lid. Each vial secured in its slot, the potions inside pulsed with radiant energy, as if begging him to use them to help. To bring hope to others.

But if anyone knew the truth—the power of the potions—there would be riots. He lifted the tube marked

Joy, and the silver-blue liquid turned a sweet tangerine at his touch. A potion that could grant someone happiness, no matter their circumstances. Could it dispel a broken heart? Could it take away the crippling grief for a lost loved one? *Or two?* An echo of the devastation he'd felt after losing his parents hollowed out his chest. The weeks following their deaths, he hadn't known who he was or how to live, as if a part of him had died along with them. As if everything in the world had been washed of color. He would never forget that horrid physical ache every time he awoke and remembered they were gone.

Could this treasure have the ability to supplant that kind of anguish, forever?

He set down the vial and secured it in the box, tangerine transforming back into ice blue. If some of the rougher sorts Andre traded with found out about the magic the potions contained, it would be worth his life. His family's lives. How could he help others without the secret getting out?

He watched Sara whirl and dance around his room, and an idea sparked. Just as he'd added a drop of healing potion to her tea, if he put a tiny measure of each potion into his elixirs, he could offer more than temporary relief without anyone being the wiser that his remedies had received an otherworldly upgrade. Magic that could grant a lonely soul true love. Time for those running out. Joy to the heartbroken. Dreams fulfilled. Healing . . . an actual cure!

His course decided, Andre threw on his clothes and planned his route based on those he knew needed the most urgent help. First he would go back to Aoannis and find Mrs. Nasside.

***

The next days flew by like a dream. People whom Andre had never once seen smile became youthful and exuberant after taking a bit of his new elixir that promised to brighten one's mood. A sweet blind man Andre had known for years regained his sight. A lonely widow found love with the local blacksmith, a man whose melancholy had locked him inside himself until Andre sold him an elixir of bergamot and lavender mixed with just a bit of magic.

"Aww, Andre, look! They're holding hands," Sara squealed from her perch on the tailgate of the wagon. She'd begun to accompany him on his route, assisting with his increased demand, now that she was so much stronger and healthier.

Andre flicked one of Sara's blond braids. "A romantic now, are you?"

She giggled. "I suspect I always have been. All those fairy tales Mother used to tell us . . . How could they not make you long for a happily ever after of your own?" Her eyes widened innocently. "Which reminds me: have you seen Maryann lately?"

Andre rolled his eyes as he straightened the shelves, making sure to place the teas and tonics that contained magic toward the front.

"Maryann's sweet on you, you know." Sara hopped down and crossed her arms in front of her narrow chest. "Just last week she brought a three-tiered cake to the cottage."

"She was checking on you, imp." Andre took off his hat, spun it on his finger, and then flicked it so it landed on her head. "Now that you're healthy, she wants to see you back in school."

"If she was so intent on me going to school, then why did she inquire as to your whereabouts no less than three times?" Sara's eyes sparkled with mischief.

Andre took his hat back and threw it onto the driver's seat. He liked Maryann. They'd attended a fair together the past month and had a nice time. She was sweet, around his age, rather pretty with her strawberry blond hair and freckled nose, and she clearly seemed smart, running the village's small schoolhouse, but he had known her all his life. Where was the mystery? The passion? He watched the widow and the blacksmith, barely able to keep their hands off each other, stroll among the merchants.

Was it so wrong to want excitement and intensity like that in a relationship of his own? Andre longed to find a challenge, a woman with so many layers that it would take him a lifetime to peel them all away.

Shaking off his thoughts, he turned back to his sister and changed the subject. "You need to take the placement tests so she can evaluate if your home studies have kept you in line with other students your age."

"Yia-Yia is an excellent teacher. I don't see why I even need to go. I want to work with you!"

"Which reminds me: I think I need to tell Yia-Yia about the potion. She didn't seem to quite accept my explanation of finding a new herbal remedy."

"Andre, no! If we tell her, she'll dump the potion into the cove," Sara protested. "You know how she feels about magic."

"I also know how she feels about you, imp." Andre shot

his sister a wink. "She asked me not to have you out too late."

Sara groaned as Andre pulled the shutters closed with a snap. Following the protocols for any new oil, he'd been giving her a drop of the potion in her morning tea each day for a week. She seemed to be growing healthier and hardier every day. Part of him enjoyed having her company and simply watching her flourish as she healed. But he knew she needed to make friends with children her own age, and the village school was her best chance for a somewhat normal childhood—something she'd been deprived of by her ailment.

As they climbed into the driver's seat, a few townies waved and called out to them. Andre tipped his hat and waved back, satisfaction bursting from his friendly grin. The last week had been like an answer to a prayer he didn't even know he'd made. And Andre often wondered if the treasure somehow knew his greatest happiness would come from helping others.

Andre flicked Ella's reins, and they traveled down a narrow lane to the road that led to their village. The dirt path cut along sea cliffs suspended between the bright bowl of a cerulean sky and an endless sheet of turquoise waters. A craggy forest rose on one side, covered in lush vegetation peppered with periwinkle and wineberry bougainvillea. The sweet scent of lemon blossoms harmonized with the salty breeze off the Mediterranean. Andre lifted his face to the hot sun, a balm to his soul, but something nagged at him, stirring up his peace.

The day Sara had shown up healed in his bedroom, he'd packed the treasure and driven straight to Aoannis to find Mrs. Nasside. He couldn't wait to tell her she'd been right about the treasure and give her whatever potion she wished for herself. He'd imagined a tea with a drop each of time, healing, and joy.

But when he'd arrived and inquired around town, the old woman was nowhere to be found. In fact, when he spoke to villagers who had lived in Aoannis for years, not one of them had heard of the Nassides. Confused and unsettled, Andre had returned home that day without opening his cart to anyone. Had the woman truly been a witch after all, as he'd accused her of the day they'd met?

But as time had passed and he'd seen the positive effects of the potions, he'd wondered more and more if Mrs. Nasside had been an emissary sent from heaven. But why him? Why now? Why their small string of villages, to distribute such wondrous magic?

Snapping back to the present, he pulled the reins

tight and sent Ella into a trot. The sharp curves of the road came up fast, and the nose of the carriage dipped as if the whole thing might careen into the abyss. Sara squealed and gripped her seat, her trust in him complete, and Andre let her carefree laughter chase away his muddled thoughts.

***

Cool salt air billowed the linen curtains on the sunporch later that evening as Andre, Sara, and Yia-Yia sat around a small table, eating their dinner. The sun painted the sky like candied oranges, sugaring the tips of the waves.

Yia-Yia had been unusually contemplative throughout the meal. She sopped up the dregs of her soup with a last crust of bread, then lowered her spoon to the table with a clatter. "What have you done to your sister, young man?"

Yia-Yia was Andre's father's mother and had lived with them as far back as he could remember. Thin as a whip, with wiry white hair and a strong Roman nose, the woman was as formidable as a ship captain, and when her memory had begun to slip, she'd compensated with a double portion of toilsome rigidity.

"This beautiful girl . . . a picture of health." A rare smile split his grandmother's face as she looked at Sara. "I'm not complaining, mind. But a change this sudden warrants a bit of investigation. I've never known essential oils and herbs to work so quickly."

Andre spooned a large bite of *patsas* into his mouth and swallowed hard.

"This soup is exceptional, Yia-Yia. Did you do something different to the recipe? Fresh basil, perhaps?"

"Andre Lucas Baros, do not think a dimpled smile and a compliment will distract me. I'm not one of your admirers." Yia-Yia pressed both her palms flat against the wooden table, her dark eyes cutting through his attempt at charm. "You're lying about something."

"I'm not lying! The soup *is* exceptional tonight." Andre lifted his brows in his best approximation of innocence.

The woman's ears flushed an alarming shade of red as she smashed her lips together so hard they nearly disappeared in the sagging folds of her face.

Sara's words spilled out before Andre could stop them. "Andre found a treasure that contains potions that heal and bring joy and true love and grant time and—"

"What?" Yia-Yia shouted as she half stood, leaning across the table into Andre's face.

Andre slumped back with a sigh. He'd hoped to prepare his grandmother before she learned the truth.

Yia-Yia came from a long line of staunch believers in

supernatural forces of evil. Unfortunately, those beliefs included a strong sense that all magic was black magic and should be avoided at any cost.

Before Andre could form a reply that wouldn't send Yia-Yia into a frenzy, Sara continued, clearly worried she'd made things worse. "It's called the Grimaldi Treasure. It's good, Yia-Yia. I promise. Look how it's helped me. And so many of the poor sick folks throughout the villages Andre visits."

Andre gripped his sister's hand and shook his head in warning, but it was too late. She'd said too much.

Yia-Yia began to shake. "You brought magic into this house! You . . . fed this *poison* . . . to your *sister*?"

He shot to his feet. "It is not poison! Look how healthy she is. For the first time in years, Sara has color and life and strength!"

Yia-Yia pointed an accusatory finger at her grandson. "You have no idea what you could've unleashed, young man. And on the villagers, you say? I thought your father taught you to help and heal, not to destroy."

Andre stepped back and crossed his arms over his chest. "You don't know what you're talking about. You should see all the positive changes in our village's people. In fact, come with me tomorrow."

"Andre, it's all right. Let's show her the box, and then

she'll understand—" Sara stood, but then her legs collapsed beneath her, sending her into a heap of skirts upon the tile floor.

Andre rushed to her side, but when he lifted her to her feet, her knees buckled again. "Andre?" She looked up at him, eyes widened in fear. "I . . . my legs . . . won't . . ."

He swept her up in his arms, his heart crashing like a storm surge in his ears. "You've had a very busy couple of days. We overdid it. You just need a bit of rest," he reassured her as he kissed the top of her head. Somehow, she grew pale in the time it took him to climb the stairs and lay her on her bed, all the healthy color leached from her small face. He placed his hand on her forehead. It was clammy.

"Give me more of the healing potion," Sara murmured. "It must have worn off."

Worn off?

Andre had not even considered that the magic might not be permanent. The possible implications ricocheted through his brain. Why grant someone's wish if it didn't last? He rushed into his room and took the box out of his closet, flipping open the lid. Most of the vials were half empty. But the healing vial contained only a third of the potion. He'd sold drops of that one in so many elixirs that he'd had to create more labels on the road. Some combinations required drops of different potions in one mixture, like the one he'd custom made for a fisherman who'd lost everyone in his crew and been paralyzed from the waist down in a boating accident. Andre had mixed several drops of healing with joy and friendship and given it as a gift for him to the nuns who cared for the man.

The next day, Andre had seen the man *standing* outside the local pub, drinking and laughing with several men from the village.

What if he needed more of that combination to keep him walking and happy? What if everyone needed more? How much of the potions would it take to continue to fuel each of the magical tonics he'd sold? There wasn't enough for everyone. Not indefinitely.

"Do not give her another drop," Yia-Yia panted after climbing up the stairs. "You've done enough damage as it is."

Andre didn't respond, but he knew deep down something was very, very wrong.

CHAPTER 5

VANESSA

A STRANGLED CRY cut through the shrieks of waking seagulls, reaching Vanessa, who still lay prone by the rocks, teaching herself to separate from the sea. The work was difficult, but the pulsing, persistent call of that elusive power she'd first sensed on coming to land motivated Vanessa to extricate herself bit by painful bit from the cradling, loving hold of her natural waters.

She searched the beach for the sound and found a tiny

girl with thin golden braids hobbling on a stick. One of the child's limbs appeared lame, and Vanessa could not fathom how the girl's spindly arms didn't break as she leaned her weight on the crutch with each labored step.

When the child reached the water's edge, she pulled a tattered bit of parchment from her pocket, her sobs quieter now. She lifted her pretty face to the sky as rivulets of water streamed down her cheeks. *Tears?* Vanessa touched her own face, wondering if she was capable of such a thing. After a moment of the girl's chest heaving, her tears retracted to pools reflected in her startlingly blue eyes. She lifted the paper and began to read aloud, her voice a broken plea.

"Save me, oh king, for the waters have come up to my neck. I sink in the miry depths, where there is no foothold. I have come into the deep waters; the floods engulf me. I am worn out calling for help; my throat is parched. My eyes fail, looking for my king. Help me, please!"

The child collapsed to her knees in the sand, crutch thudding to the ground beside her, the paper crumpled in her fist. Vanessa crawled across the rocks, as close as she dared, her human heart giving an odd squeeze. She grasped her chest, the ache fading almost as soon as it had come upon her. Like a newly healed wound, a sore spot lingered somewhere deep within her as she watched the girl's face crumble.

Her words fractured on the wind, forcing Vanessa to spell them closer to her ear. ". . . curse is too powerful! Andre did not mean to hurt anyone, I swear! He only wished to help, but now the magic has shifted to darkness and it has grown stronger and stronger, overtaking those who wished for good. Rescue us, oh great sea king, with your mighty trident, for I know you can overcome this evil!"

Everything within Vanessa grew still, her eyes narrowing on the child. Triton was the king the girl called to for help. As if he were some god or great savior? The king of the merfolk could not care less about the woes of a human child. Humans were his enemy!

Muscles quivering, Vanessa clutched the golden nautilus at her throat. Her conduit was no less worthy than that blighted three-pronged stick Triton brandished about. Its size certainly did not portend its power. In fact, she rather preferred the portability of her shell to the unwieldiness of what essentially amounted to an enormous fork.

Vanessa narrowed her eyes on the sobbing girl and, no longer sympathetic to her plight, inched forward. If she was careful, Vanessa could use such a tenderhearted one.

The dark magic the child spoke of must be terribly potent, and it explained the draw she felt toward the village on the hill. She needed to find out more.

A quick but rough plan formed. With a visualization and a touch to her shell, she covered herself with a violet dress and lavender bodice that matched her eyes. Nothing extravagant—no beadwork or crystals, as she would wear at home. Simple peasants' garb, so as not to make the child uncomfortable. Yet as she ran her hands over the soft fabric, she luxuriated in the perfect fit over her new slim waist and gently curved hips.

Vanessa crawled around the rocks and onto the beach, keeping her bare feet and the hem of her gown touching the surf. The child had ceased her wretched sobbing, and now her despairing gaze searched the waves, moisture streaking down her pale face. Her lips moved, perhaps in some sort of prayer, but Vanessa, fortunately, had muted her spell and could not hear the words.

Given how the girl begged for help with such unselfconscious abandon and on behalf of all those who had been affected by the alleged curse, Vanessa knew the child was kind and generous. These two naive traits—combined with her young age—surely meant the girl would assist her if she believed Vanessa was hurt. Perhaps even offer her a place to stay, which would allow Vanessa to dig deeper into the origins of the mysterious dark magic.

She arranged her arms above her head, legs splayed in the gentle waves, and let out a moan. Through slitted eyes, Vanessa watched the girl freeze. The child swiped at her tears with the sleeve of her dress and then looked around for the noise. *Smart girl. Just a bit farther down the beach.* Vanessa wiggled and groaned louder.

When the child spotted her, she did not hesitate but grasped her makeshift crutch and struggled across the sand.

Vanessa closed her eyes, stilling in wait. Patience never had been one of her gifts, and now was no exception. *Neptune, this girl moves slowly.* She counted in her head to keep from shouting or hissing in frustration. *Thirty, thirty-one, thirty-two . . .*

"Miss, are you all right?" the girl panted as she reached her at last.

Clearly, Vanessa had washed up on the beach and most certainly was not *all right*. She managed to continue counting for several seconds so that she wouldn't bite the child's head off in exasperation. Vanessa licked lips dry as sand and opened her mouth as if to speak, but nothing came out.

"Miss, can you hear me?" The end of a rough stick poked Vanessa's shoulder repeatedly.

With the nearly irresistible urge to snatch the crutch and snap it in half, Vanessa counted ten more seconds before fluttering her eyes prettily. The girl fell to her knees. Vanessa gasped and darted her gaze around in confusion. "What . . . Where . . ." She let her eyes fall closed.

The girl shook her shoulder. "Do not go back to sleep, miss. Please, wake up!"

Vanessa opened her eyes languidly, as if just waking from a dream. She noticed that the girl was both thinner and somewhat older than she'd first thought. Her arms were as fragile as jellyfish tentacles where they stuck out of her three-quarter-length sleeves. But her eyes, as blue as the Caspian Sea, appeared ancient in her little-girl face, as if she'd seen and experienced more in her short lifetime than most did in one hundred years.

With a soft blink, Vanessa rasped, "I don't know what . . . Where am I?"

"This is Marini Beach. Are you hurt?" The girl reached out, and Vanessa jerked back. The child's hand stilled in midair. "It's all right. What's your name?"

"I . . . think . . ." Vanessa lifted a hand to her head and let her voice pitch up in panic. "I can't remember."

CHAPTER 5

"That's all right. I'm Sara Baros." Sara glanced at Vanessa's feet, still immersed in the gentle surf. "Can you walk?"

Vanessa shook her head. That part she would not need to fake. Going from eight legs to two and actually walking on those odd narrow feet would take a bit of practice and was something she hadn't quite yet worked up to since she'd been on land.

"I'm going to get some help. Our cottage is just over the hill, but it might take me . . . a while." Sara glanced down at her crooked leg and the crutch she held in a death grip. "Can you at least move your feet from the water? The tide is coming in."

Vanessa stopped her scowl just in time. *Move out of the water?* It felt so unnatural. But land was her temporary home, so just like she'd been practicing, Vanessa lifted herself on her arms and scooted a few feet up the beach.

As soon as Vanessa had repositioned herself away from the surf, Sara rose from her knees and rearranged her flower-printed dress, but not before Vanessa spied legs like spindles. "I will return with my brother as quickly as I am able."

The girl stumbled up the beach, limping and sliding back, her progress maddeningly slow even with the crutch.

Yet Vanessa couldn't help calling out, "Miss Baros!" Vanessa watched the girl stumble just as she'd gained momentum up the sand. Sara looked over her shoulder. "Thank you for your help."

With a quick nod, the girl continued her arduous trek up the rocky beach.

Vanessa lay back down and stared into the sky. Pink tinted the edges of the white fluff that floated across the blue expanse like sea-foam. As she contemplated the vast world above, she wondered about the child and what sort of desperation it would take for a weakened girl like her to climb over rock and sand to call out for a king who would never come.

The curse must be more dreadful than any she'd concocted herself. Of course, Triton had always kept her from having too much fun. Her most recent hex had encased the merfolk in sound-damping isolation bubbles. No swimming hand in hand or giggling in shoals or singing their every thought. Vanessa rolled her eyes to the heavens. For an entire exalted week, silence had become her favorite sound.

They'd bobbled against one another like fish caught in a net. In their panic, they'd tried to piercc their bubble cages with knives, shells, coral spikes, and sea urchin spines. An especially dense group swam to the top of the castle to bounce against the pointed spires, hoping the sharp edges would pierce their bubbles and set them free. Not one had simply looked her in the eye and begged for mercy.

And then that stick-in-the-silt king had broken her beautiful spell and banished her for a month. Little did he know Ursula had built up her reef cavern over the years with furnishings and decorations discarded by fickle mermaids, along with books from the human world she'd collected and protected from the seawater with a simple charm. She felt more at home there than in her suite at the palace. It was where she devised her best spells and concocted her potions. Like the one that had brought her to this moment of exploration—an entire world without merpeople or an overbearing young king. A place where she could reinvent herself and play with no consequences. And she would return to Atlantica more powerful than ever.

Yet . . .

She stilled as a realization washed over her: Neptune had blessed her with another, more important objective. It could not be a coincidence that she'd become human and chosen to come ashore on that particular beach just as little Sara had called for help. Power simmered there, ripe for the taking. Vanessa smiled to herself. Her venture on land might just prove more lucrative than she'd ever dreamed.

CHAPTER 6

ANDRE

ANDRE HURRIEDLY saddled Ella. Sara had arrived at the cottage, ranting about a woman who'd washed in from the sea. As Andre urged Ella into a gallop, he thought he knew what to expect. A bedraggled castaway. A sickly woman in need of medical attention. Or, if his current luck was any indication, an angry witch on death's door, ready to curse him for not saving her life.

A hastened visit into the town piazza a few mornings

earlier had confirmed Andre's worst fears: everyone he had thought he'd helped by giving them a dose of the Grimaldi Treasure had had the positive effects reversed—and then some.

Andre had found Marco collapsed against the fountain. The fisherman's eyes had shifted, but he'd struggled to open his mouth. "My . . . arms . . . legs . . . can't . . . move."

Good Lord, no.

Andre had gripped the man's shoulders to keep him from falling over. The immobility had spread up to his neck. Far worse than before he'd taken the Grimaldi potion.

A shout had drawn his attention to the butcher's shop, where Daniel, the proprietor, smashed his meaty fist into a local café owner's nose. "No lamb chops today!" he shouted.

Daniel had asked for something to help him find joy and rid him of the sadness that always seemed to weigh him down. Though initially his mood had vastly improved, now it seemed as though the sadness had come back, layered with an emotion far more potent: anger.

A woman Andre barely recognized had collapsed on the front veranda of her villa. Dora had expressed her wish for the vibrancy of her youth so she could travel to see her grandchildren. He'd given her an elixir with a drop of Time, and on the spot, her cheeks had begun to glow with rosy color, her previously dulled eyes had shone, and an unmistakable spring had come into her step. Yet only a few days later, she appeared to have aged twenty years, far more shrunken and frail than the hardy middle-aged woman she'd been before taking the potion.

Andre's stomach clenched, bile rising in his throat. What had he done? All of Yia-Yia's warnings punched into his brain one after the other.

Supernatural forces of evil lurk in the shadows, waiting to prey upon our fears.

Magic is the devil's work.

You . . . fed this poison . . . to your sister?

No, Grandmother, I fed it to dozens and dozens of people, Andre thought, hysteria threatening to overtake him.

He'd believed himself a fool as he'd searched for the treasure. A dark laugh rose in his throat. He'd become so much worse than a fool. He'd turned into a monster delivering nightmares wrapped in the guise of hope. Wishes that killed dreams.

When another scream rent the air, Andre couldn't look. He had run to his horse to ride for the abbey to get help for Marco. Perhaps the priest would have some idea what to do about the . . . *curse*. He couldn't call it anything else. In his brash overconfidence, Andre had unleashed a scourge upon everyone he'd tried to help, including those he cared about most. But the priest had known no more than Andre did.

He had to find a way to stop it. Before it was too late.

When he'd found out Sara had gone all the way down to the beach alone, his temper had flared. He hadn't meant to raise his voice, but his sister was too brave by half. He'd scanned her for signs of injury, and although she'd appeared fine, he'd examined her arms and legs for his own peace of mind.

Andre reined in Ella, jumped down onto the beach, and ran. Perhaps there was finally someone he could help. When he reached the water's edge, he stumbled to a stop, his boots slipping; his breath was sucked from his lungs.

The girl, who appeared near his own age, slept with one arm behind her head, hair the color of night cascading around her shoulders, its waves entangled in the sand. She had the face of a temptress—almost too alluring to look upon. Sara, whom he'd left at home with strict orders not to move a muscle until he returned, certainly had not said he would encounter the fallen goddess Aphrodite. He swallowed hard, barely remembering the reason he'd come. His eyes swept over her body for injuries, from her delicate feet to the gentle curve of her hips to her tiny waist and full bosom.

He dropped to his knees. "Miss?"

When she didn't respond, he spoke louder. "Miss, my name is Andre Baros. I'm here to help you."

Her eyes fluttered open, and Andre fell back on his heels. Eyes the color of violets in sunshine glinted up at him. Struck speechless, he opened his mouth and closed it again, terrified his first words to the enchanting creature would be gibberish.

Brow wrinkling, she sat up and wiped sand from her cheek. "Where am I?"

Her voice, soft and rich, held a mix of accents he couldn't quite place. He cleared his throat. "This is Marini Beach. You're just outside the hamlet of Agios Limani." When that didn't seem to register a memory, Andre said, "My little sister, Sara, found you here. She said you were injured and could not walk."

The woman met his gaze and blinked several times before her red lips curved into a smile of appreciation. When she continued to stare, Andre, uncomfortable, raked back the dark hair blowing into his eyes and looked out to sea. "Did you arrive by boat?"

"I . . . believe . . . so. That makes sense, doesn't it?"

CHAPTER 6

She shook her head and then covered her face with her hands. "My head aches terribly."

"Can you tell me your name?"

Andre held his breath as he waited for her to lower her hands. As if his destiny might hinge on her answer. As if knowing her true name might reveal all her secrets.

"I'm sorry. I can't remember." Her voice broke on the last word, and her fingers braced either side of her forehead, her eyes widening with growing panic.

Clearly, the woman had sustained a severe contusion to the head, which would explain her memory loss.

In times of crisis, a familiar calm overtook him, almost as if he were on the outside of the situation, looking in. Clinical in his assessment of the steps he would need to take, he settled into that confidence and asked, "Miss, may I examine your head for injury?"

"Are you a doctor?" The woman's brow crinkled, but she nodded her consent.

"Not exactly. But I'm the closest thing to a physician we have around here." The nearest doctor was a day's ride away. If the woman was badly injured, better for Andre to treat her before making the long journey up the coast.

Andre leaned over and pushed his fingers into the

mass of her hair, following the line of her skull. When he didn't find any bumps or swelling, he asked her to sit up and then checked the back of her head. He felt a perfectly shaped skull and hair like thick silk thread.

Andre sat back on his haunches, puzzled. "That's odd. Memory loss is typically caused by a blow to the head. But I didn't feel any abnormalities."

The woman pointed to a spot near the crown of her head. "It mostly hurts right here."

Andre knew he'd already examined the spot but reached out and double-checked anyway. Sure enough, a bump the size of a small egg pushed up her skin. He had no idea how he could've missed such an obvious lump. He shook his head and rose to his feet. There was only one thing to do.

"Miss, I need to get you somewhere warm and dry so I can better treat your injuries." He reached out a hand. "Can you stand?"

"I believe so."

The woman put her hand in his, and Andre tugged her up gently. Rising unsteadily, she wobbled and crashed into his chest. The full contact of her soft body against his fissured his composure, and when she wrapped her arms around his back, her face pressed against his bare neck, goose bumps prickled across his skin. "I guess that answers that question," he said, his voice coming out in a low rumble.

Andre swallowed, took her by the shoulders, and set her a few inches away from him. "Let's try it this way." He looped his arm around her waist and tucked her arm around his. "Hold on. We'll go slow."

Her delicate jaw set hard and she offered a nod of agreement.

They didn't get far. Like a newborn foal, she lifted her feet too high with every step, which caused her to lose her balance. Andre tried not to put too much thought into why she walked as if she'd forgotten how. He'd seen it happen in older patients who sometimes lost their ability to speak and eat as well. In those cases, they had to relearn basic life skills because of an attack on their brain. Andre stopped. "Try shuffling your feet. Like this." He pushed his boots through the sand without lifting his legs.

After she tried it and they'd made a bit of progress, she gazed up into his eyes, a laugh tumbling from her throat. "It works!"

He gave her an appreciative grin. With the events of the past few days, it felt like ten years since he'd seen someone smile at him. "Just a few hundred more shuffles to go."

When they reached Ella, it took quite a bit of cajoling to convince the woman to ride the "four-legged beast," as she called Andre's beloved horse. But once he showed her how gentle the animal was, she reluctantly allowed him to lift her up, and she settled sideways on the saddle. After Andre swung up behind her and urged Ella into a slow canter, the young woman nestled her head back against his chest. Heat simmered in his blood, and he was glad she couldn't see the blush staining his neck.

When they arrived at the cottage, he helped the woman off the horse and half carried her into the house. He steered her into the front sitting room, where a fire burned behind the grate and afternoon light danced through the windows. Carefully, he lowered her into a chair near the hearth.

She sat with a stiff posture—hands gripping the arms of the chair, back straight, legs canted at an uncomfortable-looking angle—as if overcompensating for something.

"Are you certain you aren't hurting anywhere besides your head?" Andre asked as his eyes moved over her in clinical assessment.

"I am . . . fine." She swallowed, her delicate throat bobbing. "Water? Could I have some water?"

CHAPTER 6

"Of course." Andre rushed into the kitchen, grabbed a full pitcher, and poured a glass. On his way back to the sitting room, a loud crash sounded from the foyer.

He approached to find his grandmother stooped in the doorway, picking up bits of a broken vase. "Yia-Yia, what happened? Did you fall?" He squatted beside her. "I'll take care of this."

"No, I didn't fall, daft child," she snapped in a low voice. "Who is that . . . *woman*?"

"Water?" the woman croaked from her perch beside the hearth. Andre sprang up and took the glass to their castaway, who threw the liquid down her throat like a pirate on shore leave. Her pink tongue darted out to lick her lips as she lifted the glass. "More?"

"Certainly." Andre took the cup and spun on his heel. As he headed back to the kitchen, Yia-Yia caught up to him and tugged him by the sleeve. "Where did you find that . . . creature?"

"Creature?" Andre rounded on his grandmother. "That poor *woman* washed up on the beach. We believe from a shipwreck, but she has lost her memories of what happened and who she is."

"Of course she has." Yia-Yia rolled her eyes as she shuffled toward the stove, muttering under her breath, "Sirens are witches of the sea who enchant all who hear their call. Beware, all ye who draw near."

Andre poured another tumbler of water and then picked up the wavy blue glass pitcher, the one his mother had made in the village under the tutelage of Mr. Disalvo, the glassblower. He stilled. Had old Mr. Disalvo taken any of the cursed potions? Terror set his limbs trembling. He had spent every waking hour trying to find them all and doing what he could. Yet with every moment that passed he seemed to remember another townsperson who had needed a bit of hope or happiness whom he'd forgotten to check on.

Andre shook himself out of his stupor. Mr. Disalvo had passed on the previous winter. A woman in need of his help waited in the next room. Who knew how long she had gone without food or water? She could've been lost at sea for days. And there his grandmother was, condemning her as something wicked.

"Yia-Yia, stay away from her," Andre warned. "You are not in your right mind presently."

A dish towel whacked the side of Andre's face. "I'll show you who's in their right mind, you arrogant little fool!"

"Nevertheless, I'll take care of it," Andre snapped, and leaned down to meet his grandmother's eyes, which always reminded him of his father's. He offered her a conciliatory smile. "If you could prepare some food for her, I would greatly appreciate it. I don't know when she ate last, and your blueberry oatcakes are the best anywhere."

Her eyes softening, she lifted a rough hand to his cheek where she'd smacked it with the cloth. "You have a good heart, Andre. Just don't let it betray your good sense. Again."

Again.

The word rang in his head as he made his way back to the sitting room. He'd done so much harm. He clutched the glass and pitcher so hard that liquid splashed onto his boots. Perhaps helping the lost woman could redeem a fraction of his mistakes.

Sara's voice reached him as he strode down the corridor. "So you think your name begins with the letter V, like *vegetable*?"

"Let's hope it isn't that." The young castaway's voice held so much disgust that Sara giggled.

When Andre entered the room, he covered his visceral pull toward their charming houseguest by pasting on a jaunty grin and bowing at the waist as he handed her the fresh glass of water. "As you requested."

She took the cup and downed it in one long gulp,

oblivious to his gallant pose. Straightening, he set the pitcher on the table beside her. "Help yourself to as much as you like."

Her gaze flicked to the sweating pitcher. With her mouth parted, her tongue darted out to moisten her lips as she grasped the jug with shaking hands and lifted it directly to her mouth to drink.

Andre arched his brows at Sara, who guffawed behind her hand. He really couldn't judge, considering he didn't know what the woman had gone through before they found her. To throw all convention and manners aside took guts. Even in their small sitting room.

After draining the pitcher, the woman replaced the empty vessel on the table and smiled serenely. "That is much better. Thank you, Andre."

The sound of his name on her lips sent heat flaring up Andre's neck. Unaccustomed to the odd feeling, he raked the fall of hair off his forehead and shoved his other hand into his trouser pocket. "You're . . . quite welcome."

Sara cleared her throat in a not-so-subtle attempt to save him from making a further fool of himself. "You were saying that your name could begin with a *V*?"

The woman nodded. "It sounds familiar."

Sara sat a little straighter and took a notebook and

pencil from her pocket. "How about Victoria?" As she waited for a response, she scribbled down the name.

Andre sat in the overstuffed sofa facing them both and got in on the game. "Perhaps Veronica?"

The young woman twirled a strand of midnight hair in her fingers as she thought about both possibilities. After a moment, she shook her head. "No, not quite right."

Andre leaned in, elbows on his knees. "Venus?"

"That sappy goddess of love?" She grimaced in revulsion. "No, thank you."

Sara wrote furiously. "No goddesses of love. Got it."

Andre caught the young woman's gaze, the color of her eyes like a field of blooming lilacs. "Violet?"

"A bit obvious, Brother," Sara quipped even as she wrote down the name.

Their houseguest shook her head and leaned back into the cushioned chair. "No, let me think." She closed her eyes and rolled sounds around on her tongue. "Vi . . . Ve . . . Vu . . . Vo . . . Va . . . Va . . . Yes, that's it. My name starts with Va . . ."

Without hesitation, Sara guessed, "Varda! It means 'rose.' And you are as lovely as a rose."

A slow smile turned up the young woman's lips, and she cocked her head to the side. "How sweet of you to say so. But I don't believe that is correct. Perhaps if I get some rest, my memory will return."

Sara's thin shoulders drooped. His sister was like a dog with a bone. Once she set her mind on something, especially if it involved helping others, she refused to let go. Loath to see the disappointment on her sweet face, Andre thought back to customers over the years, merchants he had met, seamen he'd traded with. He had met plenty of women and girls with names that began with the letter V. But suddenly the image of a ship came to mind—one he'd seen at port now and then—and he knew he had it right. His gaze flicked to their guest, and he found her watching him with singular focus.

The name pushed from him in a rush. "Vanessa."

Her lips quirked to the side as her eyes sparkled. "That's it."

"Vanessa!" Sara cheered, throwing her hands into the air in victory. "How did you guess, Andre?"

His gaze still locked with Vanessa's, he shrugged one shoulder. "I just knew."

***

"This room used to belong to your parents?" Vanessa sat on the edge of the bed with her arm looped around one of the posts. Soft sun filtered through windows draped with buttercup cotton. In the front corner of the room, bookcases framed an empty fireplace and an overstuffed armchair and ottoman. Andre turned away. He couldn't look at the cozy nook without seeing his mother curled up in the chair, reading.

"Yes," Andre responded as he noted that Vanessa's legs were still uncoordinated and weak. But it heartened the medical side of his brain to see that her mental faculties seemed sharp. Except for her memory. She still did not know where she'd come from or how she'd arrived on Marini Beach.

"Sorry about the dust," Andre said. "No one sleeps in here. Yia-Yia's room is on the first floor, off the kitchen, and Sara and I have rooms down the hall."

Vanessa pulled her feet up and crossed them under her skirt. The movement stirred dust from the comforter, and she sneezed with a soft squeal. Eyes as round as plums, she blinked and then sneezed again. And again.

Andre pulled a clean handkerchief from his pocket and handed it to her.

Motes floated in front of Vanessa's face, catching the sun. She snuffled, her adorable nose twitching as she swatted the particles. "What is this?"

Either she'd lived in a pristine palace with a housemaid for every room, or her memory was worse off than he'd realized. "I believe we've discovered that you have a sensitivity to dust."

Her eyes watering, Vanessa swiped the liquid from her face and stared at the drop on her finger.

"It's a rather common irritant. I have raw honey and clove tea that will help soothe it."

"And I'll clean the room!" Sara announced. She'd somehow lugged a bucket, a mop, rags, and cleaning tonic, all gathered in one hand, up the stairs, using her crutch to propel her forward with the other hand. It seemed Vanessa's unexpected arrival had galvanized her spirits, if not her body. "You can rest on my bed until I'm finished."

Concern made Andre's voice sharp as he said, "Sara, I will take care of it."

His sister propped a small fist on her hip. "I found her, and I get to take care of her!"

Andre bit his lip but couldn't hold back a chuckle. "She isn't a pet, imp."

"But she needs our help. She's lost and alone and doesn't know anything!" Sara whacked the mop against the hardwood floor to punctuate her statement.

CHAPTER 6

And then Andre realized that she needed this. Her own health and life felt out of control; helping Vanessa was one thing she could manage.

"I don't wish to be any trouble." Vanessa scooted off the edge of the bed. "If you could take me to the local authorities, perhaps they can help me figure out what happened."

She rose to her feet, swayed, then took a step and tipped forward. Andre lunged and caught her just before she hit the floor. He scooped her into his arms. "I don't think you're going anywhere for a bit."

Vanessa looped her arms around his neck and snuggled against his chest.

Andre's heart gave a blip at the subtle curving of her lips as she gazed up at him with a small smile.

"Take her to my room, Andre. So I can clean," Sara called in a singsong voice.

Andre walked into the corridor, moving slowly, not yet ready to release the woman in his arms.

"You are very strong," Vanessa said, running a hand over his shoulder and down his flexed biceps.

"You are very light," he retorted. He stopped at an open doorway and shifted so she could see inside. "This is my room."

"It's so . . . small." She readjusted her hands around his neck, her fingers dipping into the back of his collar.

Chills raced down his spine, causing him to shiver slightly, an involuntary response he hoped she didn't notice. Was she doing that on purpose?

"Why don't you stay in your parents' old room?" she asked.

Andre assessed his room as an outsider might—a single bed with an iron headboard, a dark wooden dresser that also functioned as a washstand, a wardrobe he'd left hanging open with clothing strewn across the floor, and a nightstand piled with books. None of the furniture matched; the coverlet's pale green-and-blue patchwork was frayed at the edges. His parents' room was three times the size. When they'd passed, he often visited their room, sat in his mother's chair, lay on his father's side of the bed. And sometimes talked to them.

It had felt wrong to move his things in as if they'd never been.

But he simply said, "I like my own room. It faces the cove."

"But you are the man of the house, are you not?" Her voice soft and low, she gazed at him from beneath her lashes. Heat blazed across his skin like wildfire, and his stare flickered to her plush lips.

A bang sounded from the other room, followed by Sara's voice: "I'm fine!"

Andre blinked as if waking from a dream. He strode into Sara's room and lowered Vanessa onto the flowery quilt quickly, ungracefully, as though he'd been scalded by her touch. He stepped back and offered a quick bow. "I'll let you get your rest."

Andre berated himself as he exited the room. What kind of man entertained a flirtation with a vulnerable young woman with no memory? He had been acting like a lovestruck lecher. Shame flared through his chest.

No more. From that point forward, he'd do a better job of keeping himself contained. He had much weightier issues at hand. Like a potion that reversed every wish into a curse.

He could not allow it to stand. Finding a cure for the afflicted took precedence over a damsel in distress, no matter how enchanting.

CHAPTER 7

VANESSA

RAINBOW FANS of coral waved through her consciousness, anemones rippling and blooming in her dreams. Shoals of jewel-colored fish clustered and darted between light and shadow. A pair of moray eels oozed out of their hole, maws gaping. The predator, as weightless as the stars above the sea, glided among the bourgeoning burst of life. She belonged there among the singularly beautiful creatures.

A colorful little mantis shrimp scurried out of its den,

its alien eyes goggling as Ursula swam above. She reached out a finger to brush the feisty crustacean's antennae as its scarlet hammer arms slashed forward to smack and defend. She jerked her hand back just in time and spun in a circle, tentacles swirling, her laugh bubbling to the surface. Shellfish were extraordinarily delicious, but she would not consume one so unique and essential to the health of her reef—the housing of her hideaway.

She dove and pushed toward the doorway of her cavern. But she couldn't move. Her limbs tangled. Frozen, she began to sink. Her arms flailed. She fell, a spike of stony coral rising fast. Her heart hammered as she dropped. Mud and murk surged up to enclose her in darkness.

Suffocating, she jerked against the heavy mantle restraining her arms and legs. She thrashed against her captor—and then stilled as the clutches of the dream drew back and reality returned.

Her pulse pumped a primitive staccato and she cracked open an eye. White eyelet fabric above, the dastardly confinement wrapped around her was a blanket quilted with yellow flowers. Her muscles relaxed. It had all been a dream—a happy memory of home that had become a nightmare.

Blinking through motes of sparkling dust, like plankton

floating in the air, Vanessa realigned her thoughts, combing through for anything useful she'd gleaned from Andre and Sara the day before. It hadn't been much; they'd been too concerned with her health and comfort. Her thoughts went to Andre. She considered the delightful tingles that coursed over her skin when they touched, how a mere look from those jewel-toned eyes set fire to her veins. The combination of attraction and desire created a strange alchemy, an energy she wished to explore further. And perhaps use to her advantage to find the real power at hand, which had exerted an even stronger pull on her senses since she had left the beach in Andre's care. A particularly tragic aura seemed to surround the occupants of the household, a foreboding darkness that drew her in like a vortex. The call of something sinister tugged at her consciousness, just out of her reach.

A soft knock sounded, and someone called, "Vanessa? It's me, Sara. I have some tea for you."

"You may enter." Vanessa pulled herself to a seated position, the thin sleeping gown she'd borrowed cutting into her throat. A surprisingly strong fabric for something so soft, she observed as she tugged it away from her neck.

The little girl opened the door, a crutch in one hand and a steaming mug in the other. "Good morning."

CHAPTER 7

"Good morning," Vanessa replied as she took the mug and lifted it to her lips. Her entire body felt as dry as a beached starfish as she gulped down the hot liquid.

"Are you used to drinking hot tea?" the girl asked. Her wide blue gaze held a hint of calculation, as if Vanessa's answer would fit another piece into the puzzle of her missing background. Vanessa blew ripples across the tan liquid, the lie slipping easily from her lips: "The taste is familiar."

"I see." Sara smiled. "How did you sleep?"

Vanessa furrowed her brow. "Actually, I had nightmares," she confessed.

The girl tugged a chair closer to the bed with a screech across hardwood. She perched on the cushion. "What about?"

"All I remember is water everywhere. And sinking through darkness." She didn't have to fake the shudder that followed.

"That could be a memory from your accident," Sara said, raising a pale brow. "Did you see anyone else?"

Vanessa shook her head.

"What about parts of a ship or signs of a storm?"

Vanessa took another sip of her drink. It was bitter, with a hint of sweetness. "Perhaps. But I honestly don't remember."

Sara pulled a tiny notebook from her pocket and began to write. Such a weak child must find solace in journaling her feelings, Vanessa thought. The pencil scratched across paper, and Vanessa watched as the tendons in the girl's arm stood out against her pale skin, reminding Vanessa of a human fairy tale she'd read long before. Something about a destitute brother and sister who sought shelter in a house made of candy. The old woman who lived there fed the children until they were nice and plump so she could eat them. The tale labeled the woman a wicked witch, but Vanessa didn't see it that way. The delicate cycle of the natural world required the strong to prey on the weak for the survival of all. Everyone had to eat.

Sara's blond brows furrowed as she tapped her pencil against her round chin. The child had physical challenges and a soft heart, but her mind certainly did not seem frail. "What are you writing there?" Vanessa asked.

Sara paused but didn't look up. "Bits of information. I write down everything. It annoys Andre to no end."

Vanessa paused. There had to be something about the curse in that tiny book. But when she opened her mouth to ask, a call from the other side of the door interrupted.

"Sara?" It was Andre. "I have the tub."

Sara limped over and flung open the door. Andre's tall

form filled the entrance. He carried an enormous container the color of old metal coins. As he strode into the room, he nodded. "Good morning, Vanessa."

The deep, melodic quality of his voice caused Vanessa to sit up a bit straighter. He lowered the empty vessel to the floor in front of the fireplace, muscled thighs straining against the fabric of his trousers.

Vanessa swallowed and lifted her hands to smooth her hair as she addressed him in an unfamiliar girlish tone. "Good morning, Andre."

When he faced her, a half smile tugged a dimple into his left cheek. With those remarkable sea-glass eyes focused on her, Vanessa squirmed. The coverlet trapped too much heat against her body, and she threw it back, nightgown pushed up to her thighs. She watched Andre's face transform as he dropped the smile and stared. Vanessa felt a jolt of satisfaction even as she kept her features impassive, as though she had no idea what the sight of her was doing to Andre.

Vanessa allowed him to get his fill of her exposed legs before she curled them beneath the loose gown and lowered her lashes with a modest smile. "I'm sorry. It's very warm."

Andre cleared his throat. "Yes, well . . . I thought you

might like to freshen up." He gestured toward the tub. "I'll go get the water."

"I'll fetch you some of my soap," Sara piped up, following Andre out despite his protests that she stay put.

Vanessa remembered baths from her research. Under the sea, they used sponges and sweet-smelling algae to scrub themselves clean, but the human way of submerging in a deep tub of water sounded heavenly.

After Andre had hefted pot after pot of water up the stairs and into the tub, he laid a white cloth on the end of the bed and asked, "Would you like a fire started for your bath or are you still . . . warm?"

A smile played around his full lips. Moisture from his exertions slicked his face, causing his sun-darkened skin to glow. Andre Baros was unlike any merman she had ever encountered. Of course some of the men of Atlantica were handsome, kind, intelligent, or funny. She'd even had feelings for a few of them, but this human boy burned like sunbeams cutting through the sea. He moved with vigor and intention that never seemed to waver, as if he always had a plan.

An unexpected urge to unravel those plans filled Vanessa with fluttery anticipation. Like a lionfish ready to strike, she straightened her legs and focused on her handsome host as she cooed, "I'm still very warm, and I'm afraid I cannot walk on my own. Will you help me into the bath?"

Little Sara burst into the room, breaking their eye contact. She hobbled forward, oblivious to the darkening of her brother's cheeks and his stillness. "I brought two fresh bars of olive oil soap. Which would you prefer: lavender and vanilla or lemon blossom?"

Vanessa took them and lifted each to her nose in turn. The lemon smelled bright and airy, while the lavender and vanilla had depth and mystery. "I think the lavender. Don't you, Andre?"

"Either is fine." His voice sounded blasé, his eyes averted from her face as he moved a straight-backed chair close to the tub. He returned to her bedside and held out a hand. "I can assist you to the chair, Miss Vanessa."

Vanessa bristled at his formal tone but took his hand and stood. It was much easier this time. She didn't sway until she took her first step. Andre reached for her as she stumbled against the bedstead.

"I can do it," she insisted, and waved him off. Perhaps if she didn't move like a crab with missing legs, he would look at her with more interest.

"All right." He took a step back, skepticism clear on his face.

Vanessa gripped the bedpost. After a moment, she released the post and shuffled forward, barely lifting her feet, as Andre had shown her on the beach. The carpet rubbed hard against her soles, but she made it to the chair and plopped down. "I did it!"

Andre gave her a quick nod before turning to his sister. "Sara, I'll be just down the hall." Then he walked out and snapped the door shut behind him.

That certainly wasn't the reaction she had expected to her overtures. What had she done wrong? She started to ask Sara, but Sara had curled in the corner chair like a puppet with broken strings. The curious girl of the morning faded as weariness tugged her eyes closed.

Anxious to be submerged, Vanessa stripped off her gown and lowered her body into the steaming water. She rested her head on the wide lip of the tub and sighed deep. Her body was buoyant once more, her senses sharpened, serenity centering her thoughts as she analyzed Andre's earlier rebuff. He was fascinated by her; that much was clear. But perhaps she had come on too strong. Her decorum teacher, an ancient mermaid, had reprimanded her once for inviting a boy to escort her to a musical. Vanessa picked up the bar of smooth soap and ran it over her shoulder and down her arm. What was it that old eel had said? *Males like to take the lead. Allow them to make the first move and they will feel empowered.*

Allow Andre Baros to take the lead? If appearing to relinquish control won her more of that particular boy's attention, and by extension his trust, then she would play the part. She sank under the surface of the water and opened her eyes. As part of Triton's court, she'd become a phenomenal actress, hiding her true nature behind a persona of lovely lies and pleasant conversation. A little manipulation to achieve her desired outcome was practically second nature.

Vanessa took a deep breath and sank fully beneath the hot water, letting it envelop and soothe her. Eventually bubbles fluttered to the surface, and when her human lungs could take no more, she emerged into cool air. Andre was the key to unraveling the mystery of the dark magic surrounding the family. She could feel it. Vanessa grinned wide. Once she unlocked his heart, he would tell her everything she wished to know.

CHAPTER 8

ANDRE

ANDRE BREATHED deep, surrounded by fragrant bundles of dried herbs, labeled jars containing essential oils, crocks of loose-leaf teas, and rainbow glass bottles. His father had built the apothecary behind the house with his own hands. The structure consisted of a workroom with a long wooden table for mixing and bottling, floor-to-ceiling shelves, a deep hearth outfitted with a custom iron hanging rack for multiple pots, and an attached greenhouse for growing herbs and flowers.

CHAPTER 8

Quality and purity of ingredients had been important to his father. Honesty and integrity—never overpromising the efficacy of their treatments—his life's guiding lights.

What would his father say if he could see how badly Andre had messed it all up?

He'd been trying all day to come up with a fix for the curse, but to no avail. His mind was blank of ideas, same as the day before, same as the day before that. Andre grasped a vial of lemon-herb oil and, with a ragged growl, crushed the flask in his hand, barely feeling the pain of broken glass puncturing his skin. He had to find a way to reverse the dark magic. He'd tried destroying the potions by throwing the metal box off Zakyntho Cliff—the highest point for miles around. He'd watched the box fall, glass flying in sparks of silver blue as the vials exploded on the rocks. But when he'd returned to the village square, nothing had changed. It had made no difference to those affected by its malicious sorcery.

A knock on the door made Andre jump. He tossed what was left of the vial into the ashes of the fireplace, the pungent scent of thyme coating his tongue as he picked pieces of glass from his palm. The knock sounded again, more insistent.

"Hello? Andre?" a man called. "Your grandmother told me I'd find you here."

Certain another villager had come to demand he heal a cursed relative, Andre flung open the door and snapped, "What do you want?"

A man stood in the doorway in a pristine three-piece suit and top hat. Straight brown hair like strings of spaghetti brushed his shoulders, and a frown hardened the sharp angles of his thin face. Trepidation boiled in Andre's gut. Governor Zika ruled the coast with an iron fist, demanding an exorbitant 50 percent tax from every merchant within the vicinity, including Andre and his Wagon of Wonders. No one dared deny the governor his tax—even while his own mansion and grounds seemed to grow more elaborate by the year and his people grew poorer and more destitute. And for good reason. Andre had once witnessed Zika incarcerating the ten-year-old son of a restaurant owner when the owner was unable to pay funds "due" to the government. A remnant from the French occupation, Zika's control far exceeded the people's power to oust him from his role.

"Governor Zika!" Andre swung the door wide, then, thinking better of inviting the man into his inner sanctum, stepped out and shut the door behind him. "What can I do for you, sir? I believe my taxes are all paid up. Not much income to show for in these last few days."

"Well, Andre, that's just it. I've been hearing rumors that your potions have caused a bit of trouble." The governor flicked an imaginary speck of dirt off his lapel and assumed a tone of concern that rang false to Andre. "I'd like to help."

Andre studied the governor's sharp features and met his hawkish stare. Long before, Andre's father had warned him of Governor Zika's vindictive nature and advised him to give the man a wide berth, or he might offer to buy out their little business at a price too high to refuse—a command rather than a choice.

But desperation didn't allow Andre the luxury of caution at the moment. "Yes, sir. If you'll follow me to the house, you'll be more comfortable."

Andre led the way around the stucco cottage, his mind spinning furiously. How much should he tell the man? He couldn't possibly share the whole truth. And why was he showing up now? It had been days since the potions had gone horribly wrong.

"You have a lovely property here on the cove," Zika commented as they rounded the front of the house.

Was there a hint of desire in the man's tone, or

had Andre imagined it? Surely Zika didn't need to acquire additional property when he owned most of Agios Limani and the surrounding hamlets.

"Thank you. My father designed and built it himself." Andre paused at their freshly painted red front door. It was a tradition Yia-Yia insisted on each year, claiming it kept evil spirits from entering without invitation. Lately it seemed she repainted the blasted thing not annually but every other month.

Andre was fairly certain Zika qualified as an evil presence. But he needed to stay on the man's good side, so he opened the door. "After you, Governor. The sitting room is to the left."

"Thank you, young man. It is a rather hot day already." Governor Zika bowed his head to Andre as he stepped through the door. "I'm not here to condemn you, Andre. But I do need some answers in order to help."

"Thank you, sir. I would welcome the assistance. I'll explain what I can." He started in the other direction from the sitting room. "Make yourself comfortable while I find some refreshments."

Andre rushed toward the kitchen. In truth, refreshments were not his main concern; he had to find Yia-Yia and keep his grandmother's superstitious rantings of black magic in check, not wanting to make an already tenuous situation worse by having the governor thinking he'd put a hex on his village.

He found a pitcher of fresh lemon water on the counter; there was the sweet nutty fragrance of pignoli cookies cooling on the stove. But Yia-Yia was nowhere to be found. Andre searched the pantry and the washroom before walking down the short hallway to his grandmother's bedroom.

"Yia-Yia?" Worry tightened his throat. The woman only stopped moving when she slept. She cooked, cleaned, made meal plans, tended the flowers, homeschooled Sara. She never rested during the day, claiming something about the devil finding work for idle hands.

Despite their vast differences in thought on the powers of magic and its abilities, he didn't know what he would do without her. And not just because she took care of the house. Yia-Yia was their only link to their parents, the only family he and Sara had left.

Her bedroom door stood ajar. Andre knocked and called her name again as he pushed inside. His grandmother knelt on the hardwood floor, her hands folded on a chair, a weathered Bible at her elbow. Whispered prayer reached his ears and touched his soul with its desperation.

He walked over and placed a hand gently on her shoulder. "Yia-Yia."

She finished with a fervent "amen" and then lifted her head, eyes damp.

"Grandmother, let me help you up." Andre lifted her easily. So much strength in such a frail package. Just like Sara.

She sank in the chair and stared up at Andre. "We are surrounded by trouble on all sides. We need protection, my boy." She wrapped her arms around her waist. "I know that Zika man is here. I saw him come up the walk. Something is wrong with him, Andre." She began to shiver. "It's so cold. I'm so cold."

Andre placed a palm to her forehead, checking for fever, but her skin felt cool. "Let's get you to bed. I will take care of the governor." He tried not to worry as he tucked his grandmother under the coverlet. Surely she just needed a bit of rest.

"What of the girl?" Her eyes drifted closed and then fluttered open again. "She's not what she seems. . . ."

He placed his palm on her wrinkled cheek. "Just rest, Yia-Yia. We're safe. I promise."

As soon as her eyes closed, Andre retreated to the kitchen, where he poured lemon water into cups and dumped cookies onto a platter. He had a strong suspicion his guest wasn't accustomed to waiting. Perhaps plying him with Yia-Yia's famous pignoli cookies would help.

Offering in hand, he approached the sitting room to the sound of conversation. Sara sat in a chair opposite Governor Zika, who appeared captivated by her sunflower smile and animated chatter.

Following his sister's lead, Andre pasted on a pleasant expression and said, "I apologize for the delay. The cookies were just about finished baking, but it's worth the wait, sir, I assure you—my Yia-Yia's specialty."

"What a gracious host." The governor took a sip of lemon water and smiled. "If I had known the Baroses were such charming company, I would have visited sooner."

Andre perched on the edge of the sofa, bit into a cookie, and waited—a sales strategy he'd learned well over the years. If you had a difficult customer, you made them feel welcome and then shut up. The silence and space to think prompted them to speak more honestly.

"These cookies are quite delicious. Do you grow these pine nuts on the property?" the governor asked.

"Yes, we have several pine trees, and Yia-Yia dries and hulls the seeds herself," Sara explained.

"So your grandmother lives here? Anyone else besides

the beguiling Sara?" Governor Zika threw Sara a friendly wink.

Andre straightened his spine. "Just the three of us since my parents passed."

"I see." The man rubbed his fingers over his mouth and then tapped his stubbled chin. "Okay, Andre. Tell me what happened to cause the horrific reactions to your tonics."

"A bad batch, I suppose." The lie churned in Andre's gut. *A bad batch indeed.* But most believed that magic existed only in stories, and Andre knew if he told the whole unvarnished truth, the governor would have him locked up for lunacy and he'd never get the chance to reverse the nightmare he'd created.

Governor Zika set down his water glass. "From what I understand, a wave of miraculous healings preceded the . . . extreme decline of your patrons. How do you explain that?"

Andre crossed his legs and then uncrossed them, setting his feet firmly on the floor. "I . . . well—"

"Andre bought a box of various oils from a woman in Aoannis," Sara cut in. "When he incorporated them into his tonics, they seemed to help at first, but as you said, sir, the shocking deterioration affected many." She touched her crutch, which rested against the chair. "Including me."

CHAPTER 8

Governor Zika leaned forward. "Are you saying you weren't crippled before you took these . . . potions?"

"I've been ill for a long time. That's why I volunteered to try the new tonic first." Sara swallowed. Her narrow throat bobbed, and Andre wanted to tear out his own hair as he watched her struggle to hold back tears. "I . . . felt wonderful for several days and then became weaker than I had been before. My muscles are shaky at best, and when I'm tired, I can barely walk."

"So you didn't have a degenerative muscle disease before you took the elixir?" There was no doubt of the accusatory tone Zika spoke with, his gaze trained on Andre even as he questioned Sara.

She shook her head and then lifted her chin. "No, sir. But it isn't Andre's fault. That old crone never should have told him about the trea—"

"Treatments." Andre talked over her. "The woman insisted her treatments had incredible results."

"I see." The governor linked his fingers in front of him. "Do you have the woman's name?"

"She claimed to be Fani Nasside," Andre replied. "She said she was visiting her son. But when I looked for her later, no one in Aoannis knew anyone named Nasside, and I—"

Andre cut himself off as Zika stiffened, his bushy brows meeting over his nose before he shot to his feet. Andre followed his gaze to Vanessa, who stood at the entrance to the sitting room. She was backlit by the sun, her damp hair braided over one shoulder and her bare toes peeking out beneath violet skirts.

"Good morning," Vanessa said with a soft smile, her gaze angled demurely to the floor.

Andre arched a brow. Although he'd known her less than twenty-four hours, *demure* was not a word he would use to describe the mysterious woman. Andre stood, walked to her, and offered his arm. "Please join us, Vanessa." He turned to the governor. "May I present our houseguest, Miss Vanessa." She placed a hand on his elbow, and that familiar sparkle returned to her eye as she nodded her thanks. When Andre led her into the sitting room, he noticed that she walked with small steps instead of shuffling. He gave her an encouraging nod. A return of her mobility was a good sign for her healing.

Zika's hawkish gaze followed as Vanessa made slow progress to the sofa, lowered herself to the cushion, and perched on the edge like a bird about to take flight. Her deep purple eyes met Andre's as he sat beside her, something in their depths tugging out an instinct to place a hand reassuringly on her back.

"It's nice to make your acquaintance, Miss Vanessa." The governor bent in a low bow, then returned to his seat across the room. "Are you a friend of the Baros family, or . . . ?" His words trailed off as he awaited Vanessa's answer.

Andre studied the man thoughtfully. Did he mean to come off as intimidating or was it merely habit?

Vanessa's spine straightened beneath Andre's fingers, the heat of her skin burning through layers of cloth as she said, "I am not."

Several beats of silence followed. Politeness dictated that Andre allow his guest to continue her explanation. When she didn't, he opened his mouth, but Sara beat him to it once again, saying, "She has no memory, Governor. I found her on Marini Beach yesterday."

"Is that so?" Governor Zika crossed his arms in front of his chest, skepticism written all over his stubble-covered face. "No memory at all, you say?"

Vanessa shook her head in reply and then winced, lifting a hand to her scalp.

Andre addressed the older man. "She sustained a rather brutal hit to her skull that resulted in a large hematoma.

Such trauma has been known to cause temporary mem-ory loss."

Zika nodded. "Then she should be treated by a real doctor." Disdain dripped from his voice. "There is a hospital in the city. I will arrange to have her taken by ship first thing tomorrow."

"That's up to Vanessa," Andre replied, crossing his own arms. Certainly this man was accustomed to getting his way, but in this case, his overbearing manner would not serve him well. Andre might not have been a doctor, exactly, but he knew how to treat a simple head injury.

"No, thank you," Vanessa replied. "I have no money to pay for medical care. I'm sure I'll remember something soon."

"The nuns at the abbey—"

Andre cut the governor off. "Are overwhelmed with victims of the . . . bad tonics." *Victims of the curse*, Andre mentally corrected himself. "Which brings me back to the point of why you are here, sir. You mentioned wishing to help. If I may suggest, the abbey is running out of resources quickly. If a man of your influence could make a donation and encourage others of means to do the same, it would go a long way in replenishing their food stock and medical supplies."

CHAPTER 8

Neatly backed into a corner, Governor Zika gave a terse nod but then practically snarled, "And what of the cause of this epidemic you started, Mr. Baros? Surely you don't expect me to believe your story about an old woman, whose existence cannot be confirmed, giving you tainted oils or some such."

Andre stiffened. "I cannot make you believe me, sir. But I'm doing everything I can to find the cause of this disaster, and I *will* find a cure for those affected."

"You'd better," Zika growled, and stood. "My profits are suffering while so many of the villagers tend to the *ill* or fall sick themselves. Fix it. Or perhaps I'll throw you into the bowels of Eterna with the monsters you created."

The only penitentiary in the district, the Eterna prison was rumored to have been carved into the cliffs of Pilos by the gods of Olympus themselves to contain the Titans who opposed their supremacy. A few of the especially violent victims of the tonics were being kept there for their own protection and the protection of others.

Andre's hand tightened into a fist, white-hot flames coursing through his veins. A small part of him recognized the irrationality of his fury, yet he welcomed the heat's cleansing fire, as it burned away the guilt that had been plaguing him day and night. His muscles tensed, and he leapt to his feet. "I'd like to see you try."

"Andre!" Sara barked, her tone part shocked, part angry as she limped over and stood between the two men. "Governor, please excuse my brother's rude behavior. This catastrophe has been extremely hard on him. Not to mention the damage it has done to our family business." She threw a glare at Andre over her shoulder and then turned back to Zika with a bright smile. "We appreciate any help you can give the victims, and please inform us of any information you may hear about a local shipwreck or a missing woman."

The man's face softened—a testament to Andre's little sister's powers of persuasion—and he knelt so he was eye level with Sara. "What of you, young Sara? How can I reverse your misfortune?"

Sara's face paled even as she set her slender shoulders. "Just help my brother find a cure, please."

Zika straightened up and adjusted his immaculate suit. When he spoke to Andre, his voice reverted to its normal, albeit irreverent, tone. "There is someone you could talk to. A savant who has spent his life studying the ancient philosophies and folklore."

Equal parts intrigued and skeptical, Andre gritted his

teeth before asking in a neutral tone, "Why would you think a philosopher could help me? I've combed through every related text at the library in Cyrgos and found nothing useful."

Governor Zika tilted his head and stared at Andre, his sea-blue eyes glinting. "Because, young sir, I suspect you have run into a bit of witchery, and this particular scholar is also the protector of the magical archives on Omis Island."

Before Andre could formulate a response to the disturbing bits of information in the governor's statement, Vanessa exclaimed, "Omis Island! No one has lived there in centuries!"

Three sets of eyes locked on the woman perched on the sofa with a cookie raised halfway to her open mouth.

"I mean . . . it's an island that cannot be found except by those who already know where it is hidden." Vanessa swallowed. "I don't know how I know that."

Andre blinked at the mesmerizing girl he'd invited into his household, who he knew absolutely nothing about, and dread eddied into a greasy mire in his gut. How did she have knowledge of a supernatural isle that most believed a myth?

He considered himself savvy to the ways of the world and a darn good judge of character, partly because he'd traded with merchants from far-off lands, outwitted pirates, and dodged brigands intent on indenturing him into their service. He'd evaded thieves and thugs up and down the coast and outfoxed bullies, some of whom he'd converted into loyal customers.

Andre had never believed himself naive. But in that moment, as he thought back over his recent misguided decisions—starting with Mrs. Nasside and her cursed treasure—he began to doubt himself. Was there more to Vanessa than met the eye? Was it too much of a coincidence that she'd washed up on their beach in the midst of the curse while the village people were being struck down and Sara was in a desperate state? Could she be a captivating con artist? An enchanting siren?

Was there truth to Yia-Yia's fears that they were surrounded by evil?

Andre blew out a breath and fingered the Saint Raphael medal at his throat. One problem at a time. He would have to deal with their castaway later.

He faced Zika. "What is this scholar's name, and how do I find him?"

CHAPTER 9

VANESSA

VANESSA HAD some damage control to do.

She'd seen the stark surprise cross Andre's face when she'd blurted out that no one had lived on Omis Island for centuries, and then his skepticism as she'd tried to backtrack and downplay her reaction. *Idiot.* Why hadn't she been more careful? To be fair, it wasn't her fault; she'd been preoccupied with those divine sugary pine nut pastries from Andre's crazy Yia-Yia, not to mention thrown off by Governor Zika, who had simmered with repressed magic.

To the man's credit, he hid the sorcery well. So well that Vanessa could not discern the level of his power. But a bigger question remained: had he recognized her magic . . . her *otherness*? How much he could detect from one meeting she couldn't say, but as two supernatural creatures passing themselves off as human, they both stood to lose if their secrets were exposed.

Vanessa would worry about Zika later. Right then something about Omis Island was niggling at the back of her mind. For years during Ursula's lonely childhood, she'd been obsessed with the Greek gods and their outrageous stories. She had studied the massive tomes in the royal library—one of the only rooms in Atlantica contained in a bubble of air, so as to keep the books dry. Ursula had spent hours devouring everything she could find about the ancient all-powerful beings most considered fiction. But even then she had known better—had felt it in her soul that they had walked the earth.

Vanessa paced across the creaky floors of her temporary bedroom, gaining confidence and becoming more sure-footed with every step. Normally when she faced a problem, she figured out a solution by swimming through the sea as quick as her tentacles would take her—which was faster than any mer ever hoped to fly. Now, as a land dweller cooped up in the tiny space, she felt like a fish in a net.

She threw open the drapes, raised the window, and leaned out into the fresh air. When she breathed deep, she could taste the salt on the breeze, and she heard the splash of the surf. Almost as good as the real thing. She forced herself to breathe deep and focus.

According to human myths, Omis Island was home to La Befana, the benevolent witch. Many believed that the night before the Feast of the Epiphany, Befana flew around on her broom, shot down chimneys, and delivered gifts to good little children. At each house she used her broom to sweep up the ashes after her before flying back up the flue and heading to the next house. In the folktales Vanessa had read, Befana began using her magic to grant gifts to children because she'd lost her only son and wished to find a way to honor his memory.

But Vanessa knew the truth: Omis Island had birthed one of the greatest enchantresses the world had ever known—Circe the witch-goddess. When Odysseus, envious of her great magic, went after her, she turned his men into pigs and then seduced him away from his wife,

Penelope. After Circe bore him several children, Odysseus grew bored and decided to return to his wife. Circe agreed to help him on his way home and instead sent him to the Underworld. Then, in her grief, Circe used her magic potions to bring her late lover back to life.

The old stories portrayed a magic so powerful and undiluted that it saturated the land of Omis Island, and that even centuries after the gods and goddesses had vanished, any creature who set foot on its soil became forever entwined in the enchanted fabric. Ships crashed into its rocky shores even on blue-skied days. Thus, the legend of La Befana had been created to keep curious mortals away from the deadly island. Parents told their children if anyone found Befana's true home, they would receive no more candy or toys for the rest of their lives and their children's lives. In actuality, Circe was the real threat. Vanessa wasn't scared of anything, but unnecessarily drawing the ire of the gods gave pause even to her.

A few years back, when a young merman disappeared in that area, a team was sent to investigate. They had never returned, leading many to suppose not all the gods of ancient myth had vanished into antiquity. But Vanessa didn't believe for a moment that the gods were alive, because if they were, surely they would still be ruling earth to that day.

So how did their power still protect Omis Island, keep it from being found? Unless it was like the wards around Atlantica that shielded the mer-world from unwanted visitors. The magic used to protect their underwater city was embedded in the fabric of Atlantica itself and linked to the king's conduit. As long as the original spell lay undisturbed beneath the city and Triton's fork remained uncompromised, the spell would hold for eternity.

So perhaps a magical relic left by the ancient gods remained on Omis and served as a protection against intruders.

She straightened and turned from the window, staring into nothing as she searched her memory for a clue. Something she'd read eluded her—something important about the witch-goddess and her ensorcelled island. Vanessa's recollection failing her, she turned to the information she'd learned.

If the so-called scholar Zika had referenced really did exist and the curse Andre believed he'd unleashed was real as well, perhaps they could both find what they needed on Omis. A shudder traced down her spine at the thought of facing such ancient magic. But Vanessa had never considered herself a cuttlefish, hiding from danger, and this payoff could be worth the risk.

She slipped on a pair of black shoes from the wardrobe, using a quick spell so they expanded to fit her feet, and then stood and checked her appearance in the mirror above the dresser. Hair like midnight seas waving around her shoulders, honey-smooth skin, wide twilight eyes. She arched a winged brow and pursed her full pink lips. With a flash of the shell at her throat, her unruly curls wove into a set of narrow braids that joined at the back of her head, leaving loose ringlets to tumble down her back. She smiled wide, exposing rows of white teeth.

Divine.

First orders of business: dissuade Andre of any skepticism that might have popped up thanks to her display and find out more about that wicked little curse that had him so torn up. Then persuade him that the only way to stop it resided on Omis Island, and that they would need to go there. Together.

Her decorum teacher's instructions in mind, she practiced lowering her eyes and looking up through thick lashes, lips bowed down in an attractive pout. Modest was a bit too much to ask.

Coquettish. Genial. Persuasive. She could do that.

CHAPTER 9

It wouldn't kill her to collaborate with the human—this once.

***

By the time Vanessa found Andre, her stomach was growling with hunger and her limbs were growing weak. At home she ate when she was hungry, and she always had her main source of food readily available. After all, she didn't subscribe to the fish-free mermaid diet that Atlanticans favored after a prior queen's "adopted flounder son" had been served as the main course at a banquet. Ridiculous. If something tasted good, she hunted it and ate it.

But here it seemed nourishment came at the discretion of Yia-Yia, the wretched woman. Vanessa looked around at the foliage surrounding the small glass building where she spied Andre's shadow, and, comporting herself as a prim young woman would, she knocked on the door instead of barging in.

"Yes?" Andre called from inside.

Vanessa stepped into the hot, humid air of a veritable jungle: fledgling trees grew in tall pots; rough tables were covered in containers that sprouted with leaves of every shape and size. Piles of moist soil overflowed from buckets and clay containers. Pointed metal tools hung in a neat row beside a burlap apron. Vanessa took a deep breath and choked. Earthy, pungent vegetation coated her throat. She thought she'd adjusted to breathing with her new human lungs, but this air went down hard.

A ringing smack sounded from farther inside. She coughed, covered her mouth, and continued deeper into the foliage. Another hard thwack shook the wall to her right.

Vanessa brushed back a thick palm leaf to find Andre with his arm arched back, a silver-handled knife clutched in his fingers, and a perfect row of matching blades buried in a wood support beam.

Andre whirled and lowered his weapon. "Vanessa?"

Sweat coated his exposed bronze flesh, showing off broad round shoulders and defined arms. The tissue-thin fabric of his undershirt stretched across the muscles of his chest and the flat ridges of his stomach.

Vanessa tried to commit to playing coy and demure, but she couldn't take her eyes off him or prevent the rush of heat that flooded her cheeks. She had seen young mermen shirtless—many of them larger and more powerful than this human man. But none of them had enticed her like Andre Baros did now, standing before her. The desire to run her hands over his bare skin, to watch what her touch would do to him, threatened to overwhelm her. Eyes locked on to his, she stepped forward, the harsh scents of vegetation and dirt no longer registering.

He watched her approach, those verdant eyes taking her in from head to toe. She had been wrong to compare his eyes to dead sea glass: his gaze was fertile, with ever-evolving greens and golds and rich browns. His strong, full lips pursed as he blew out a slow breath and raked a hand through his hair.

But then he stepped back, gaze shuttering. "Your walking has improved."

The cold tone of his voice washed over her like an icy current, and the color drained from her face. *Neptune's blood!* He clearly didn't trust her.

She touched the petal of a scarlet flower. "Ah . . . yes, I've been practicing." She tried a half smile and gestured to the row of knives buried in the wall. "What are you doing there?"

"Target practice." He yanked the silver blades from the wood. "My father gave me these daggers and taught me to throw with accuracy. Protection for myself and my family." A muscle in his jaw flexed as he grabbed a shirt hanging behind him and shrugged it on.

Such a shame. In Atlantica skin was nothing to cover up.

"What can I do for you, Vanessa?" Andre asked as he tilted a can with a long spout, sprinkling droplets of water over a flower.

"I wanted to explain my earlier outburst." When he didn't so much as look up, she continued, "I don't want you to think . . . It's just that I've been having odd snippets of memory. They make little sense. Like this morning, when I heard Sara's cane, an image of breaking open crab legs and eating the meat made my mouth water." Absolutely true. She'd nearly limped down to the cove to dive for crab, the taste so vibrant on her palate. "It's all making me rather jumpy, I'm afraid."

The tension eased from Andre's shoulders as he focused on plucking a yellow leaf from a vine, but he didn't speak.

Vanessa tried again. "When I awoke this morning, a song played through my head. But I have no idea when or where I heard it."

He glanced up at her and then refocused on his task, that lovely seal-black hair falling across his brow. "What song was it?"

His tone was innocent, but Vanessa knew that Andre was no dummy. Her answer might give him a clue as to her origins. But he couldn't possibly know that he'd given her the opening she needed. "Let me think." She turned her back to him and began to sing.

Sparkles of sunrise, hope, and fathomless longing flowed from the core of her nautilus and interlaced with her voice. The melody was sweet and seductive, and she spun around just as the shimmer flashed gold in his eyes. The spell could not conjure true feelings; it was just a bit of help to overcome his distrust. But by the time the spell wore off, she would have replaced it with moments that would supersede his doubt.

She finished singing the chorus with an irresistible mix of allure and persuasion. Then she asked, "Do you recognize it?"

Andre blinked, his mouth hanging partway open, then seemed to come to and shook his head. "It sounds familiar, but I don't know why." He smiled, his eyes soft and gentle, dimples appearing in both his cheeks. "Are you hungry for some lunch?"

Vanessa's grin showed all her teeth. "Ravenous."

***

"Yia-Yia isn't feeling well, so I hope you don't mind cold shrimp pasta." Sara hobbled to the table and set the plate of chilled pasta in front of Vanessa.

"Looks delicious," Vanessa said as she watched Andre pick up his fork, twirl the pasta in the tines, and shove a bite into his mouth. She mimicked his movements, still unsure how particular foods were eaten on land. After consuming several bites and wishing for less linguine and more meat, she asked, "When do you plan to travel to Omis Island?"

Andre reached for a slice of bread and used it to dredge seasoned olive oil. "I'm not sure if that's a good idea."

Sara looked up from her plate. "Andre, you have to try! This is the only lead we have."

He took another bite, chewed slowly, and nodded. "Even if this is the right course of action, I'll need to hire a boat, and we're short on funds at the moment."

"Are you?" Vanessa could transform shells into gold if need be, but she couldn't risk the suspicion it would spark if she turned up out of nowhere with a small fortune.

"Since this . . . sickness has happened, I've been unable to sell my tonics," Andre explained, his shoulders slumping.

"Why?" Vanessa already knew the answer but hoped her perceived naivete would prompt Andre to talk about the curse.

"No one wants to buy tainted elixirs, do they?" Andre

stared hard at his half-empty plate before setting his fork on the tablecloth.

"What exactly were they tainted by?" Vanessa asked. "You said something about an old woman giving you oils. What reactions did they cause?"

Sara picked up a piece of bread and pinched off a crumb. The little girl frowned. "I felt amazing for several days. No weakness or pain in my muscles. I had boundless energy for once in my life. Then it all returned tenfold. My legs refuse to work properly, and I ache constantly."

Andre reached over and covered Sara's pale fingers in his large hand, grief rolling off him in palpable waves.

"I think Governor Zika had it right." Vanessa forked a piece of shrimp. "It sounds like magic to me."

Two sets of eyes stared at her as she popped the crustacean into her mouth and chewed slowly. Magic must be a dark and shameful thing on earth, just as she'd learned it was in Atlantica. When a young king used it to protect the city or create a useless underwater rainbow, he was applauded. But helping those guppies with their mundane problems had cast her as a pariah. All she'd asked for was a tiny little price: their most precious memories. One girl had given her all the details of her first kiss. A boy had relinquished a favorite bedtime story from his late father.

A mother had once surrendered her fondest memories of her son to save him from a deadly parasite.

Vanessa had gathered all the priceless moments and filed them away in her reef cave for later use. They had come in handy many times in trade or in earning an individual's silence. Some called it blackmail. But she thought of it as a simple transaction. A means to both her and her customers' desired ends.

Andre leaned forward, his elbows on the table. "Why do you speak of magic?"

"Because anything worthwhile—anything magical—comes at a great cost." Did they really think that healing was free? That a potion practically handed to them by a strange woman would come at no price? Her own transformation from sea creature to enchanting human had taken five years off her life span. It was a price she'd gladly paid. Growing old and decrepit had never been part of the plan. She'd much rather go out in a blaze of light and thunder.

Andre wilted back in his chair, his gaze lowered as he spoke in a low rumble. "She said the treasure would only appear to the desperate. To one with a pure heart who didn't seek gain for himself. I thought . . . I thought . . ."

"You thought you were special," Vanessa suggested

softly. "That because you truly sought only to help others, there would be no price."

His eyes lifted, shining with dew. "I wanted to believe it. I did believe it. Urgently and stupidly!" He shot up from his seat and stalked toward the bank of windows.

Vanessa exchanged glances with Sara, looking to the girl for guidance on how to react. Empathy had never been her strong point. Nor had she ever encountered such an altruistic soul as Andre Baros. She stared at his broad back. He had sought to help everyone else and had taken nothing for himself except the satisfaction of watching them thrive.

She didn't understand him in the least. But Neptune help her, she wanted to.

Sara bobbed her head and then tilted it toward her brother, encouraging Vanessa to do something. But what? She stood up and walked over to join him. For a moment, she soaked in the cool, briny breeze blowing off the cove through the open windows. She thought back to when she'd witnessed merfolk comforting one another, their platitudes, their false encouragement and soothing phrases. Well-intentioned, perhaps, but Vanessa refused to speak such empty words. When she encountered a problem, she found a way to solve it.

Striving for a comforting tone, she whispered, "How did you acquire this . . . treasure?"

Andre didn't look at her when he answered. "The old woman gave me a map. I followed it to a nearby lagoon and eventually found a metal box shoved inside the underwater crevice of a boulder."

"What was inside the box?" Vanessa held her breath in anticipation of his answer.

"Vials of glowing liquid with a message that read 'Wishes that money cannot buy.'" He rubbed the back of his neck. "When I speak it aloud, it sounds like a ridiculous fairy tale."

"And you used the potions to help your family and your clients?"

"Yes, miraculously, it brought some happiness, some love, some healing. Whatever they needed most. I witnessed so many extraordinary results right away that I continued to dole them out. But in a few short days, the cures backfired, leaving devastation." Andre hunched over and gripped the windowsill so hard that Vanessa could see shadows of bone beneath his skin. "I created atrocities."

Vanessa breathed in deep. Now they were getting somewhere. She placed a hand reassuringly on his back and asked what she really wanted to know. "What did you do with the rest of the potions?"

"I threw them off Zakyntho Cliff and watched them shatter into a thousand pieces against the rocks," he practically growled.

Vanessa tried not to show her shock—and anger—at his response. "None of the potions are left? Not even diluted in your tonics?"

Andre shook his head. "I destroyed them all. Every last tainted bottle."

Vanessa lowered her hand and clenched it into a fist. It was gone. The beautiful, vicious curse discarded without a thought. What a dolt.

She let out a slow breath and regathered her focus. "What . . . happened then?"

Andre whirled to face her and snapped, "Nothing, Vanessa. Destroying them changed nothing. Just like Sara, everyone it affected remains broken."

Vanessa bit her lip to keep her expression passive, but her insides clenched with excitement, the pieces finally falling into place. If destroying the potions didn't kill their effects, that meant there was another source for the curse.

One she could still harness.

A muscle spasmed in Andre's jaw. "If Zika is right, my

only hope is to talk to this . . . savant on Omis Island. But I have no money for passage. And because of the blighted curse, I can't work to earn more."

Vanessa's first thought was to steal a boat, but she pushed that aside. Andre's ethics would never allow it. Yet coin was no object for one with the means to acquire it.

A corner of Vanessa's mouth lifted. "Well. Perhaps I can help."

CHAPTER 10

ANDRE

AS A NEW DAY dawned, with the ocean tipped in waves of gold, Andre steered the wagon around a sharp bend and through the arched gates of the fishing port of Aio. Vanessa sat beside him, preoccupied with the sea to the point that she turned and watched it disappear from view. Aio was the best option for their endeavor to make enough for a boat trip to Omis Island. It was far enough away from Andre's village that they might attempt sales without the pall of the curse hanging over them. They'd discussed traveling even farther, to the northernmost town of Saxos, with its arid olive groves and rocky shores, but the sparsely populated village was a day's ride away and would have required an overnight stay.

Yia-Yia had awakened that morning with no signs of whatever had ailed her the day before, and she served them yogurt with fresh fruit and nuts. She didn't talk much, and her eyes followed Vanessa's every move. When Andre had pulled Yia-Yia aside and told her they were taking the wagon out, her eyes had widened; then she'd simply pressed her lips together and nodded in resigned silence. It might not have been the approval Andre was looking for, but it was enough.

Andre's gaze shifted to the magnificent woman seated beside him. Hair layered in shades of the night sea fell in natural waves to her waist and met in a peak over dark arched brows. She'd dressed in a white peasant blouse and a skirt of rainbow silks stitched together in a riotous pattern that fluttered around her trim ankles when she moved. He envisioned himself lying beside Vanessa next to a campfire under the stars, and the cozy night that would have awaited them on a journey to Saxos. Instantly, a blush crept up his cheeks.

CHAPTER 10

Penetrating eyes locked on his, almost as if she could see the images in his mind of their imaginary sleepover in the forest. He glanced away.

Vanessa clasped his hand in her delicate fingers. A rush of energy traveled up his arm, and Andre's gaze lingered on her pink mouth before he forced his eyes away again and shifted on the bench. A spontaneous smile broke across his face as he pulled the reins back and clucked to Ella, slowing the Wagon of Wonders to a halt in a shady spot.

Hands discreetly linked, they watched the town come to life, and Andre was reassured by the seemingly unaffected village morning. The fishmonger set up shop under a round tent as ruddy-faced seamen delivered crates of their daily catch. Flower girls sashayed past in matching petal-pink skirts, their arms overflowing with blooms for sale.

Yet trepidation turned Andre's stomach. "This is a bad idea," he muttered.

A slow grin tilted Vanessa's mouth as one of her brows arched high. "Do you doubt me so soon?"

"It isn't you that I doubt exactly. . . ."

She squeezed his fingers, effectively silencing his protest. "Open the cart for business and leave the rest to me."

Reluctantly, Andre tied up Ella's reins and opened

both sides of the wagon. Then he began to unpack a crate of Middle Eastern pottery he'd recently obtained from a buccaneer ship. He removed each piece and dusted the bold painted surfaces. Then he rearranged the shelves to better display each bowl and vase.

Loud laughter drew Andre to the front of the wagon. When he peeked around the front, he saw a small group gathered near Vanessa, listening to a story she told about a merman and the beautiful princess the sea creature had lured into the ocean. The crowd listened with bated breath as Vanessa painted a vivid picture of an underwater world. When she finished her story, the group leaned in, and a merchant asked, "Well, did the princess make it back to land?"

Vanessa pursed her lips and then replied, "I've heard once you've had a merman, you'll never want a seaman."

Those gathered laughed uproariously. But more significantly, they lingered, some chatting with Vanessa. Their lighthearted banter drew others until a veritable crowd surrounded the wagon.

Andre, still in shadow, leaned against the front edge of the wooden frame and watched Vanessa work. She took various canisters of tea off the shelf and announced a "buy two, get one free" sale. She danced and sang a limerick about a girl who was partial to gin but drank tonics instead.

The crowd seemed to grow. Enchanted by the melody of Vanessa's voice, burly fishermen who normally would have laughed off Andre's wares as fanciful indulgences gathered close and stayed to watch the sway of her hips. She charmed them with an intimate smile or a fleeting touch to the arm, all while touting the benefits of Andre's elixirs and oils. On the drive, Andre had given her an overview of each oil's curative properties. However, what she said didn't seem to matter as much as how she said it, using the lure of her vibrant voice and charisma.

Money exchanged hands faster than Andre could track.

When she motioned him to her, he spoke to the customers, learning about their various ills and making suggestions. In the comfortable rhythm of diagnosing and recommending treatments, he lost track of time.

"I think we've sold enough for one day. It's getting late," Vanessa said as she wrapped up a bottle of vetiver and orange blossom for a customer. "We should go home."

We should go home.

The words reverberated in his mind.

For so long Andre had taken care of everyone. Customers up and down the coast looked to him to fix their problems, saw him as their doctor and their counselor, blamed him when he didn't have the quick answers they desired. Since his parents passed, he'd been responsible for his grandmother and sister. It had never felt like a burden; he provided for them out of love. They were the brightest joys in his life.

Yet at times it seemed as if everyone needed him for something. He was the strong one, without wants or needs of his own. He could admit only at his weakest moments that he felt utterly alone.

He clasped Vanessa's hand, and she squeezed his with an encouraging smile.

Yia-Yia had it all wrong. The tides were turning for him, all starting with this brilliantly daring woman.

***

"Flour's on sale, sir. We received an extra shipment intended for Cyrgos," the young salesclerk said. They'd stopped in Agios Limani for groceries on their way back to the Baros home. Vanessa, spent from her brilliant sales spiel, rested in the back of the wagon in the town square.

"I'll take two bags, then, Beatrice." Andre added the flour to his basket of supplies and then checked the list Yia-Yia had given him. He reached into his pocket and pulled out a large pile of coins, then stared at them in semi-disbelief. Had Vanessa truly been so successful? Perhaps she had been a saleswoman by trade before losing her memory and landing at his shore.

Forcing his attention back to his list once more, Andre asked, "Do you have any potatoes?"

"They're in a barrel out back," the clerk's disembodied voice called from the stockroom.

Andre pushed open the alleyway door. A salty wind whistled through the narrow passage as he looked out over the steep incline to the sea beyond. Most of the villages along the coast were built into the cliffs like mountain goats overlooking the ocean. Agios Limani had few streets wide enough to drive a cart through, and none of them were straight. Stone steps wove in a maze up and down the hills and between stucco buildings. If one hadn't been raised in the village, it would be easy to lose one's way.

Andre bent over the barrel nearest the door and picked through the dirt-coated tubers. Roasted potatoes with feta were a staple in their household, and Yia-Yia was particular about the produce she used. She would be furious if he brought home half-rotten vegetables.

A sudden shift in the air tugged Andre upright. He whirled around to see a clenched hand flying toward him.

The fist smashed into his jaw, and Andre stumbled against the opposite wall, groceries flying. Stars reeled in his vision, and he threw up his arms instinctively, partially blocking another hit.

The next blow arched pain down his shoulder, his right arm going numb. As Andre staggered backward, his sight clearing, he saw three figures in front of him. One lifted something large and metallic, and Andre spun away, his back hitting a delivery cart that blocked the exit to the alley.

The first man advanced, barrel-chested, his arms corded with the muscled tendons of a dockworker. The two others, with similar builds, flanked the first attacker. Like a murder of crows, they were dressed in black from head to toe. But the inky swirls on the leader's face and the golden rings hanging from sunburned ears distinguished them as the worst kind of ruffians.

Pirates.

No way could Andre outfight them, especially since he'd left his daggers in the wagon. The tattooed man lifted a pipe.

"Wait!" Andre raised his hands. "I think there's been some mistake."

"No mistake," the man grunted. "We know who you

are. You turned my niece into a lunatic." And with that, he swung the pipe.

Andre lunged to the side, but metal connected with his left kidney, the pain driving him to his knees.

The cursed potion. He'd known this was coming, and part of him almost wanted to submit to the punishment. Didn't he deserve it, after all?

Then again, if they killed him, who would find a cure?

Andre leapt up, drove his head into the leader's gut, and shoved with all his strength. The man fell back into one of his mates, and Andre kicked the pipe down the stairs and out of sight.

Panting, he stumbled back, fists up, and faced the third man. "I didn't mean to"—the guy swung, and Andre ducked—"hurt anyone!"

"But you did!" the leader growled as he regained his stance, his friend still dazed on the cobbles. He swung, his meaty fist connecting with Andre's mouth. Blood and pain exploded across Andre's vision. Another punch to his temple sent him down hard, his skull bouncing off flagstone.

"You've made some important people very angry with your little witch's potion." The leader slammed his foot into Andre's ribs, stealing his breath. Andre curled into the fetal position as blow after blow smashed his ribs and back.

Hands tugged him to his feet and threw him against the hard wall. An ale-soaked voice growled close to his ear. "Stop selling your poisonous concoctions, or it won't just be you we come after."

"I'm not selling poison. I destroyed all of—" The resounding smack of a fist silenced Andre's protests. His head rocked back, limp on his neck. He attempted to say, *I'm trying to find a cure*. But no words would form as the final wallop sent him into a black pit of pain, down, down, and down further still.

CHAPTER 11

VANESSA

"DON'T SIT UP YET."

Andre's eyes snapped open, and he jerked awake with a gasp.

Vanessa searched his beautiful, battered face. She'd grown bored waiting for Andre in the wagon and had gone to seek him out only to find him alone, passed out in a pool of blood, behind the store. "Why would someone do this to you?"

He moaned in response.

"Who attacked you, Andre?" Anger flared in her chest. She would make them pay. "Who hurt you?"

"Pirates," Andre garbled around his swollen mouth.

"Pirates?" Vanessa exclaimed, not having expected that answer. They couldn't have gone far. She rested his head on a half-empty sack of flour, shot to her feet, and ran to the stairs that led down the hill and toward the wharf.

"Stop!"

Vanessa pivoted as Andre, pushed up on one elbow, called to her.

"I need to find them," she said, but as she watched him grab on to a nearby cart and struggle to his feet, every movement clear torture, she knew she couldn't leave him.

He hobbled toward the stairs where Vanessa stood, and fell to his knees with a groan. The world spun before Vanessa's eyes, heat flashing over her skin, as she watched the strong, capable young man, who had done everything in his power to help her, crumble at her feet.

This would not stand. Whoever had done this would wish they'd never been born.

Vanessa knelt beside Andre and used the edge of her skirt to wipe the blood from his cheek. "What did they want?"

"Revenge for a niece who took the Grimaldi potion.

But they also said I'd made some important people angry." He quirked a crooked smile. "I don't know any important people."

"What ship were they from?" she asked, a hint of steel entering her voice.

"I'm not sure. I've never seen them before today. I have to find that cure as soon as possible." His face paled. "But I'm not sure Omis Island is the answer. I need to stay with my family. Protect them."

Gently, she combed his dark hair out of his eyes as he blinked up at her, and she noticed striations of gold and darker green in their depths. He had to be delirious with pain. Omis Island and the savant were the only leads they had. She needed to keep him on course. "Don't you see? Threats won't stop coming for you until you find a cure. Going to Omis *is* the only way to keep your family safe."

And the only way she could explore the possible source of magic there.

Suddenly, his eyes flared open. "The wagon!" He pushed to his feet, moving quicker than she had thought possible under the circumstances.

They left the store, and he began to half hobble, half run down the steep path that led to the village square, where he'd left his wagon to venture to the grocery. Vanessa sprinted past him in a swirl of rainbow skirts.

When she finally reached the piazza, she gripped Andre's arm tight. Colorful glass shards littered the street like a sunburst, all his handmade tonics leaching between the bricks. Shelves hung loose and broken. A beheaded porcelain doll rested among shattered bits of hand-painted pottery. Books lay scattered facedown in pools of oil. The carriage roof caved inward.

The Wagon of Wonders had been destroyed.

Andre began to shake as he shuffled forward. "Ella!" he cried. But his horse was nowhere in sight.

Vanessa whirled around and, when she didn't see the animal, said, "I'll find her."

But in that moment, Ella rounded the fishmonger's stall, chomping on a bunch of yellow daisies.

A young girl held Ella's lead and glanced at Andre shyly. "I didn't want to see her hurt, so when I saw what those brigands were doing, I lured her away with a snack."

Andre nearly collapsed as he stumbled toward his horse. "Thank you." He threw an arm around Ella's neck and pressed his face against hers. "Wagons can be replaced. But I don't know what I would've done without this girl."

Vanessa, her jaw set hard, approached and took Ella's

lead. "Let's see if that wagon can still roll. We need to get you home."

Andre allowed her to help him into the driver's seat, and he instructed her on how to hitch Ella to the wagon. As Vanessa tightened Ella's lead, something Andre had said drifted back to her.

They also said I'd made some important people angry.

If the pirates had really wished to destroy Andre's livelihood, they would have taken out the wheels and the hitch. Even the beating they'd given him seemed methodical. True vengeance didn't show restraint. That kind of anger didn't stop until forced.

The job reeked of money.

When Vanessa reached the back of the wagon, the young girl who'd brought Ella back still hovered, tears welling in her gray eyes.

Vanessa pulled a few coins from her pocket. "Thank you for your help. If you'll clean up this mess, I'll pay you handsomely." She dropped the money into the girl's small hands. "Can you tell me anything about who did this?"

The girl looked reluctant, then said softly, "They're from the ship the *Striker*."

Vanessa nodded. "Do you know when the *Striker* plans to embark?"

The girl hesitated. Vanessa glanced over her shoulder, didn't see anyone, and reached into her pocket once again, this time to transform a bit of lint into a gold piece. She handed it to the girl, wanting to keep her talking.

Eyes wide at the valuable coin, the girl answered more quickly. "I heard them talking just now. Their ship leaves tonight. They were saying that this stop in Agios Limani had been more lucrative than they'd ever imagined."

Vanessa nodded crisply. "Well, then, I'd better act quickly."

CHAPTER 12

VANESSA

THE *STRIKER* bobbed low in the night-black sea, its sails frosted in moonlight. Vanessa pulled the deep cowl of her cloak over her head and, with the stars as her guide, observed the quiet wharf. Her senses reached out to soft splashes of waves against the quay, a silent patrol of bats above, swirls of mist rising off the ocean, and the light breeze stirring her cape, so buoyant she thought she might float if she lifted her feet. The exquisiteness of the night was interrupted only by voices that rose in a bawdy shanty, echoing across the water.

Vanessa followed the song, her slippers making little noise as she stalked down the wooden dock. She pondered the best approach as she neared the vessel and watched the pirate crew climb into the rigging, load provisions, and unfurl sails. It seemed she'd timed her arrival perfectly.

Who were these crooks that beat and robbed an innocent man? And she *did* believe him innocent. Despite all of Andre's self-righteous blather, Vanessa knew he'd been set up. Whoever had crafted the curse had chosen him to do the dirty work. But who had created it, and what did the creator hope to accomplish? Sure, Vanessa liked to cause a bit of havoc now and again, but she mostly used her magic in transactions that achieved a specific and profitable end. Or at least to obtain leverage for later use.

Nothing about this curse seemed logical. It appeared to hurt indiscriminately for hurt's sake. Using Andre to deal out harm to random individuals made no sense. When he'd destroyed the potions, it should have broken the thrall on the afflicted. Since it had not, the curse had to be part of a larger plan, a long game that she needed to understand. Cornering the pirates and figuring out who they'd been working for might be the first step to unraveling the mystery.

Vanessa sashayed up the gangway and paused at the top, her hand on her hip. "Good evening, gentlemen."

One by one, the seafarers froze and glanced her way, some with mouths parted slightly in surprise, others with their hands on the weapons strapped to their waists. Vanessa scanned the faces. Andre had described the ringleader of the group who had attacked him as huge and bald, with a wave tattoo rising above his collar.

The silence crackled with tension until a nimble young pirate swung down from the rigging and landed in front of her with a graceful thud. His almost cherubic appearance, with his bronze curls, upturned nose, and freckles, made him appear the least likely pirate Vanessa could imagine. "Ignore the horrible manners of these miscreants," the boy said with a dismissive wave toward the rest of the crew. "What can we do for you, ma'am?"

Vanessa stepped forward, the air buzzing with anticipation. She breathed deep, luxuriating in the nectar of vehement emotions swirling on the night air—like fuel for her power. Pitching her voice so all could hear, she said, "I'm looking for someone you might know."

"Who's that, sweetheart?" A gap-toothed, red-faced mariner swaggered forward. "I'm sure I can help ye out."

Rancorous laughter circled around the deck, followed by a few coarse suggestions of how they might assist her.

Magic crackled from Vanessa's nautilus to her fingertips as she stepped forward and took down her hood, prompting a series of low whistles, which preceded a fall of rapid-fire comments.

"Well, hello there, darlin'."

"Praise be to the saints for answerin' my prayers!"

"No way, Ratty. Ain't no saint gonna listen to your debauched self."

The one called Ratty threw back his greasy head and guffawed. "A truer statement ain't never been spoken!"

The elfin boy interrupted. "Quiet, you lot! We gots a lady on board."

Vanessa graced him with a smile. "I'm seeking a tall man with a wave tattoo."

A voice boomed from somewhere above them: "Who's askin'?"

Vanessa followed the voice up to the quarterdeck. A mountainous man scowled at her from above before loping down the stairs. Andre's description of the man had been generous. Years in the wind and sun had burned his skin to wrinkled leather, and his nose made a hawk's beak seem dainty. Dead-looking eyes narrowed on her face, his lips set in a cruel slash.

He crossed meaty arms in front of his chest. "I'm captain of this here vessel. Most call me Krill, pretty lady. We're about to set sail. But you're welcome to join us if you're looking for a bit of entertainment—" Whoops of approval interrupted him before he raised a single fist and all fell silent. "If not, I suggest ye disembark whilst ye still can."

Power flared through Vanessa's veins, and she clenched her hands tight against it as she lifted her chin and said, "I need some information, and I won't be leaving until I get it."

Krill widened his stance. "And what might that be?"

"A friend of mine was badly beaten today."

"Oh, you mean that bludger from that blasted Wagon of Wonders?" Ratty stepped forward. "We got him good, didn't we, Cap? He won't be sellin' nothin' from that cracked-up rig for quite some time."

"Not bloody likely," said the pirate with the missing teeth.

The expression of devastation on Andre's face when he'd seen what they'd done to his vehicle—his livelihood—flashed across Vanessa's mind. Magic burned for release inside her chest. "Tell me who paid you to do it. Then I'll be on my way."

"You came all this way for that lout?" Krill pulled a leather scabbard from his pocket and slid out the hilt of a tarnished knife in a not-so-subtle threat. "Not happenin', doll."

Three men towered over her, and she noticed Gap-tooth had a swollen lip and Ratty's eye was ringed with purple. One side of her mouth quirked. Andre hadn't gone down without a fight, and neither would she.

"I'm nobody's doll." Vanessa whipped a hand from her cloak and snapped her fingers. Ropes of light flew into the air and curled around Ratty's arms and legs. She yanked and he fell like a rock. Cries of "witch" were in the air; men converged to back up their mates. She threw out her palm and froze them in place as Gap-tooth pulled a wicked blade. With a flick of her chin, a burst of wind slammed into his jaw like the crack of a fist. The man's head flew back, and he crumpled to the deck.

Krill lunged for her, his dirk raised in a meaty fist. Vanessa whirled out of his reach with a laugh. She'd saved the best for last. Lightning crackled over her knuckles, and she lifted her hands like claws. He blanched and stumbled to a stop, palms held up in surrender.

But it was too late to appease her. Intoxicating splashes of frantic fear and waves of mass hysteria thrummed in her blood, searching for release. For a target.

She flung out her arm, and lightning flashed from her fingertips, splintering across the captain's flesh. He stiffened, eyes wide, and fell to his side on the deck.

Vanessa walked toward him, her power coursing through him growing more intense as she reached his side. She knelt down, tilted her head, and watched him convulse. "I'll ask again. Who hired you to hurt Andre Baros?" Scarlet blood began to pour from the captain's ears and nose, his big body jerking like a fish out of water.

She closed her fist and withdrew the shock from the captain's body. "I'm waiting."

His head flopped toward her, his eyes unfocused, as a gurgle escaped his throat. "Off . . . shore."

She curled her fingers, her magic slowly strangling the captain as she leaned in close. "That doesn't answer my question."

Krill's mouth moved, spit leaking out, as he clawed at his throat, trying to speak.

Vanessa rolled her eyes in disgust at his weakness and released him. "Fine. Say it again, big boy."

"A letter . . . arrived by boat," he choked out. "Anonymous . . . with gold . . . lots of it."

Somehow, she believed him. But she wasn't through with this lot yet. She straightened and smoothed the fabric of her skirts and addressed the entire crew. "Tonight you've learned that women are *not* dolls for your entertainment. Do you understand?"

They blinked, but none of them could move.

Vanessa lifted sparking fingers over Ratty's face, and he nodded vigorously.

"Good." With a wave of her hand, the rest of the pirates were released from her spell. Each of them moved as if drugged. Her eyes found the bronze-haired boy who had retreated to the corner, untouched by her magic. He offered a trembling smile, his charm his best defense. A good strategy. She smiled back. "What's your name, boy?"

"Spiro."

"Spiro, I require passage to Omis Island. And I don't believe your captain will be capable for some time. Rally your crew, and I will return midmorning." The idea had come upon her, and she had to admit it was a perfect one: wrangling the wretched pirates to take her and Andre to the island so he could keep their day's earnings for himself and his family. Thanks to the pirates, he'd now need that money more than ever.

His smile wavered. "I . . . I can't."

With a twirl of her hand, ropes of kelp flew around the stunned crew, including the unconscious captain, pinning them all against the mainmast. And then she stepped toward the boy. "You . . . can't?"

He blinked wide mesmerized eyes. "I don't know where the island is. No one does. They say it moves by moonlight and rises with the sun."

"Lies," Vanessa said, scoffing. In her experience, the young held the capacity to see beyond the facts to the fantastical. Through the years, many adult humans who had spotted her at sea had simply shrugged off the appearance of her aquatic form as the tentacle of an octopus or a giant squid, whereas a child, who had not yet learned to doubt, could glimpse the otherworldly, see everything for what it was—even a magical island that had remained hidden for centuries.

"Ships that have found it are dashed against the rocks, the crews' bones stripped clean by kelpies," Spiro insisted.

Vanessa pursed her lips. "Myths and legends to scare off the timid. You don't strike me as timid, Spiro."

"No, ma'am." He lifted his pointy chin.

"Then you must have some idea how to find the island."

Spiro gripped his curls in a tight fist, his eyes shifting to the befuddled crew as if he feared repercussion.

"Don't you do it, boy," Gap-tooth growled, waking from his stupor.

"Enough!" Shell conduit sparking, Vanessa sent a string of kelp leaves skittering down Gap-tooth's throat. She turned to Spiro. "I will not free them unless you help me."

The older pirate gagged, his eyes bulging. The boy rushed to him and tugged the vine from Gap-tooth's mouth. But the more he yanked, the longer the weed grew.

Panicking, Spiro spun on Vanessa. "Stop! You're killing him!"

Vanessa splayed out her hand and stared at her broken thumbnail. "What a shame."

"Please!" the boy screeched as the pirate writhed and fought for breath.

Vanessa blew on her thumb and watched the nail grow back. "Take me to Omis Island."

"Yes! I'll try. Make it stop, please!"

She would like to have certainties, but she knew the boy could do it. She felt it in her bones. She nodded, the kelp withered, and the old pirate gasped, then gagged as

CHAPTER 12

Spiro pulled the vine from his mouth. Vanessa moved to the top of the gangway, where she faced them all: belligerent stares from the captured pirate crew and a mixture of awe and resignation on the face of the youngest among them. "I will return shortly. Be ready to travel to Omis Island or suffer the consequences."

Several "ayes" and rapid nods confirmed she'd gotten through to them.

Feeling triumphant, Vanessa practically skipped down the plank. But as she lifted her hood and made her way down the dock, a chant reached her ears. It was weak at first but built with each hateful word. The grin melted off her face.

"Witch! Witch! Burn the witch. Find a ditch and toss her in it!"

A ringing sounded in Vanessa's ears as the pirates' voices cut through the night.

A long-ago memory of a merchild's birthday party. Her first-ever invitation. They'd gone into the garden, full of iced kelp cake and sweet seagrass shakes. The birthday girl had instructed Ursula to stand still as all the other children formed a circle around her and held hands, the girl leading them in song. *"Witch, witch, she lives down in a ditch. Feed her a feast and she'll turn into a beast. She gobbles up shrimp and bloats like a blimp. That's our sea witch! Sea witch!*" They'd swum faster and faster around her, their words stinging as they churned up silt until she couldn't breathe.

That was the last party she'd ever attended that she hadn't thrown herself.

Vanessa came back to the present with a jolt, and as she reached the main pier, the chant carrying over the midnight water, she turned back, gripped her necklace, and whispered, "Pop. Pop. Pop." Their chorus cut off abruptly as her spell enclosed the seamen's heads in bubbles half filled with water. Let them struggle to breathe until she returned the next morning.

She was not that child witch being tortured in the garden any longer.

And she never would be again.

***

Satisfied with the evening's work, Vanessa strolled along the uneven boards and lifted her face to the sky. Suddenly, the silver stars spun, streaking into a dizzying swirl. She stumbled to the side, just catching herself before tipping off the dock. She steadied her footing and continued, an inescapable weariness pulling at her every step.

CHAPTER 12

It made no sense. What she'd done to those scallywags should have been as easy as breathing, yet it seemed to have taken the very life force from her human bones.

Vanessa's head spun, and she focused on the hills where the village loomed, the stucco buildings like broken fingers reaching for the empty sky. Dread slithered through her.

By the time she'd trudged back to the Baros cottage, the sky had begun to lighten in the east. She lurched to the kitchen door, which she'd left unlocked. She just needed to make it inside. Sleep would restore her—if she could make it up those blighted stairs.

Then Vanessa stopped, her hand on the doorknob. Something tugged at her consciousness. She closed her eyes. The gentle lap of water, brine, fish, and sediment wrapped around her, drawing her like a siren's cry.

The sea called her home.

She stumbled away from the cottage and toward the cove. Seagrass waved, tips peeking through the surface, enticing her forward. Every ligament and muscle in her body ached, her breathing was labored, and her skin itched terribly.

Vanessa slipped out of her cloak, kicked off her shoes, and dove.

Water caressed and soothed her, soaking into her pores. Her brain sharp once again, she understood. This human body could not conduct her power as well as her aquatic form. She needed regeneration. Replenishment that could come only from her beloved ocean.

She swam deep down into the water and sat among the plants, crabs clicking at her skirts. Too soon her human lungs burned, and she kicked back to the surface for a gulping breath. She dove back down and swam toward the opening to the sea, her legs itching and tingling, pain blooming. Light danced behind her eyes.

Then a surge of joyous magic.

Vanessa pushed up in one powerful motion, her legs no longer human but eight glorious tentacles that unfurled around her. She moaned in relief. Her true form strained for full release, but with her magic restored, she easily managed to keep the rest of her human body in place.

It was enough.

As she bobbed across the pool, one suckered tentacle curled around a passing anchovy and lifted it to her hand. She ate it in one bite. Using magic always left her ravenous. Another tentacle plucked up a clam and squeezed it open, then carried the pulpy flesh to her mouth. She slurped it down, and sinking below the surface, she continued to hunt.

"Hello? Is someone there?"

Vanessa froze, a crawfish halfway to her mouth. As she looked up through the glassy water, she realized dawn had crested the horizon. The pool she swam in was so crystal clear that on a sunny day, one could see all the way to the bottom. She pushed deeper into the weeds and spotted a wavering image of a gray-haired woman peering over the edge.

Yia-Yia.

That old turtle had never trusted her. With good reason, but still. Vanessa had caught the woman's look of rage and blame as she'd taken in Andre's battered state when they'd returned from their journey. She suspected Vanessa of being something other than what she claimed; that much was obvious. If she spotted Vanessa in the lagoon now, she would never stop filling Andre's head with her obnoxious rantings of evil creatures and black magic.

The grandmother dipped a bucket into the water to fill and then set it on the bank. Vanessa's chest caught fire, her vision growing dim. She could transform the rest of the way, trading lungs for gills, but it would take weeks, perhaps months, to re-create the spell that had made her human. She'd lose the trail of magic she'd happened upon, and by the time she made her way back to the shores, it would be too late.

Vanessa slithered through the cove to the far bank and lifted her face to the surface. But as silently as she tried to move, her larger form caused a splash.

"Hello?" The old woman's voice shook as she rounded the edge of the pool, nearing the spot where Vanessa had left her cloak and shoes.

Vanessa could not allow the old granny to see her true form. She took a big breath and then sank and rolled to face the seafloor. Grasping her shell to keep its light from reaching the surface, she called back her human legs. Pain lanced her core as the transformation ripped through flesh and sinew. A groan bubbled from her lips just as Yia-Yia approached in the dawn light.

What Vanessa needed was a distraction.

With a wave of her hand, she sent a school of guppies jumping on the far side of the pool. Her stupid human lungs burning again from lack of oxygen, she glanced up through the water to find Yia-Yia standing directly above her. But Vanessa's diversion caught the woman's attention, and instead of looking down, she hobbled away to investigate the sudden noise.

CHAPTER 12

Vanessa's heart pumped like a typhoon in her throat, in her ears, and in her veins until her limbs felt numb and darkness closed in. She pushed her head above the water, inches at a time. As her eyes broke the surface, she watched the old woman pick up the bucket of salt water and hobble away toward the house.

Finally.

Vanessa emerged with a gasp, a realization washing over her: using her magic on land came at a much greater cost than she'd anticipated. It was dangerous and risked her exposure. In the future, she would need to use it judiciously.

Her arms and legs still shaking like jellyfish streamers, Vanessa swam to the embankment and crawled up onto the rocks. She scooped up her cloak and shoes and snuck around the side of the house to the rear entrance, already crafting in her head an excuse of an early-morning swim in case she ran into Yia-Yia. But she made it undetected to her room, and after stripping down, she collapsed onto her bed. Eyes heavy, she crawled under the covers and dreamed of the mysterious Omis Island and its potential power, nearly within her grasp.

PART 2

OMIS ISLAND

The killing witchery that lies
In her soft, black, delicious eyes,
When gather'd in one amorous glance,
Pierces the heart, like sword or lance;
The prey that falls into her snare,
For life must mourn and struggle there.

—Nezami Ganjavi

(translated by James Atkinson)

CHAPTER 13

ANDRE

ANDRE GRIPPED the railing as they crested a steep wave and splashed back down. Blue skies and calm seas became darker and more tempestuous the closer they drew to Omis Island. As the volatile weather tossed the *Striker* about, Andre's stomach lurched, and he glanced over his shoulder at the pirate manning the ship. The captain ignored Andre, as did all the other pirates, which he found a bit odd, given the nature of their last interaction. Gingerly, Andre rubbed his sore jaw. He was loath to admit how nervous it made him to be dependent on the very ruffians who had attacked him just a day before.

A spray of sea misted Vanessa's face, and a sharp wind whipped her emerald skirts into a frenzy as she joined Andre at the prow of the ship. Beside him, she clutched the railing tight, her knuckles white. Shooting him a thin smile, she said, "Circe must be angry today."

Andre furrowed his brow. Though he thought she'd meant it as a joke, there was no mirth or lightness to her usually playful tone. "What if the rumors are true?"

"Which ones exactly?" She faced him.

"That Circe inhabits the island, and not La Befana," he said, squinting through the fog. They had to be getting close—to a cure or a cursed death. Either way, it was too late to turn back. If the island housed magical archives and a hermit savant, as Governor Zika claimed, Andre would need to keep an open mind. It was the only chance at redemption for the people he had inadvertently hurt—including Sara.

Vanessa bit her lip, seeming hesitant to speak. "The story I remember is that although Circe is long dead, the island is still protected by her magic, and the very land is steeped in it. That's why the island is uninhabitable." Her eyes were full of the same dread that consumed him.

"Are you sure that's all you've heard about the island?" he asked. He didn't know her well enough to prove it, but Andre's gut told him Vanessa knew much more than she was letting on.

Vanessa shifted her stance, the wind sending her dark hair flying out like a flag. "Well, they also claimed Omis Island was the love nest of the goddess Circe and Odysseus." She arched her brow flirtatiously.

Andre smiled at her attempt to lighten the mood of their situation, but when he looked beyond her humor, her shoulders were tense, and darkness lurked in her eyes. He wondered again about her eagerness to accompany him on the journey. Clearly she believed danger lurked ahead.

A sour taste coated Andre's mouth. Whether due to the rough seas or dread of what was to come, he couldn't be sure. He cleared his throat and moved to another disturbing topic. "I'm still confused about how you convinced the pirates who attacked me yesterday to take us to Omis Island today."

"Just a bit of leverage here and there." When Andre lifted a brow skeptically, Vanessa swiftly added, "They agreed to transport us for a bit of coin and a promise that I wouldn't turn them in to Governor Zika. They rely on trade up and down the coast."

Andre could tell she was withholding the full story, but before he could press her, a boy who appeared to be in his early teens approached. "There's land ahead, Miss Vanessa. Brace yourselves."

"Brace ourselves with what?" Andre sputtered.

The boy ignored him, his wide eyes drilling into Vanessa as he asked, "Our deal is still in place?"

"If this is truly Omis Island and Captain Krill transports us back to Agios Limani safely once our business is finished, then you can count our bargain fulfilled, young Spiro."

Spiro nodded and then scampered back to the quarterdeck, shouting orders to tighten the sheet and prepare anchor.

Andre glanced over his shoulder and up to the wheelhouse. The captain stared straight ahead, his expression blank yet focused. Taking a cue from the man, Andre shifted his attention to his own area of expertise, where he, too, was confident and sure, asking Vanessa, "Are any of your memories returning?"

"Snippets, but they don't add up to anything." She

shrugged her slim shoulders. "It's like I remember random stories from my childhood, but I don't understand the context."

"There haven't been any reports of downed ships or missing women," Andre said. "I asked around at the docks."

She stared into his eyes but didn't respond, their hands nearly touching as they both gripped the railing. A tingle shot up Andre's arm as another large wave pushed them together. Neither of them moved away. Andre cleared his throat and continued, "It must all be terribly frustrating for you."

Her lips tilted in a half smile. "Yes, it is, *Doctor*." Her voice was teasing but not unkind. "But what about your poor face?" She lifted her hand and brushed his cheek just below his blackened eye. The swelling had gone down, leaving a garish purple discoloration in its place.

He offered a dimpled grin. "I think it makes me look rather rakish."

Vanessa dropped her hand and held his gaze. "I don't believe you need any help in that department."

Heat built in Andre's chest until he had to look away. A heavy silence fell between them as the whitecaps diminished and the mist thickened. He fingered the hilt of the dagger strapped to his waist. If he was being honest, he'd found Vanessa discovering him beaten to a bloody pulp rather humiliating.

Each day—each hour—with her, he walked a tightrope between distrust and awe. True, he had longed for a partner, someone he could rely on. But he'd done things on his own for so long he didn't quite know what to make of her help. The practical, perhaps even cynical, clinician in him warned that becoming too attached would be a mistake. He needed to prepare for the day her memories came back and stole her away from him. But he was drawn to her all the same; she seemed to turn his hardships around with the blink of a lovely violet eye.

The boat slowed, and they both looked up at the island towering over them. As if from a great oozing cauldron, vapor slithered over the water, rolling in feathery wisps onto the shore. As the boat drifted closer, the fog shifted to reveal a dense forest, a crumbling pier, and a partially submerged boat bobbing in the thick haze.

"That's it. I go no further," the pirate captain announced from the wheelhouse.

"The dock looks secure enough," Andre said. "Just take us to the end."

"Ain't no way I'm risking the *Striker*." The pirate glanced at Vanessa and then quickly away. "Even for her."

CHAPTER 13

Andre had opened his mouth to protest again when Vanessa's warm hand lightly gripped his forearm. "Let me speak to him."

"I don't think it'll make a difference, and you can't swim in those heavy skirts." Andre leaned over the railing and stared down into the churning indigo waters. The notion of what creatures lurked beneath nearly closed his throat. But he had to get to that island. Even if the chances were slim that the answers he sought rested in its mist-covered hills, he had to try, for every single person he'd harmed with the curse.

For Sara.

"I'll go alone. I'm a strong swimmer. Wait on the boat. . . ." But when he glanced over, Vanessa was no longer by his side. He turned to see her approaching the captain. Under normal circumstances, Andre would've bet a mountain of coin the pirate wouldn't budge. But he'd witnessed the power of that smile. He surrendered to it gladly. And it appeared this man could do no different.

The captain gave Vanessa a stiff nod, then signaled to his crew. As the sails caught the wind, the craft glided forward, enveloped once again in the viscous haze.

***

The boards of the dock creaked, and thick mist eddied around their feet, making every step a guessing game. "Ready?" Andre asked, offering his arm to Vanessa. "You should hold on to me."

"Or you should hold on to *me*," Vanessa retorted with a small smile.

"Perhaps we could hold on to each other," Andre suggested as she linked her arm around his elbow. He set his hand on hers, forcing them to walk in tandem.

Andre peered back just in time to see the boat disappear into the miasma of fog and waves. He tugged Vanessa around and raised his hand, but the call for the ship to stop died on his lips. It was no use. Clearly the pirates had never intended to wait for them as they'd agreed.

Vanessa gripped her shell necklace, a look of utter rage dissolving into a muttered curse: "May drought plague Krill by day and storms ravage him by night for the rest of his short but miserable life."

Andre laughed, a little nervously. "Oddly specific, wouldn't you say?"

"But necessary." Vanessa's free hand was propped on her hip as she whirled around, brow quirked. "I could be much more explicit for that bloody bug—"

"All right," Andre said, cutting her off as their shuffling

steps led them to the end of the dock. Her intensity was something to behold.

They stepped onto solid ground and stared up at the impenetrable wall of swirling fog as tall and wide as the eye could see. Sunbeams sparkled in whorls and then disappeared as if swallowed whole.

Vanessa took a step forward, and Andre pulled her back. "I'm sorry. I never should have brought you here."

"Why?"

"What if . . ." His throat closed, and he fought to get the words out. "What if we never get off this island?"

Her gaze locked on his in challenge. "Why are you here?"

He swallowed, and his voice was rough when he said, "To find a cure for the cursed potion."

"Do you have any other ideas how to reverse it?"

"You know that I don't."

"Then we're wasting time." She took his hand and tugged him into the shroud of shadows.

It was like stepping from day into night, the peels of mist coating his skin and reaching into his lungs. Vanessa coughed, then rasped, "Hold your breath."

But it was too late. He'd already consumed the mist, causing him to wheeze like his customers with breathing disorders. If only he had a cloth saturated with lemon or eucalyptus oil . . . By the time he'd thought through which tonic would help him best, the cloud had thinned, and light glistened on the other side.

They began to run.

Stars winked in Andre's vision as they emerged from the poisonous mist. He bent double and sucked in clean air. Once the pain in his chest eased, he straightened. Vanessa stood as still as a statue, her eyes wide and unblinking. He followed her stare.

Flowers of every shape and color bloomed across the ground, on lush hedges, and on trees. He looked up to find a canopy of snowy petals, vines bursting with pink, and vivid green leaves framing a periwinkle sky—close to the shade of Vanessa's eyes. He stepped closer to a sprawling tree, its branches reaching out as wide as it was tall. He fingered the delicate moss that dripped from it like verbena curtains as it flowed in the gentle breeze. "Amazing," he breathed.

There were species of plants Andre had seen only in books and some so exotic he'd never seen anything close. As in the biblical Garden of Eden, enormous fruits grew in profusion, each one plumper and more vibrant than the last. He walked over and plucked a deep red apple, the globe nearly as large as Sara's head.

He didn't dare take a bite of the monstrous fruit, although by touch he could tell the flesh would be firm yet juicy. He wandered to a row of vines covered in dark purple clusters of grapes, each one three times the size of what the vineyards grew in Agios Limani. Then he moved to a plant and stopped short. The bush was as tall as he was, with leaves that appeared gossamer, each one made of iridescent strands knit together like spiderwebs. He drew closer and cupped a leaf in his palm, studying the geometric pattern. He looked at another and another, each one as unique as a snowflake.

His heart racing, he ran to the next exotic tree, covered in clear stars, like bubbles that disconnected in the breeze and floated into the air. He spun around to show Vanessa this earthly—or maybe otherworldly—wonder, and his heart plummeted.

She was nowhere in sight.

CHAPTER 14

VANESSA

VANESSA PEERED into a shallow pool. She could smell the salt as if the creatures within had washed in on the high tide. Rich green grass surrounded each irregularly shaped pond that dotted the vast field, wildflowers and thistle growing in profusion, which told her salt water had not touched the land in ages.

She sniffed. The air smelled acrid and invasive, like oil in water, with a pulse reminiscent of a heartbeat. Like magic. A smile came to her lips. The power she was sensing could easily have spawned Andre's cursed potions.

A shape darted beneath the surface of a pond at her feet. She knelt and reached slowly, then struck with predatory speed, snatching the creature out of the water. It squirmed, but she held tight to the slick skin, cold and hard like metal. Shaped like a fish, the thing had a humanoid face with floppy ears like a dog. She flipped it over and poked its soft silver underbelly. It jerked out of her grasp and dove back into the water.

Atlanticans were educated from an early age on every body of water and its life-forms. But nothing like these creatures, as far as Vanessa knew, existed on earth or in the oceans.

She ran to the next pool and found a linear thing, its body divided into three finger-width appendages of orange, green, and white, connected by a vertical face with no discernible mouth. When she tried to turn it over, something sharp stuck into her palm. "Ouch!"

The thing fell into the water with barely a splash. Rubbing the sting from her hand, she leaned in to find a delicate creature with wing-shaped fins flitting just below the surface.

Suddenly, she realized Andre hadn't followed her to

the ponds. Had the magic drawn them apart? For what purpose?

She stood and moved in a slow circle, searching for his tall form, and spied something big not far from her. She spun and grasped the shell at her throat. Two large beasts—one snow white, one black as night—stood side by side at the edge of the forest and stared in her direction.

Vanessa gaped, captivated by their equine beauty. Then they moved, their steps in eerie syncopation, heads shaking at the exact same angle, manes flying, every hair in perfect harmony. She tripped backward as the horses pranced in spine-chilling unison. As if they were one being, not two, they turned, and eyes like liquid stars stared across the meadow.

A man emerged from the forest and stopped beside them. "Welcome," he called.

Vanessa stiffened as he walked across the field, his animals close behind. Surely he was the one she and Andre had come looking for.

He stopped a few feet away. His ebony skin contrasted with light golden-brown eyes that flicked over her and paused on the nautilus around her neck. "Well, aren't you a remarkable creature," he noted, his tone casual.

She raised a brow. "Aren't we all?"

CHAPTER 14

The man threw back his head and laughed long and hard. "Right you are, dear. Right you are!" He smiled. "Excuse my manners. We so rarely get visitors here."

"You said 'we.' Do other people reside here as well?"

He shook his head of twig-brown curls. "Oh, no, I meant myself and the other creations who live on the isle."

Other creations?

He pointed to the beasts beside him. "Do you like them? They're echoes. Mirrors, if you will. Light and dark. Salvation and destruction. Some would consider them aberrations. Like most things on Omis Island." He smiled wide. "But I see them as my pets."

Goose bumps rose on Vanessa's skin, but curiosity got the best of her. "I've never seen creatures like these." She swept her hand to indicate the tide pools. "Where did they come from?"

"Here and there. They are each one of a kind. As are many of the plant species." He moved closer, and she noticed he was quite a bit shorter than her human form and younger than she'd realized.

"Do you collect them?" she asked.

Those unnerving gold-brown eyes settled on her. Still, she could not detect a hint of magic in him. Power flittered around his person, but Vanessa could not home in on it long enough to determine its origin. Was it the magic of the island itself she detected? Or was he the source of it all? She stared harder and stepped toward him.

"Mmm," the peculiar human hummed, not answering her question. "It always interests me where people pop up on the island. You see, the specific point of entry caters to their particular fascinations."

"What do you mean?" she asked, growing more confused by the minute. He spoke as if the island had a mind of its own.

"Well, the man back there"—he waved his hand away from where they stood—"clearly has an interest in flora."

"Andre?" Vanessa's eyes narrowed. "What have you done with him?"

He gave her a benign smile. "Nothing. The island showed him those specimens first. But you were drawn right away to the tide meadow and our unique sea fauna, which tells me a bit about you."

Vanessa's pulse quickened. "Are you saying this island has a consciousness?"

"Of a sort." He hopped over a nest burrowed in the tall grass, a step closer to her.

CHAPTER 14

Vanessa fingered her shell, sparking her power. Opening his mind and simply extracting what she was after would possibly save him from bodily harm. "Answer me directly," she said, her words an enchantment. "What is this island's source of power?"

The savant just laughed. "Forcing others to your will is not the way to find your true self."

Vanessa whirled on him, her eyes flashing and her magic lashing out. "You will answer me. Are you the savant?"

He was beginning to appear a bit bored. "Don't exhaust yourself, dear. I am immune to magic. It is how I exist."

She lowered her hand, and the shell's light winked out. "What *are* you?"

"What are *you*?" he returned, his mouth curling up.

Vanessa clenched her hands into fists. How could this average human be immune to her power? It didn't make sense. Guardian or scholar, the little pundit would help them, whether he liked it or not. She longed to sink into the salt water of a nearby pool, regain her full power—already she could feel the earliest signs of it dwindling—and show him who he was dealing with.

Just then, Vanessa heard Andre calling her name.

He jogged to her, sweat dampening his tan skin and

turning it gold in the sun. Great Neptune, he was beautiful. Even in that exotic paradise, he practically glowed.

She rushed to him and met him halfway. They talked over each other.

"There are plants I've never seen here—"

"I think I found the savant."

His green eyes widened. "You what?"

She nodded toward where she'd left the human and his otherworldly mirror pets. The beasts tipped their heads down, their manes falling over starry eyes in perfect unison.

"Holy God, what are those things?" Andre gasped.

"They're his pets," Vanessa whispered.

Andre recovered quickly, calling out, "Hello. I'm Andre Baros, and this is my friend Vanessa. Who are you, kind sir?"

Vanessa had to give Andre credit. Although she could feel the tremors of trepidation buzzing through him, his voice did not waver.

"I am the caretaker of Omis Island." He lifted a hand. "Weir Adamos. A pleasure to meet you."

"Now he's pleasant and forthcoming?" Vanessa grumbled. Andre had gained more information with a single question than she'd garnered in an entire vexing conversation. Perhaps anemones did catch more plankton than barracuda, as the old adage said.

Andre threw her a curious look before he moved around her, blocking her view with his large body. "We seek the guardian of the magical archives. Can I assume that is you?"

Vanessa skirted Andre and his misguided notions of gallantry.

"Guardian, you say." Weir scratched his curly head. "I suppose on some level that's true. I like it." He swept his arms wide. "Guardian of the archives!"

"So there *are* magical archives?" Vanessa asked.

The savant grinned. "Follow me and we'll chat over tea and cakes."

Weir pivoted on his heel and walked toward the tree line, expecting them to follow—which, of course, they would. Wouldn't they?

Vanessa looked at Andre, who widened his eyes and raised his brows high. She nearly laughed out loud, his expression communicating her own mix of amusement and trepidation concerning the strange savant.

Vanessa and Andre followed until Andre suddenly stopped dead to examine a metallic blue flower. "Incredible," he breathed, bending down and gently caressing its silky petals. Vanessa rolled her eyes—really, what was so compelling about a bunch of plants?—and kept walking. Taking the opportunity to catch up to Weir, Vanessa jogged to his side as they circled around a tide pool.

"I'm sorry." She nearly choked on the words as she tried to take a page from Andre's book. "For my earlier behavior."

"That's quite all right, dear."

Searching for a way to ask what she wished to know, she hedged. "Do you live here alone?"

After a pause, he replied, "Yes. For a very, very long time."

Vanessa's pulse quickened as she asked, "Do you know why we're here?"

"I have my suspicions."

They walked in silence for a moment as she watched him covertly. He almost bounced as he walked, anticipation radiating from his countenance. He was excited by their presence. If what he said was true, that he'd lived there alone for that long, then he had to wish for companionship. She glanced over her shoulder to find Andre following at a distance and decided to take a calculated risk.

CHAPTER 14

Vanessa stopped walking. "Tell me what you are, or we leave right now."

Weir slowed and faced her, his expression grave, his eyes shimmering like golden galaxies. Vanessa found that she could not look away.

"My dear," he said, "I *am* the island."

CHAPTER 15

ANDRE

ANDRE PAUSED, breathless, at the wide veranda and stone columns soaring several stories above their heads. He couldn't help grinning when Weir announced with a flourish, "Welcome to my humble abode."

Andre paused on the porch and gestured for Vanessa to precede him as Weir opened a set of double doors and waved them inside. The austere stone facade had not prepared Andre for the luxurious interior. His feet sank into plush carpet as he lifted his face to a hundred-point crystal chandelier, glowing with an undetermined light source. He stepped into the enormous entrance hall and walked over to inspect a tall vase full of colorful flowers, their blooms as unique as everything else on the island.

"Come, come, follow me." Weir strode past him and into a grand sitting room. Andre returned his focus to Weir as he trailed behind him and Vanessa.

As Andre joined them, he marveled at the room, papered in forest green and claret paisleys, floor-to-ceiling windows framing a roaring fireplace as wide as Andre was tall. The blaze put off no heat, and as he drew closer, he reached out a hand to the mystical river-green flames.

"I wouldn't do that if I were you." Andre pulled his arm back just before his flesh met the fire. "Those flames have a mind of their own."

Andre took a huge step back and muttered, "Of course they do."

"Please, take a look around. I'll be right back." Weir slipped from the room like a ghost.

Andre turned to Vanessa, who hovered in a corner of the room, staring out the window. She'd been unusually quiet since Andre had caught up to them in the field. "Vanessa?"

She turned to him, but her wide eyes didn't seem to focus on his face.

In two strides, Andre was by her side. "Are you all right?"

"Yes," she whispered. "I just think we should go as soon as possible."

"But you were so sure we should come here." He looked at her in confusion. "And besides, the pirates left us, remember?"

"There has to be a boat somewhere on this godforsaken island," she spat, digging her fingers into his arm almost painfully.

"Okay, okay." He placed a hand on hers and removed her clawlike fingers from his flesh, still bemused by her sudden desperation to get off the island. "Let me speak to him and then we'll . . . find a way to get home."

Just then, Weir reentered the room. He beckoned them near with a wave, perching on the brocade sofa's arm. "Now, what can I do for you?"

Andre led Vanessa to the settee facing their host. After they were seated, he noticed that a three-tiered silver stand had appeared on the table. It was covered in tiny cakes iced in rich chocolate, sparkling lemon yellow, and glazed strawberry pink. The top level held finger sandwiches that looked to contain hummus, cucumber, and glistening olive oil. Where the food had come from was as big a mystery as everything else since they'd arrived.

Having had enough of the enigmatic, Andre got straight to the point. "We need to see the magical archives."

The young man's otherworldly eyes twinkled. He scratched his curly head and said, "Hmm."

Andre selected a sandwich, stretched an arm across the back of the sofa, and crossed a leg over his opposite knee. Then he settled in to wait. The little man was decidedly odd, but a bit of sales psychology just might work here again, like it had with the governor. Let the customer come to him.

Weir stood up and paced in front of the hearth for several moments before pausing to face them. "Tell me why. Please make it a compelling argument. I've been on this island too long for some boring treasure hunt story."

Vanessa seemed to have finally returned to herself as she patted Andre on the knee and rose to her feet. "We've come for your help to counteract a curse that is preying upon innocents up and down the coast."

"Tell me more," Weir said, beginning to pace again.

"An old woman sent Andre after a treasure she claimed would grant wishes that money could not buy. He found it and chose to help his villagers with their various ailments and hardships. The potions worked at first."

"Even healing my little sister, who has been ill for years," Andre interjected.

"But then," Vanessa continued, "each wish turned—"

"Bad." Andre spoke up again. "My sister Sara's health markedly improved, but then in an instant, her condition worsened to the point that she can barely walk. One poor man who wished for prosperity for his family of ten children happened upon a bag of coin, but then lost his entire crop of apples in a rare frost that seemed to affect only his orchard. Without the sale of his harvest, he and his family will lose everything." Andre ground his back teeth until pain made him stop. "And it was all my fault."

"I see, and what sent you on a mission to Omis Island for help?"

"Governor Zika," Andre replied.

"Governor . . . *Zika*?" Weir shook his head in disbelief and plopped down on the stones of the hearth. "You can sit down, dear," he said to Vanessa. "I need to think."

Andre finally took a bite of the dainty sandwich in his hand and nearly groaned in pleasure at the combination of flavors. He was suddenly ravenous. Vanessa poured herself a cup of tea and, after taking a sip, sank into the cushions of the sofa with a sigh.

Weir looked up, noticing her appreciation for the brew. "Cherry hibiscus tea with a bit of cane sugar. My proprietary blend."

Andre's gaze flicked to the man. "You own it?"

Weir chuckled. "I own everything on this island."

"Do you know Governor Zika?" Andre asked, not wanting to be distracted even as he stuffed a delectable chocolate cake into his mouth. Raspberry filling and layers of ganache nearly made his eyes roll back in his head.

"Let's say I know *of* him, and I can tell you he does not have your best interests at heart."

Andre glanced at Vanessa, whose eyes narrowed in suspicion. Was Weir saying they were in danger? Or . . .

"What do you mean? Are the magical archives even real?" Andre rose to his feet, but suddenly the room spun around him, and he dropped back onto the sofa. His limbs felt like glue.

"Did you"—he could barely form the words, his tongue sticking to the roof of his mouth—"poison me?"

Vanessa stood with the lethal grace of a panther. "Weir Adamos, I swear on Neptune's grave, if you've hurt him, I'll tear you apart limb from limb."

The man gave a small mock shudder. "Like you tear into a meal of crab, no doubt."

Vanessa stalked forward, gleaming like a sunrise. Andre squeezed his eyes closed, but when he opened them again, she stood before Weir in a halo of gold and lavender, like an avenging goddess. Anyone could see that she had as many thorns as petals. That her passion for life sometimes overrode her sense. But that unpredictable nature, that bit of wildness, attracted Andre like the anticipation of a storm.

"No need to get angry, my dear," Weir said soothingly.

"Don't call me 'dear.'"

"Don't be so testy. Your beau will be fine. . . ."

Andre fought to stay conscious, but his blinks seemed to last longer and longer as he fell into a night-dark cloud, tucked in by the warmth of the stars. He smiled a stupid, senseless grin at nothing. The last thing he heard before drifting away could have been real or imagined.

Weir's voice floated as though they were underwater: "The archives are too dangerous for humans to traverse. And Mr. Baros here is much too chivalrous to allow you to accompany me alone. . . ."

"No," Andre moaned. He refused to abandon Vanessa to the machinations of Weir and the perils of the island.

CHAPTER 15

He gave one final Herculean effort to fight against the darkness and forced his eyes open a slit. Vanessa, no longer sparkling like sunbeams on the ocean, tersely nodded assent to Weir just before sleep swallowed Andre whole.

CHAPTER 16

VANESSA

WEIR LED Vanessa through a dense jungle, vines dripping from enormous trees, leaves as big as her torso shading their heads. The vast change in topographies, from the mountainous coast, resplendent with tide pools, to an enchanted forest full of fantastical flora, and now this tropical jungle, could only be the result of layers upon layers of magic.

She stuck close to Weir down a narrow dirt path that would have been dark but for the preternatural glow lining both sides of the walkway. Vanessa had only ever seen bioluminescence created by strange creatures swimming in the farthest depths of the ocean. She knelt and reached out to touch the pulsating blue-and-purple radiance, but Weir snatched her hand back.

"Those insects burrow into your skin."

Vanessa sprang away with alacrity. There were enough burrowing parasites in the sea that she knew to keep her distance unless she wished to play host to a bloodsucking organism.

"Is the archive close? I don't want to leave Andre alone too long." She was still furious with Weir for what he'd done to Andre, but she decided to overlook it for the time being in favor of getting what she had come for. She'd deal with Weir later. Perhaps he was, in fact, immune to magic, but Vanessa would bet that his precious pets were not.

"Not near. Not far. Up here." He gestured in a direction vaguely ahead of them as they walked.

Vanessa unclenched her teeth to ask, "What will I be looking for, exactly?" She doubted the answer to finding the source of the curse—and utilizing its power for herself—lay in some dusty old tombs.

"There *are* books, but . . ." Weir's voice trailed off as he pushed through the leaves of an enormous fern. "There is also a singular object with immense power. If you are lucky enough to find it, I believe it will solve many of our dilemmas."

An object. Vanessa thought back to her notion that there must be something magical on the island, keeping it hidden away from those who would seek it unless it wanted to be found. Perhaps that was the object Weir was referring to.

She was about to ask him, but just then, the path opened to a ripe green hill. A confection of white stone that appeared to exude light perched at its pinnacle, its abrupt beauty stealing the breath from Vanessa's throat. As she climbed, a pulse of energy that could not be seen, like the tides of the moon or the coming of a storm, tugged at her senses, seeming to exert a stronger pull on her with every step.

Vanessa broke out in a cold sweat. Moisture drenched her hairline and ran down her spine. She knew it was only a building, but for a moment, a premonition screamed that if she walked through its doors, she could be stripped down to nothing—made as average as a human. She subconsciously gripped her shell for security.

They reached the top of the slope, and Vanessa sensed

a change; sorcery radiated beneath her feet and into the very air. Energy so potent she could taste it on her tongue, feel it entering her pores. Magic so concentrated it didn't need a conduit, like her nautilus.

The essence of a true deity.

Need rose in Vanessa like a ravenous beast, empty and clawing with hunger. *This* was the power she needed to possess. To wield. To rule.

Without hesitation, she stepped into the throb of radiance.

"Wait!" Weir called.

But it was too late.

***

Vanessa paused inside as the door closed, encasing her in darkness. A lock turned with a loud click. She spun back and grasped the handle. It didn't budge. Fine. Whatever the place held, she could handle it. She'd faced powerful beings in Atlantica and beyond.

With a snap, light appeared on her fingertips, illuminating an empty room. Didn't human libraries have cozy furniture and warm light and shelves spilling over with old dusty tomes? The desolate square space looked more like a stone cell fit for creatures that skittered in the shadows.

Or a tomb harboring the dead.

Her conjured flame flickered out, and a chill resonated from deep in her bones.

A bang sounded on the door, making Vanessa jump.

"Vanessa!" Weir called from the other side.

"I'm here. The door won't open. Where are the archives?" Her hunger for the power she'd sensed outside the structure returned in force, overruling her trepidation.

"There's a door on the opposite wall that leads belowground."

Vanessa rolled her eyes. A tomb indeed.

"Be honest about your intentions. And do not use your magic. It will anger her," Weir warned, his voice sounding muffled.

Her?

Vanessa pounded a fist on the door, tired of his games. "Do you mean Circe?"

Her question was met with silence. But Weir didn't need to say her name. The unending power Vanessa had sensed outside could only be from the witch-goddess Circe, who, according to legend, had vanished along with all the other ancient Greek gods. Though apparently Circe had only made it as far as Omis Island.

Vanessa walked across the small room and carefully felt along the walls for an opening. Excitement tightened her chest.

Her fingers found a turn in the brick, and she felt open air with her other hand. Without her magic she could see nothing. But she took shuffling steps and felt along the stones until her foot slipped over an edge and she wobbled. Her arms flying out, she felt walls on both sides, and she braced herself against them as she felt her way downward. The air smelled of damp mist and a trace of something rotten.

As Vanessa advanced, she reviewed everything she'd read about the witch-goddess in her bespelled library of human culture. Circe was the daughter of Helios, the Titan of the sun, and Perse, an ocean nymph. Circe had the ability of transfiguration and had been known to turn her enemies into animals. Did she still reside there? Hidden for centuries? Could that explain all the unique mystical creatures on the island?

Then a memory froze her in place.

Circe's conduit, the Rhabdos. A thing of legend.

Could it still exist on the lost island? Was that the

object Weir had spoken of? If she could find the magical staff, she wouldn't need some dusty old text to unlock a higher level of power. She could do it on her own, with the staff as her aid.

Vanessa stumbled down another step before righting herself against the slime-coated wall. She jerked her hand back and paused to take a breath. Surely a fellow sorceress would not protest her conjuring a bit of light so that she didn't fall and break her neck. No matter what that eel Weir said, Vanessa felt a connection to the ancient goddess and knew she would understand, one powerful female to another. With a quick snap, flame shot from her fingertips and lit the passage.

The crumbling stone staircase angled down into darkness. Vanessa resumed her descent, lifting her fingers high to illuminate her way. Rivulets of water coursed down between the bricks. The scent of brine grew stronger. She ran a finger through a slow stream and then touched her tongue. Salt. That made sense, of course, as she was likely below sea level at that point.

An arched opening loomed below, and an eerie silence flowed over her like the fathoms of the Hellenic Trench. She rushed down and through the doorway and was greeted by the rough-hewn walls of a cavern.

CHAPTER 16

She turned in a slow circle. Empty. No tomb or magic staff or even shelves of dusty old books. Disappointment extinguished her light. She reignited it and walked the perimeter, searching for any sign of charmed compartments hidden in the rock. Either sleeping or dead, Circe's spirit lingered. That much was clear.

A narrow passage branched off the main room, and Vanessa hunched over to follow it, emerging in a round cave bisected by a waterfall. Vanessa tiptoed toward it, unsure at first why its presence raised the hairs on the back of her neck. Then she realized the water flowed silently, up out of the floor and toward the ceiling.

Vanessa reached out her hand toward the falls and whispered, "Circe, I am a fellow sorceress from the sea." Her fingers edged closer to the silent rushing river. "I seek your wisdom."

A sour taste burned the back of Vanessa's throat just before an explosion of water pushed her into the air. She slammed hard against the far wall, the breath knocked from her lungs.

"You lie, little fish."

That voice, like an abyss—bottomless and void—burrowed into Vanessa's mind.

Vanessa scrambled to her feet and spun in a circle,

searching for the source of the voice. "Show yourself!" she gasped.

When there was no response, her stomach sank. She needed the goddess's help. "I didn't lie. This human body is a temporary form. I am of the sea."

"I see your true self, Cecaelia. But you seek wisdom from no one." The fearsome voice spoke in her head.

Cecaelia was her real form, the sea-dwelling hybrid of human and octopus. "Who are you?"

"You know exactly who I am." The voice hissed and pounded in her blood. Vanessa covered her ears, knowing it would do little good. If Andre were there, he could persuade anyone of his innocence. Of his intention to help others.

"That is because it would be the truth." The witch-goddess's voice boomed again, reading Vanessa's thoughts.

Vanessa walked forward slowly and carefully, searching for a visual sign of the being. When she detected nothing, she decided to try again. "I wish to find a cure for the Grimaldi curse."

Circe didn't respond. The silence stung.

Vanessa's focus wavered. The call of Circe's magic intoxicated her. Beckoned for possession. She closed her eyes and fought against the darkness in her soul, the selfish creature who had come ashore to amass power for herself; she pushed down the greed and searched for a pure motivation, suspecting it was the only way to engage with the goddess. She visualized Andre again, his beautiful face etched with pain over what he'd done to inadvertently hurt others, his forest-green eyes shining with unshed tears. Brave little Sara hobbling around on her painfully thin legs, helping Vanessa any way she could manage. Longing and grief and hope tangled together in Vanessa's chest, her heart splitting in two halves. It started to feel more real to her than not.

She dropped to her knees before the waterfall and bowed her head. "The man I came with would like to find a cure for a curse, and I am told a magic library resides here. Will you help us?"

Water crashed over Vanessa's head, and she scrambled back as it flowed onto the ground, spreading out and surrounding her like a curtain dropping. Braced on her arms, she now stared up at a wall full of artifacts and ancient tomes, faded with time and use: murky jars, opaque crystals, and leather- and cloth-bound books, some wrapped in fish scales.

The magical archives.

What great potions and terrible spells those texts must contain, Vanessa thought as she gazed upon the library of a goddess.

Vanessa swiped the sodden hair from her eyes and stood, her legs unsteady beneath her. "Where do I start to find the curse?"

"Roots," Circe replied calmly, as if she hadn't flung Vanessa into a rock wall moments before.

"What do you mean?"

"Power is one thing. Origin is another. The curse lives and breathes beneath the ground, its roots growing and spreading like a fungus. You must rip it out from the source. The more time passes, the less time you will have to stop it," Circe said, her tone now almost conversational.

"And what of possessing it? Andre wishes to stop it, *and* I want to take its power." If the deity could read her mind and had still given Vanessa access to the library, perhaps the witch-goddess understood her divided heart—and her separate intentions—in seeking out the curse's source.

"Why?" The question echoed in Vanessa's mind. "Why do you need more power? Will it grant you happiness? Eternal life? Love?"

Vanessa had a distinct feeling the goddess spoke from

experience. "I do not need love. I wish for . . ." She paused, her heart pulsing loudly in her ears. Love was a fairy tale she'd given up on long before. If not love, what reason could she find that would buy her favor with the goddess?

Stalling for time, Vanessa turned the question back on the ancient witch. "What do you want, Circe? Why are you here, alone in this desolate place?"

"Waiting. We're all waiting for something, aren't we, little cecaelia? Waiting for rescue, for purpose . . . for escape."

Vanessa's stomach turned cold. "Are you waiting to die?"

"No, I am waiting for the one who will carry out my legacy."

High color flushed Vanessa's cheeks. If the staff still existed and held even a trace of Circe's magic, Vanessa could step into her greater destiny and return to Atlantica triumphant. *She* could be the witch-goddess's legacy.

Vanessa moved closer and craned her neck to see the shelves towering at least a story over her head. All that knowledge, locked away, vacant and dead, when it could be used and brought back to life in her hands. She pushed back the thought and refocused on the cure for the curse.

But a notion foraged for purchase in her mind: if she

found the cure for the curse, how could she harness its power for herself? As she scanned the library, her eyes landed on the answer.

Nestled on a high shelf, a carved wooden stick, the length of her lower arm, rested inside a case of glass.

The Rhabdos.

There it was, exactly as Vanessa had hoped.

Without thought, Vanessa grasped her shell with her left hand and reached for the staff with her right. The bookcase trembled as tomes rattled and fell with a splash into the pool below the shelf.

"Stop!"

The ground shaking beneath her feet, Vanessa ignored the voice and reached for the staff again, shouting, "*Come to me!*"

The glass case didn't budge from its perch, even as tome after ancient tome splashed into the water. A reverberation whipped out as the felled books flew from the pond back onto the shelves. The cave shook harder, bits of the ceiling crashing down. Vanessa braced her legs and tried again, gripping her nautilus tighter. "*COME TO ME!*"

But the staff didn't appear in her hand, as the spell dictated. Instead, huge sheets of glass slammed down around Vanessa, boxing her in.

CHAPTER 16

"My legacy is not for you to own." Circe's voice crashed through Vanessa's brain. "But now you are mine to possess."

Vanessa was caged like an animal. A scream tore from her throat.

CHAPTER 17

ANDRE

THE MANSION trembled and Andre's eyes popped open. Tiny cakes and finger sandwiches flew as the serving tree crashed onto the table. Menace raced down his spine, an anger like he'd never felt blazing through his mind. He bolted up.

What has Weir done with Vanessa?

The tremble became a shattering quake. Priceless paintings crashed to the floor. Bricks tumbled into the fireplace. Weir raced into the room, panic stark on his face.

CHAPTER 17

Andre leapt to his feet and then wobbled, clutching his spinning head. "What's happening? Where's Vanessa?"

A horrendous crash and bang sounded, and the stone floor cracked open. Andre grabbed Weir's arm and yanked him away from the fissure.

"We have to get out of here!" Weir yelled. "Follow me."

Andre staggered after the savant into the hallway and out the front doors. His legs and arms tingled as if asleep, and he tripped over his own feet. A massive pillar shook loose, and Weir whirled around as it fell. Andre froze, his eyes wide, the stone column plummeting toward him. Weir raised his hands and stopped the pillar mid-fall. "Go!"

More fury than fear dampening the aftereffect of whatever sleeping draft the savant had given him, Andre leapt up and jumped off the porch. Feet pumping, he ran from the crumbling building.

Weir released the column with a devastating crash and caught up to Andre. They raced down a forest path and then through the tide pool field. Branches splintered from the trees. Andre wove and leapt over a tide pool that boiled like lava.

Without warning, the shaking stopped. Andre's head spun, and he slumped against a giant oak. Helplessness and rage pounded in his ears. He'd brought Vanessa to

Omis Island against his better judgment; if something happened to her, he would never forgive himself. "Where is Vanessa?" Andre launched off the tree, grabbed Weir's arm, and spun him around.

"She's . . ." Weir's eyes darted back and forth, as if he saw something Andre couldn't.

Andre grasped the servant's shoulders and shook him. "Did you take her to the archives? Is she still there?"

"Archives?" Weir blinked at Andre as though he didn't recognize him, his eyes swirling with pinpricks of ethereal light. Andre's heart squeezed. What manner of creature was this man?

The earth gave a mighty quake, and Weir's gaze seemed to snap back into focus. "Yes, the archives . . . but it might be too late."

Andre leaned down and growled in Weir's face: "Too late for what?"

"She's dislodged the staff. . . ." The savant nodded sharply and then ran up the path, but the ground heaved, and he fell hard onto his hands and knees. Staring at the ground, he muttered, "This is either very good or very, very bad."

"For whom?" Andre snarled as he took Weir by the arm and lugged him to his feet.

CHAPTER 17

"For Vanessa . . . bad. For me . . . good." He shook his curly head. "Or good for you and bad for me."

Andre had no clue what the man was rambling about. He leaned down to peer into his face and said with measured slowness, "Just show me where she is."

"Right." Weir turned back to the path and began jogging.

The trail widened into a steep hill, and they raced up toward a small white building. As they neared the top, the earth gave an enraged judder, and Andre fell to his knees, fighting back a wave of wooziness from Weir's cursed drug. Andre glanced back to find the man rolling back down the hill.

A macabre screech rent the air as brick and mortar cracked and the earth writhed in agony. Andre slid back down the grass, the ground pitching and tossing him into the air.

Weir bowled back onto his feet and pointed up to the tiny building that seemed perched impossibly far above them. "Vanessa's in there."

Andre turned back. Digging his fingers into the dirt, he struggled to find purchase as his feet slipped out from under him. Methodically, he clawed his way up the quivering mound. He'd unwittingly surrendered so many to the curse and there had been nothing he could do to stop its toxic repercussions. Now Vanessa had put herself in danger to help him find a cure.

He scaled his way inch by inch up the hill, pain flaring and blood flowing as his fingernails tore and his skin was gouged by falling rocks. Andre paid no mind to his physical discomfort, setting his sights on the building at the pinnacle. He would not give up until he saved Vanessa from the nightmare he'd dragged her into.

CHAPTER 18

VANESSA

VANESSA FOUGHT her way to her feet, visions of being trapped for Circe to possess and use for her every whim fueling her fury. She threw out a hand to crack the glass, but the ground tilted beneath her and her spell flew wildly overhead, knocking more rocks from the ceiling. As the last books lifted back into place from where they'd fallen, a lid slid over the top of Vanessa's cage. Panic gripped her as she pounded her fists uselessly against the glass walls.

"I'm so very glad your greed brought you to me, beautiful cecaelia," Circe hissed.

Salt water rushed into the sealed box, soaking Vanessa's shoes and then her skirts. "You tricked me!"

"No, I warned you that more power would not bring you what you wished. And still you reached for my beloved staff." Circe's vile voice drilled into Vanessa's brain, every word a nail in her prison. "Once I have you weakened enough to inhabit you, my spirit will be free to roam the earth once again, inside your magnificent body. You will be *my* conduit, Cecaelia."

For a long moment, Vanessa forgot how to breathe as water leached up her bodice, locking her in a watery coffin. She closed her eyes.

The first thing she saw was not the Rhabdos in her hand as she ruled Atlantica. Not even her beloved ocean. Her mind filled with visions of Andre Baros's beautiful face and the wild notions of her heart that seemed to gain strength with every hour they spent together. The flash of his dimpled grin that made her feel like she'd been shoved off a cliff. The connection when their eyes met that told her he might become the only creature on earth to understand her if they had more time. She'd never felt that way about anyone—that tangle of tenderness, admiration, and longing.

Her heart shuddered. She would never see that noble, brave, selfless man again if she didn't do something. *Now.*

Vanessa realized she would need to trick the goddess, distract her by thinking about one thing while really plotting her escape. So she focused on something completely benign that made her smile every time she thought about it: all those little merpeople bouncing around Atlantica in the magic bubbles she'd created.

Water reached her neck as she focused on all the mundane objects the merfolk had used to try to break out of their prisons—sharp cupolas, stingray barbs, lava rocks, their teeth. She simultaneously gathered her power, calming her mind while activating her body, drawing on the rage of the sea, the power in a storm, the fire under the caverns of the earth.

She gripped her nautilus and sent a burst of energy into the glass. A hairline crack splintered as the water continued to rise over her head.

Nearly there. She swam in a circle, fighting the cry of her body to transform, keeping the memory of the merfolk foremost in her mind to distract the goddess. Her insides screamed and pulled on every dark spell she'd memorized, every enchantment she'd stolen from Triton's study.

Then she faced the wall of the deity's precious books, and as she muttered a hex, lightning crackled out of her palms, shattering the glass. More bolts, almost uncontrollable now, blasted into the magical archives. The bottom row of old tomes burst into flame.

With every reserve of magic she had left, she flung a fork of light behind her and ran. An ungodly scream filled Vanessa's head as Circe raised the water curtain, but it was too late. The books had caught like kindling.

Vanessa spun and sprinted through the tunnel, the entrance swimming before her eyes. The goddess's screech sliced through her brain. She aimed right and hurtled up several stairs before they appeared to tilt, and she fell against stone. Vanessa pushed off the wall, legs pumping harder. Circe's cries of protest faded and the mental connection between them seemed to weaken with Vanessa's every step forward. But so did her human form: depleted of energy, she fell to her knees as her legs buckled. She needed to reach the sea, to immerse and reenergize. As she crawled, her human heart stuttered in her chest.

But Circe's outrage grew fainter the farther Vanessa climbed. She kept clambering on hands and knees. Murky waves crashed over her vision, and for a moment she clawed up the stairs practically unseeing. Her movements grew sluggish, and she felt her pulse speed up, then slow.

She'd pushed this mortal body too hard.

CHAPTER 19

ANDRE

ANDRE BACKED UP several paces, tightened his muscles, and aimed his shoulder toward the door for the fifth time. But before he reached it, the handle turned with a soft click and the door swung open. He barreled into the dark room.

"Vanessa!"

The interior looked like an empty concrete cell. He rotated in a circle before spotting a narrow passage in the far corner. Without checking if Weir followed, he raced through it and nearly tumbled down a flight of stairs swallowed by shadows.

"Vanessa?" Andre's voice echoed back to him.

He stepped into the abyss, arms out and using both walls as a guide. Something heavy lay in the air, separate from the acrid smell of smoke and burning rubbish, reminiscent of the tingles of power he'd felt while handling the Grimaldi curse. But infinitely more potent.

He continued to descend, fingers tracing slime-coated stones. What, or who, resided in this place? The archives must have been guarded by someone—or something.

"Vanessa?" His voice sounded shaky even to him as it bounced off the cold surfaces.

A light flared behind Andre, and he whirled to find Weir at the top of the stairs. "Did you find her?" the man asked, his voice more command than question. "We have to go before this place self-destructs . . . now!"

"No, but—" Andre broke off as he spun around and saw a body sprawled on the stairs just below him.

He raced into the gloom, any trepidation gone at the sight of her prone figure. "Vanessa!" He placed a hand on her back. Her clothes were drenched and icy cold. Andre shook her, then checked for a pulse. When he found it, he placed a hand on the side of her chilled face. "Vanessa, please wake up," he whispered. But she remained motionless.

He faced Weir, and as he did, something zipped past his head. Andre ducked down as Weir caught whatever it was in his right hand. A disconcertingly wide grin on his face, the savant tucked an oblong glass box inside his coat and then said, "Andre, we must leave, or we may never be able to."

Andre reached down and scooped Vanessa into his arms. As small as she was, her wet gown and limp body made him stagger. His already bruised shoulder crashed against the stone wall just as the ground began to shake again.

"This building is not long for this world," Weir called. "Now, run!"

With a final rally, Andre pushed off the wall and sprinted up the quivering stairs, Vanessa hanging limply from his grasp. A large stone fell from the ceiling, and he ducked out of the way just in time as he made it to the top of the landing.

Weir waited outside the main door, motioning frantically. "Go! Let's go!"

Andre's survival instincts kicked in and adrenaline propelled him outside. Once they reached the hill path, the quaking gentled. Andre leaned back to counteract Vanessa's weight and half stumbled, half ran down the slope. "How are . . . we . . . getting off . . . the island?" Andre panted.

Weir's face split in the demented grin of a jester. "I have a boat."

They reached the bottom of the hill and Weir sprinted through a stand of trees, Andre close behind. "I thought you couldn't leave Omis?"

"I created the *Mermaid* for the eventual glorious day." He swept his arms wide as they cleared the forest, and indicated a boat, tied to a short pier, bobbing in the water. "That day has finally arrived!"

A horrendous crash, like the side of a mountain sliding into the earth, jolted the ground. Andre shifted Vanessa in his arms and followed Weir to the waiting boat.

***

"Are you sure she's going to be okay?" Andre asked as he leaned over Vanessa, her face in perfect repose. Her breaths were shallow, skin sickly pale, and she lay as still as death. He brushed a strand of wet hair off her cheek and took her cold hands, warming them in his. Clearly, some trauma had befallen her. And he'd been in no state to assist her in the archives, thanks to the cracked little savant who'd spiked his tea.

"She will be fine, dear Andre!" Weir cackled from the wheelhouse. He'd been as giddy as a child with a gaggle of puppies since they'd left Omis Island.

Currently, they traveled across the channel with no crew, the craft propelled by some invisible force. Not suspicious at all, Andre mused as he searched the open waters, relieved to find there were no boats near enough to question their supernatural passage. Calling to Weir over the wind, he demanded, "How are we moving through the water?"

"A bit of magic that I'm afraid will leave me soon."

Andre didn't trust Weir. Nor did he care for his cryptic ways. But he had helped rescue Vanessa and procured them passage off the island. For now, Andre had no choice but to put their lives in the strange man's hands. "What happened back there?" he asked.

"Don't know, exactly." Weir steered the boat over a large swell and let out a whoop as the bow lifted into the air and then smashed down with a gargantuan splash.

Andre threw his upper body over Vanessa's and gripped the nearby railing, water soaking the back of his coat. "Take it easy, would you?" he yelled over his shoulder.

CHAPTER 19

But Weir's response was to toss his head back and laugh uproariously.

Andre wished he could force the savant to talk and tell him something, anything, that would shed some light on the situation, but he didn't dare leave Vanessa in her helpless state. She bore no wounds, bumps, or bruises that could clue him in to what had happened to her down in that pit.

Andre waited a moment for Weir's laughter to subside, then tried again. "Did she find the archives?"

"Oh, yes, she definitely did," Weir replied, eyes on the horizon.

"And?" Andre ground out between clenched teeth.

"I don't believe the outcome is how you would wish it." The slight smile never left Weir's lips as he said, "But I'll allow your girl to explain."

"*My girl* is incapacitated, thanks to you."

"She did all of that herself." Weir gestured into the air. "The island took control."

"Saints, man!" Andre growled. "Are you ever going to give me a straight answer?"

They hit another huge wave just then, and Andre lost his footing as Vanessa nearly rolled off the bench. He tucked her neatly under his arm, anchoring them both in place.

"You know," Weir said conversationally, "I did not think your visit to the island would end well. I foresaw that destruction would follow you. And that much is true. But it turns out I am in your debt."

Andre placed a hand on Vanessa's forehead. Her skin still felt unnaturally cold. He leaned back and worked to digest everything the savant had said. Vanessa had found the magical archives, but until she awoke, Andre wouldn't know whether she'd learned something useful that could help them. But what was this about Weir anticipating their visit? He clearly had some sort of magical ability, but the rest didn't make sense. "If you knew we were bringing destruction, why did you welcome us onto the island?"

"Because, my new friend, there are risks worth taking. Now, for the first time in centuries, I am free."

Done with Weir's half answers, Andre focused on how best to get them home. They had walked to get to the port that morning. Had it only been a day? It felt like weeks since they'd sat around the table at the cottage eating a light breakfast of muffins and tea.

As the peculiar craft sped across the water, the skies cleared into a big bowl of blue, the churning seas quieting into layers of turquoise glass as they approached Agios Limani Harbor. Andre geared up for his next move; he didn't have any money to pay for transportation, but perhaps he could find a friendly face and entreat upon their kindness to help him get Vanessa home.

Suddenly, the boat banked sharply to the right, away from the port. "What are you doing now?"

"Where can I dock this thing that isn't so public?" Weir asked.

Good point. Andre imagined a boat with no sails or oars *would* cause quite a ruckus. As he thought over the possible places where they could make land, he remembered the short dock at the end of the cove near their cottage. They hadn't used it since his parents' accident. The memory tried to surface, the shroud of pain and terror and grief that had encompassed him as he'd last stood on that dock. He pushed it all down deep, willing himself to remain in the moment, to stay strong for Vanessa's sake, if not his own. "Follow the coast and I'll tell you where to turn."

Andre stared down at Vanessa, his eyes drifting over her thick dark lashes, shadowed cheekbones that swept up like wings, lush lips that begged to be kissed. But his connection to her went deeper: it was the way she made him feel, her fearlessness and unpredictability, that intrigued him like no other. In the short time they'd known each other, they'd been through so much that their bond felt strong. Unbreakable. He couldn't lose her now.

Andre entwined their fingers and leaned in close to her ear, his whisper laced with urgency. "I'm here, Vanessa. I've got you, and I'm not letting go."

CHAPTER 20

VANESSA

THE DAY AFTER Andre and Vanessa had traveled to Omis Island dawned with bright sunlight in a cloudless blue sky. The opposite of Vanessa's mood as she threw back the covers and began to dress, ignoring the sharp, persistent ache in her temple.

The Rhabdos had been within her grasp, and instead of fighting for it, she'd run like a cuttlefish under the spear. Shame splashed over her at the memory of her weakness. The only information she'd found out about the

Grimaldi curse before destroying the archives was beyond discouraging: Circe had said that not only did the curse live beneath the village and have roots that grew like a fungus, but the more time that passed, the less time there would be to stop it.

And absorb it.

Andre would be devastated.

After dressing in a royal blue skirt and soft peasant blouse in pale lilac, a periwinkle lace-up bodice embroidered with swirls of golden thread completing the ensemble, Vanessa ventured downstairs, where she found Weir chatting up Yia-Yia at the kitchen table. She rolled her eyes to the heavens. "What are *you* doing here?"

When Weir Adamos saw her in the doorway, he shot to his feet. "Vanessa, you've recovered, I see."

"No thanks to you," she grumbled as she pulled a chair out and plopped into it. Her head hurt worse than when she'd stayed up all night spelling lobsters into tango dancers as a gift for the king's coronation. He hadn't even appreciated the dozens of shellfish in tiny ruffled dresses and formal suits performing synchronized twirls and dips when it had upstaged his acceptance speech.

Vanessa rubbed her temples, trying to soothe away the ache.

CHAPTER 20

"Andre has a mixture of lavender, peppermint, and lemongrass that can help with that," said a soft, weathered voice.

Vanessa's hands stilled and she looked up to find Yia-Yia watching her with a neutral expression. It was the first time the woman had addressed her directly.

She didn't have to wonder what had precipitated the change for long. Weir set down his teacup and said, "I was just telling Mrs. Baros how you risked your life to try to find a cure for the curse."

"*Try* being the operative word." Vanessa sat back and crossed her arms under her chest. Had she tried? At first, perhaps, but she'd soon been distracted by the greater prize—the power of a goddess's staff—as Circe had known she would be. Admitting defeat did not come easily. Yet she had escaped with her life, avoiding the appalling outcome of her body's becoming a puppet for a cranky goddess.

Yia-Yia placed a bowl of yogurt and berries with fresh honey in front of Vanessa. "Eat. You need to rebuild your strength. You'll send Andre into a tizzy if he sees you so pale."

The old woman's tone was far from warm, but she was right. Vanessa's ordeal had drained her human form to the point that even the simple acts of dressing and walking down the stairs made her limbs feel heavy and her mind fuzzy. "Where is Andre?" She found herself longing for his steady gaze and solid presence.

"He and Sara are in his workshop bottling new tonics."

Vanessa nodded, feeling unaccountably annoyed at Andre's absence. Wasn't he worried about her? He usually hovered like a protective . . . what? Friend? Suitor? Lover? She swallowed a bite of the overly sweet berry mixture. She had no idea what she was to Andre. Or how he felt about her. All she knew was that when she'd been trapped in Circe's box, the fear of never seeing him again had motivated her to fight until she couldn't hold on any longer.

Vanessa's stomach churned uncomfortably. Was this what insecurity felt like? Perhaps it was her physical weakness playing with her mind. She tossed her hair over her shoulder and downed a cup of tea. Ridiculous. Of course Andre wanted her. How could he not?

Weir and Yia-Yia's chatter blurred into nonsense as Vanessa drank two more cups of tea. But it wasn't enough to stave off the persistent weakness of her body. She needed the salt water of the cove. Her eyes drifted out the window to the mirror pool. Could she slip in without being noticed? Likely not before dark.

"Miss Vanessa, will you accompany me on a walk?" Weir's request jolted Vanessa from her distracted thoughts.

CHAPTER 20

"Yes, visit the workshop. Andre will be relieved to see you up and about," Yia-Yia chimed in, her voice syrupy.

Vanessa gave a nod and stood to find the old woman assessing her, lips pursed, head tilted. But Vanessa could work with skepticism. It was a vast improvement over outright suspicion. She offered a smile as sweet as her breakfast. "Thank you, Mrs. Baros. I feel much restored."

Outside, Weir offered his elbow and Vanessa reluctantly placed her hand on his thin arm. When they were out of hearing distance of the house, Weir exclaimed in a low voice, "I have to know what happened! How on earth did you defeat her?"

"Weir, I'm too tired for your games. You have to know that I didn't defeat anyone."

He led her over to a flat rock on the edge of the cove. "It's a hot day. Let's put our feet in the water."

Vanessa spun on the little man. Could he have discerned her secret? It was as though he'd heard her innermost thoughts, wishing for the cool balm of her native sea. She sniffed as if the idea disgusted her. "I think I'll go find Andre."

"If you sit, I will explain why I am forever in your debt," Weir said as he gestured toward the rock ledge.

Vanessa sat at the edge of the cove. The sea shimmered

in layers of seductive aqua blue. Desire welled in her heart, and, too desperate to hide her need, she kicked off her shoes. The moment her toes touched the water, revitalizing energy rushed into her veins. Vanessa leaned back on her hands, feet dangling in the soft current, and sighed. "Now, tell me how it is that you owe me a debt when I burned your magical archives to the ground."

"Don't you wish to know why the island flows—flowed—in my veins?"

Vanessa shot him a sidelong glance, nodding for him to continue.

"I am a direct descendant of Circe and Odysseus. A piece of the witch-goddess's magic was born inside of me."

Vanessa sat up straight, and her head whipped toward him. "What?"

Weir looked at her knowingly. "Before you get any devious ideas, my power is nontransferable."

Her heart sped up even as her shoulders slumped. "I wasn't thinking about that."

"Don't lie, dear. It doesn't suit you." Weir waved a hand in the air in dismissal and then continued. "When I was twenty years old, the island lured me from Benin to become its guardian. To mesh with the enchantment. To learn. And protect it.

CHAPTER 20

"I'd been an orphan, begging for crumbs in the streets, for as long as I could remember, with no familial ties. No notion of who my parents were. Still, to follow a mystical call was not an easy decision. But the moment I accepted my fate, money and transportation fell into my lap, making the journey easy." Weir's eyes grew wide and shiny. "I've been on that island for centuries. Not aging. Never changing. Alone, save for my pets. You freed me."

Caught up in his swirling gold gaze, Vanessa whispered, "How?"

Weir stared out across the turquoise pool in contemplation before saying, "Circe's spirit resided in the archives. Whatever you did, Ursula of Atlantica, severed her hold over the island and allowed me to leave."

Cold fingers wrapped around Vanessa's throat. "How do you know me? Who I really am?" Her voice sounded strained. Then the realization hit her all at once: he could read her thoughts, just like Circe. "Can you still see into my mind?"

He shook his curly head and chuckled. "No, thank Zeus! I can sense its energy, but I can't see inside any longer. Your brain is a wriggling mess of dark and light contradictions. Not easy to navigate, I can tell you that."

"What about Circe's magic? Are you cut off from that now as well?"

"Yes. I had enough to power the *Mermaid* and get us off the island, but the longer I'm separated from Circe, the more quickly it fades." He rubbed his curly head. "I have to admit I miss that bit. But my freedom is worth the price."

"Do you . . ." She stumbled over her words. "Will you tell the Baroses who I really am?"

Weir leaned forward and stared down at the brightly painted triggerfish and fairy wrasses playing at Vanessa's feet, visible through the glassy water. "That depends."

Vanessa pointed her toe, touching the squishy head of a brilliant blue-ringed octopus. "Depends on what, exactly?" She didn't feel threatened by the little man. However, his next words could change that in an instant.

"I have seen into Andre's mind on the island. I think you know he would do anything to help the people he's inadvertently harmed through the Grimaldi curse. I also know your intentions are divided. If I feel you are going to harm this sweet family, I will do what I need to do."

Vanessa had no desire to hurt them—in fact, without a doubt, she was falling for Andre Baros. The way he looked at her made her feel reckless, all her carefully laid plans to gain power unraveling with a single touch. But if he found out who she really was—what she was—she didn't know if he could move past it. He would never trust her again.

Deciding it was best to move on from the topic of the Baros family, and her intentions, she asked, "Did I . . . kill Circe?"

"She was already dead. An ancient curse tied her spirit to the island through the archives. You actually did her a favor, as well, by freeing her so she could move on. She may have resisted it, but it was what was best for her."

A tiny octopus tentacle wrapped around Vanessa's foot, its slick caress tickling her sensitive skin. She squirmed, and a sudden euphoria to be alive following her brush with death made her laugh out loud.

After her laughter died down, she gave her foot a shake, and with a quick promise to return later, she sent the mollusk back to its den before turning her attention to Weir. "If you were connected to Circe, you probably know what she tried to do to me down there."

"Actually, no." Weir shrugged a shoulder. "The archive building is protected by enchantments that cut off my mental connection with you. And I've never been able to read Circe's thoughts. How did you escape?"

Vanessa shuddered, not wishing to relive the ordeal. "Let's just say she tried to use me to come back to life, and I made the difficult choice to destroy her glorious staff and centuries of magical knowledge in order to save myself."

"And how, exactly, did you save yourself?" Andre's deep voice called from behind them.

Vanessa whipped around, pulling her feet from the water, to find Andre and Sara approaching. Surely they hadn't heard anything of what she'd said except for the last bit, or Andre's smile would not be quite so wide.

Andre walked straight to her and extended his hand to help her up. She took it, the now-familiar tingle at their touch electrifying her veins as he pulled her to her feet. Their chests nearly collided, and she placed a hand on his jacket as she gazed up into his glowing green eyes.

"I'm so relieved to see you are well," he murmured as he looped one muscled arm around the small of her back.

Heart racing, she smiled into his eyes. "Much better now that you're here."

"Vanessa!" Thin arms wrapped around her, breaking the moment between them, and Vanessa tore her gaze from Andre to find Sara hugging her waist. "We were making a special tonic to revive you. I'm so happy that you don't need it!"

An odd thickness coated Vanessa's throat, her eyes stinging as she swallowed. In that moment, held in the arms of people who seemed to actually care for her, she knew without a doubt that she'd made the right choice by escaping with her life. Even if it meant leaving the mythical the Rhabdos and all its magnificent power behind forever.

Love held a magic all its own.

***

"What happened when you were down in that cave, with the archives?" Andre asked as they walked side by side back to the house. "Weir won't tell me anything."

Vanessa glanced over her shoulder to see Weir hanging back with Sara, asking her a million questions as she hobbled along. There would be no help from the little man. Not that she wanted any of his unpredictable input.

They reached the shade of the cottage and Vanessa pulled Andre to a stop with a hand on his arm. His muscles tensed beneath her fingers and she resisted the urge to squeeze, to feel the tendons that made up his limbs, the pulse of his blood. Instead, she dropped her arm and plucked at a coral-colored blossom.

"What is it, Vanessa? I'm not stupid. We barely escaped the island with our lives intact—I know it didn't exactly go well." He stood close enough that the intoxicating scent of his skin muddled her senses.

Calculating that their attraction would distract him,

she threw her arms around him and pressed her cheek against his neck, breathing deep before exhaling a sigh. "Oh, Andre, I—" Her voice broke off. How could she tell him enough of the truth that he would understand and forgive her for what she'd done?

His large warm hand pressed into her back. "It's all right. You can tell me."

And oh, how she wanted to spill it all, every secret she'd kept from him since the moment they'd met. Yet she knew the truth would drive a wedge between them—kill the love and acceptance she'd felt for the first time in her life.

"We'll let you two lovebirds have some privacy," Weir teased as he walked past. "Right, Sara?"

"Yes, but do hurry," Sara said amiably. "I need to know what happened, too."

Vanessa kept her head buried in Andre's shoulder, his voice a rumble as he replied, "We'll be right there."

When Weir and Sara's chatter moved around the corner, Andre wrapped Vanessa in both of his arms, and as they pressed together like perfectly matched butterfly shells, every thought eddied out of her brain. He didn't speak but stroked her hair, his hand running down its length and then up to cup the back of her neck. When his thumb began to move in slow circles against the sensitive spot behind her ear, Vanessa decided she never wanted to move.

Electricity sparked between them like an approaching storm. Andre peered into her eyes. "Are you truly well, Vanessa?"

Her name, whispered from his lips, amplified the heat spiraling through her by a thousand. "I am," she murmured back against the strong column of his neck. Gods, she wanted more of this—of him.

She breathed deep, threaded her fingers through the thick hair curling at his collar, and pressed her lips against his throat in a soft kiss that sparked all the way to her toes. She leaned back and gazed into his eyes, dense black lashes lowered over green irises that had gone dark as the deep sea. And in that moment, she knew she would make every one of this man's dreams come true if given the chance.

She let her gaze fall to his strong lips, and her entire body lit up with urgency to seal their connection. He lowered his head and she lifted her face, lips tingling in anticipation.

"Andre? Are you back here?"

Andre released her and Vanessa stumbled with

surprise, nearly falling back into a bush. He grinned and grabbed her hand, pulling her back to her feet with a wink.

A pretty girl with strawberry blond hair falling in ringlets down her back strode toward them. "Oh, there you are!"

"Maryann." Andre dropped Vanessa's hand and straightened his waistcoat. "What brings you here?"

Vanessa would have liked to know the same thing, along with who this chit was to Andre and how fast Vanessa could get rid of her. Her gaze raked over Maryann's gingham skirt, ruffled blouse buttoned up to her slim throat, rounded cheeks sprinkled with freckles, rosebud lips, and wide blue eyes fit for a porcelain doll. The young woman was sweetly attractive in a fairy-tale princess kind of way that made Vanessa squirm.

Maryann handed a cloth-covered basket to Andre with a wide smile. "I brought over those butter walnut scones that your grandmother loves so much."

"I'm sure she will be grateful." Andre turned to Vanessa, an odd formality in his voice. "May I present our houseguest, Miss Vanessa. Vanessa, this is Maryann Aprílios. She teaches school in the village."

Of course she did. Vanessa's lips curled at the edges as she gave Maryann a cursory nod.

CHAPTER 20

The girl dropped into a curtsy. "Nice to make your acquaintance, Miss Vanessa. From whence do you hail?"

Vanessa's brows winged in amusement. Had the girl learned English from a Chaucer novel? Or been raised by silent nuns? She crossed her arms under her chest and gave Maryann a wan smile. "Oh, I hail from here and there. I don't like to stay in one place for too long."

Andre stiffened at her lie but did not correct her.

"Oh? Like a nomad? How exciting!" Maryann exclaimed.

"Maryann, Sara's health has had a turn for the worse," Andre said, a slight hitch in his voice. "I'm sad to say she will not return to the classroom anytime soon."

"How devastating!" Maryann's pale brows furrowed over her disgustingly cute button nose. "Perhaps I could provide some home tutelage."

"I believe Yia-Yia has Sara's schooling under control, but you could speak to her." Andre stepped forward into the full light of the sun, and Maryann gasped.

"Andre, your poor face!" She rushed over and lifted a hand to his bruised cheek. "I had heard about the attack but did not realize the extent of your injuries. You should have sent for me."

Andre did nothing to discourage Maryann as her fair fingers brushed his tan cheek.

Vanessa propped a hand on her hip. "I'm quite capable of caring for all of Andre's needs."

Andre's eyes shifted to her face, a dark glint sparking there as he bit into his bottom lip to stop a grin.

Maryann dropped her arm, blue eyes wide. "Oh, erm, yes, well . . . I didn't realize you two had an understanding."

An understanding in human culture could mean anything from a romantic attachment to a betrothal, and although it wasn't true, Vanessa had no intention of correcting the schoolmarm's assumption.

"It's not like that, Maryann. I just . . ." Andre scraped the black swath of hair off his forehead. "I'm fine, is all." He reached out and took the basket. "Here, let's take these in to Yia-Yia. I'm sure she'll be thrilled to see you."

"That is very sweet, Andre." Maryann smiled, placated, showing rows of small pearly teeth as she placed a hand on Andre's arm.

The pair began to walk side by side, and Andre motioned for Vanessa to follow before disappearing around the corner of the house.

Had he just left her there like a bucket of chum? An afterthought?

Brows drawn, Vanessa stomped after them and observed their interaction. They were a study in contrasts,

Maryann's hair sparkling in the sun as she gazed up at her dark, handsome companion. They gossiped like old friends, throwing out names of mutual acquaintances, their conversation easy and light. Kind, thoughtful, generous, prim, Maryann Aprílios was everything Andre deserved. Everything Vanessa could never be.

Vanessa's gut burned as if a cluster of lampreys squirmed in her stomach, biting her insides.

Before she knew what she was doing, her hand closed around her conduit. She barely kept herself from spelling pustules all over the schoolteacher's porcelain skin. Vanessa slowed her steps and forced herself to think. She could not bind emotion or create it, but she could conjure outside forces that influenced feelings. As Andre leaned closer to better hear Maryann's soft voice, a memory took shape of a jilted merman who'd come to her once in secret, for help. The spell she'd crafted for him would do nicely.

She pulled back and lifted her shell, whispering, "Repulsion and repugnance, fill the air, and divide with a gulf no rapport can repair."

A shadowy rush of nausea-inducing disgust filled the air, wrapping the couple in an invisible stench of grief and calamity and something akin to rotting flesh.

Andre and Maryann abruptly stopped walking and

pulled apart. A deep frown etched Andre's face as he said, "I just remembered I have to, er, paint the wagon today."

Maryann's freckled forehead scrunched, and she walked backward, nearly tripping over the ground. "Yes, I must study . . . to . . . teach." With a quick wave, she spun and race-walked down the driveway.

Vanessa gave a crisp nod, her task complete, and stalked forward; but the release of power so soon after her ordeal caused her to stagger like a drunkard. Andre rushed to her side and looped an arm around her shoulders. "You need to lie down."

She smiled up at him, his lovely face swimming dizzily as she steadied herself on his arm. The spell had been well worth the effort. "I'm not tired. Let's walk a bit."

"I think not." His tone was firm as he took her hand and tugged her after him.

But she dug in her heels. There was something important she needed to say, and it would go down better without an audience. Especially since she'd made some sort of headway with Yia-Yia that morning, even if it was thanks to Weir.

With a sigh, she tugged him through the sunny garden and into the cool forest and leaned against a massive tree. "You asked me earlier how I saved myself on Omis Island.

I wish to explain, but I must request that you keep an open mind."

"Of course, Vanessa." He moved close and placed his large hands on both of her shoulders. "However you escaped, I cannot resent it."

When he stood so close, she couldn't think straight; more specifically, the temptation to lie to keep him there grew too hard to resist. Not that she was averse to lying if need be, but in this case, Weir would surely fill in whatever blanks she left in her story. She would need to choose her words carefully.

She took his wrists in her hands and moved them off her shoulders. He stepped back, eyes searching her face for answers.

Vanessa took a deep breath and then let the story she'd prepared while he'd been distracted by Maryann rush out of her. She'd tell him everything—almost. "The magical archives were deep underground and guarded by a spirit—the spirit of the goddess Circe. She told me something about the curse."

Andre gave her hands a squeeze. "What did she say?"

He wasn't going to like any of what she was about to say. "Circe claims the curse lives beneath the village and grows like a fungus. She said that the more time that passes, the less time we will have to stop it. That it's rooting."

His brows lowered and he opened his mouth, but she barreled on with the rest before she lost her nerve.

"Before I could investigate the books, she imprisoned me in a glass cage. The goddess intended to take over my body and use it as her own."

"Saints!" Andre muttered as he tugged the collar away from his neck.

"I broke out of the glass prison, but she attacked me with magic. Drained my energy. My very life."

A muscle jumped in Andre's jaw. "Why didn't Weir help you?"

"She locked him out. I had to go in alone. But, Andre, that's not all." She clutched his hands hard in hers. "There was a magical artifact, a magical staff that could have helped us. In order to escape, I had to set the archives on fire, including Circe's staff. The books . . . they're all gone, too. I never had a chance to search for a cure to the curse."

He flinched as if she'd slapped him. "I thought . . . I assumed we'd be able to return together and try again." He tugged his hands away and clenched them into fists as he stared into the distance.

CHAPTER 20

"I'm sorry, Andre. You must know if there was any other way—"

"I understand." He was short with her, but not angry, as he cut her off and rammed his fisted hands into his trouser pockets. "I just need a minute to think things through, come up with another plan. It sounds like we're running out of time."

With that, he stalked off into the forest.

Vanessa pushed off the tree and walked aimlessly. Telling the truth—at least partial truth—was more difficult than she'd imagined. She'd been tempted to enchant Andre so he would forget his anger and frustration right away. But her weakened state would not allow for such quick spell work, as she'd found out the hard way.

She plucked a leaf larger than her hand from a low-hanging branch and stared at the pattern of veins within. Life on land continued to surprise her. Especially the people—the humans. She hadn't cared what others thought of her for a long time. It hurt too badly when they let her down. She traced a vein inside the leaf and its path connecting it to the others. So simple, yet so complex.

Just as her life had become. Her goal for power convoluted with emotions. Feelings that clouded her judgment and stole her resolve. All of a sudden, it seemed Andre's wants had become her own. He'd said he needed to come up with another plan. Well, so did she. For him, and for herself.

She crumpled the leaf and threw it to the ground. She would start by investigating some of those afflicted with the curse. Perhaps it would give her some clue to the source.

"Psst!"

Vanessa whirled around to find Sara's head poking out the back stable door, blond braids dangling.

"Come on." She motioned Vanessa inside. "Hurry!"

Curious, Vanessa ducked into the barn. "What's going on?"

Sara's eyes twinkled. "We're going to town. I got a lead that Sheriff Kush knows more than he's saying. I think you need to talk to Governor Zika."

CHAPTER 21

ANDRE

ANDRE STOPPERED a clear blue flask and dripped melted wax around the lip to seal it. He did his best thinking in his workshop, the scents of herbs and flowers wafting in from the greenhouse, windows open to the sea air. But he couldn't escape the fact that no matter how many tinctures he bottled, not one of them could reverse the curse. And with the disaster at Omis Island, they'd lost their only lead to how to stop it.

If only he could create a time travel potion to go back

and tell Mrs. Nasside to shove off instead of falling into her snare. Who had the old woman been in actuality, and what had she hoped to accomplish by tricking Andre into distributing the poison?

He'd thought back over whom he could have offended, or who might have a grudge against him. But until all of this had happened, he didn't have a single enemy. Nor, it could be said, a friend. Since his parents had died, he'd pulled away from all his old schoolmates and rarely participated in any social activities. He hadn't met his friends at the pub or joined the village rugby matches he used to enjoy. The fair he'd attended with Maryann felt like years ago instead of weeks. Funny that he hadn't even realized he'd separated himself until now, when a specific attachment threatened to overpower his senses. As incredible as it felt to hold Vanessa in his arms, to share some of his burdens with her, to laugh with her, he could not allow the luxury of blind belief again. Not when the lives of so many of the villagers—not to mention his family—were at stake.

He poured jasmine oil into a green bottle, his hand shaking so badly some of the precious liquid spilled over the side. A memory had haunted him ever since they'd returned from Omis Island. In Weir's sitting room, just before the sleeping potion had taken effect, Andre recalled the savant saying, *The archives are too dangerous for humans to traverse. But I knew Mr. Baros would not allow you to accompany me alone. . . .*

Andre leaned both hands on the worktable and hung his head, weariness pressing heavy on his shoulders.

If the archives were too dangerous for humans, what did that make Vanessa?

CHAPTER 22

VANESSA

VILLAGERS BUSTLED around the town square, heads down and focused as a fierce wind whipped up skirts and captured hats. Vanessa watched an older man chase his cap across the soot-covered cobbles as Sara tied up Ella and their two-seater carriage to a post beside the general store. A food cart adorned with dirty streamers sat broken and abandoned, a group of ragtag children playing in the overturned booth. Trash littered the square and broken pottery bobbed in the central fountain.

The square held an odd juxtaposition of neglect and struggle. Some businesses, like the fishmonger and a few merchants, pressed on to make their livings and provide goods and services, despite the dark shadow the curse had cast on the formerly idyllic village.

Glad Andre was not present to witness the deterioration of his hometown, Vanessa turned back to his little sister, who didn't seem fazed. "Things are much worse here than even a week ago."

"Yes," Sara commented as she took her cane firmly in hand. "The cursed require so much time to care for that some everyday businesses have shuttered. But not all, thankfully. We have supplies to purchase." Sara reached into Ella's pack and handed Vanessa a leather satchel. "But first, you'll find the governor and charm a bit of information out of him."

Vanessa's eyes widened. "Oh, really? And how do you propose I do that?"

Sara waved a slim hand in the air. "Your womanly wiles or some such. It works on Andre. He turns into a googly-eyed puppy around you."

Laughter burst from Vanessa. She liked this girl and her irreverent sense of humor. Vanessa straightened her bodice and pulled down the arms of her blouse to show a bit of shoulder. She stuck out her chest and posed with a hand on her hip. "Do you mean like this?"

"Meanwhile"—Sara rolled her eyes and spoke over the last of Vanessa's chuckles—"I will visit Miss Aprílios and get the rest of my schoolwork that she failed to give me. Odd how she ran off so quickly."

Vanessa suppressed a smirk. Miss Perfect Proctor wouldn't have any inclination to return to Baros Cottage for quite some time.

On the ride into town, Sara had explained that Yia-Yia had said something about the governor bearing a grudge against their family that went back years, and was worried Zika might be behind the curse as a way to ruin the Baros family. Their grandmother hadn't wanted to mention it to Andre for fear he'd confront the powerful man and land himself in jail as the governor had threatened. So Sara had decided Vanessa was the best person to delve deeper.

She was not wrong. Vanessa had a few things she'd like to discuss with the governor herself. He'd sent them to Omis Island. But why? Had he been involved in hiring the pirates to threaten Andre because of some rusty old vendetta? Or did it go deeper?

"Also, I'd like to interview one of the cursed," Vanessa said as she looped the satchel over her shoulder. "What is this hideous bag for, anyway?"

"That is for the meat we're picking up from the butcher, who also happens to be one of the cursed."

"Where will I find Zika?" Vanessa asked.

"Follow the stench of ale and lazy men," Sara replied as she began to hobble away. "He likes to play poker with the sailors during the hot part of the day when most are napping."

Daily *ypnákos* were ingrained in the culture along the coast. During that scorching part of the day, Vanessa usually slipped into the cove to refresh herself in a different way. Odd that the governor didn't follow the traditions of the village.

"Zika is the worst kind of opportunist," Sara offered over her shoulder in response to Vanessa's bemused expression. "Taking advantage of the broke and destitute is his specialty."

Vanessa shook her head. The child was too smart for her own good.

***

As promised, Poseidon's Pub polluted the briny breeze with a pungent mixture of fried seafood and acrid spirits. The sounds of riotous laughter and clinking glasses spilled out onto the cobbled street. As Ursula, Vanessa had spied on ships and overheard enough sailors' prattle to know that they came to port to blow off steam, get a real meal, and gamble away their earnings, or trade them for a bit of companionship.

As she walked into the pub, she witnessed a little of each pursuit. Seamen, still in their caps and ragged deck pants, bellied up to the bar, shoving food into their mouths with both hands. Groups gathered around tables, fondled cards, puffed on cigars, and threw coins into piles while scantily clad women leaned cleavage into the poker players' faces and ran fingers through their greasy hair.

Having no desire to trade for her own company, Vanessa pushed up the sleeves of her blouse and scanned the room but didn't recognize any of the men as the thin, steely-eyed governor. With a lift of her chin, she headed to the roughhewn wooden counter. The barman stopped polishing the glass in his hand as he met her gaze. "What'll ye have, sweets?"

Vanessa smiled. "I'm looking for Governor Zika."

CHAPTER 22

"Governor don't wish to be disturbed. When I see him, who should I say is lookin' for him?"

Vanessa hesitated, not expecting an interrogation from the likes of this toadstool. She lifted her chin and spoke with authority. "Miss Vanessa. We met at Baros Cottage. He *will* wish to see me."

He gave her a dark look, then walked away. Had she imagined that he stiffened when she'd mentioned Baros Cottage? Likely not, considering how the curse had affected so many in the tiny hamlet.

In a far corner of the room, a two-man band struck up a cacophonous tune with a concertina and a battered fiddle. Vanessa leaned against the bar, grimacing when her sleeve stuck to the grimy surface. She lifted her arm and walked toward the window, a few of the men casting looks her way. She clutched her nautilus and stared over their heads. Smoke and the odor of unwashed bodies clotted the air, scratching her throat and turning her stomach. She didn't like this place.

"Miss Vanessa, what can I do for you?" Governor Zika, hands bracing his narrow waist, swaggered up to her side.

Something about him seemed off, as if he wasn't the

same man she'd met previously. The impression, combined with the putrid atmosphere of the pub, overwhelmed her human senses, dulling her brain. "Governor. May we step outside?"

"As you wish, Madam." Zika gestured for her to lead the way.

Vanessa strode quickly out the door and onto a shallow patio dotted with tables and chairs. As much as she loathed to spend too much time with the man, she took a seat in a shaded spot under the awning. The governor perched on the chair across from her and met her gaze.

Remembering Sara's advice to use her *charms*, Vanessa lowered her eyes and toyed with the laces on her bodice. "I suppose you heard about the attack on Andre Baros? He was badly beaten and his merchant wagon destroyed. Which is the sole source of income for his family."

She glanced up from beneath her lashes, unsurprised to see the man's gaze dart away as he shifted in his seat. "Yes, I heard. I placed an inquiry with the sheriff in Aoannis."

"Any word on what might have prompted such an attack?"

Zika shrugged.

Vanessa grasped her shell conduit but then

remembered how weakness had overtaken her after she'd cast the repulsion spell. She certainly couldn't afford to be vulnerable in this putrid place. Her wits would have to do. "Surely, such an honorable government official such as yourself would not wish to see anyone in his jurisdiction harmed."

He stood and straightened his jacket. "I have places to be."

She shielded her eyes from the sharp rays of the sun as she looked up at him. "You sent us to Omis Island. Told us about the savant and the archives. Why offer help to Andre only to leave him to the wolves? Perhaps vengeance . . . ?"

"So now we get to it," the governor said, his face still in shadow, magic thrumming around him like the discordant notes of a song. "Ask me what you really want to know."

Vanessa picked up the hem of her skirt and stood.

This man—or whatever he was—set off alarm bells in her body. Like the instinct she felt when a great shark lurked.

"You sent Andre to Omis Island on a doomed mission, never expecting him to return. Why?" Vanessa hissed at Zika. "What's your stake in this curse? You had something to do with it, didn't you?"

A strange shift eddied in the air like a whirlpool, guttering everything in its wake. Numbness spread down Vanessa's back and arms, the sensation ending in tingles at the tips of her fingers—like the feeling after waking from a nightmare. She pushed against it, her will strong enough to hold off the invasion. Someone was attempting to infiltrate her mind.

Vanessa stared hard at Zika, and the flicker of something dark slipped across his gaze before he lifted a brow and tilted his head. Then it was gone.

She took a step back, having entirely lost the thread of their conversation.

"Are you quite all right, Miss Vanessa?" Zika asked with a wry sneer. "Too much noonday sun, perhaps?"

On a good day, she would take this man on without hesitation, but her residual weakness from Omis Island and the public setting worked against her. Not to mention that she'd entirely forgotten why she needed to speak to the governor at all. Odd. What had he done to her? She blinked to clear her thoughts. Best to retreat with a bit of dignity. "Excuse me, Governor. I need to meet Sara at the school." She bobbed her head and walked away.

"Oh, Miss Vanessa," Zika called.

She stopped but didn't turn back around.

CHAPTER 22

"Any luck with the return of your memory?"

His tone held more curiosity than concern. She glanced back and their gazes locked. "Why do you ask?"

The man did not look away as he said, "I'm quite interested to learn more about your origins." He took a step closer. "In fact, I—"

"Vanessa! There you are," Sara called as she limped her way to where they stood, stopping in the middle of the square, pain lancing across her face.

Still disoriented, Vanessa took the opportunity to escape and, with a quick nod to the governor, rushed to join Sara by a tiny food cart run by a vendor who had been spared the curse. With a deep exhale, Vanessa pushed away her strange encounter with Zika and breathed in the mouthwatering scent of roasted nuts coated in sugar and cinnamon that swirled in the air.

When she glanced back, Zika was nowhere to be seen.

Sara handed the vendor a coin in exchange for a brown paper bag full of toasted walnuts. The girl took her snack and slumped onto a barrel. "I'm so tired. Please tell me you learned something useful."

Vanessa squatted down in front of the girl. "Not much, I'm afraid. Except that Zika knows more than he's telling."

Sara gave a solemn nod. "About Andre's attack?"

Vanessa told her everything except for the fact that Zika radiated magic and had caused her to lose track of her thoughts midway through their conversation. The nasty bottom-feeder. Vanessa had to unclench her fists and force her focus back to the girl beside her.

"I still don't know exactly what happened on the island. Weir won't tell me," Sara said with a pout.

Vanessa dug her hand into the paper bag and popped a few nuts into her mouth. Flavor, warm and earthy, like a cool evening by the fire, burst on her tongue. In that moment, happiness coursing through Vanessa, her magic surged in a natural response to her joy. She stiffened, barely holding it back. Wide blue eyes met hers with concern and Vanessa realized her power tingled through her right arm—the hand that rested on Sara's knee.

She jerked back and stood up, taking Sara's hand to help her to her feet. "Um . . . those nuts are delicious. I don't think I've ever tasted anything like them."

She steered the girl away from the crowds and they walked side by side in the shade of a three-story villa. "As I was saying, I think Zika knows something he's not saying. But I don't know if he paid the pirates to attack Andre.

They implied their benefactor came from somewhere offshore."

Sara offered Vanessa more nuts. "If it wasn't Zika, though, who else would be rich enough to afford such a thing?"

"Aren't there other wealthy families in the area? Like whoever lives in this glorious building." Vanessa gestured to the villa towering over them, bright red shutters framing clear glass windows that dotted the fresh white stucco. They paused at the doorway to a lush courtyard, a fountain tinkling in a stone pool behind the locked iron gate.

"That's the governor's residence," Sara said.

Vanessa stared at the fountain. The statue spewing water in its center depicted a man, standing on two feet, with leonine features and a wild mane. An image superimposed over the figurine faded before she could fully grasp it. Perhaps something she had read in her research of Earth's history. But she'd read books on human folk tales, mythology, historical accounts, literature, and poetry, and it all blurred together.

"We should get moving so we can head home before we're missed," Sara said, and tugged on Vanessa's sleeve.

"Wait, I still need to speak to one of the cursed."

"You're about to."

The stench of blood and raw meat as they entered the butcher's shop nearly pushed Vanessa back out the door, but she forced her feet to follow Sara. A long counter divided the customer area from the butcher's workroom in the back. Sara shuffled to the counter and tapped on a metal bell.

The sickening thwack of steel slicing bone made Sara jump. Then a huge man with thick arms and long hair tied into a tail came lumbering out of the back room. Scarlet spattered his long white apron, and the dark grimace on his face suggested he would slaughter anything—or anyone—at the slightest provocation. "What'll it be?" he asked gruffly.

He addressed Vanessa, but Sara answered as she set coins onto the counter. "A pound of lamb chops, please."

The man's gaze slashed down to the blond girl, raking over her bent leg and candy-striped cane. "I don't serve cripples. Never have, never will."

Sara straightened. "That isn't true, Daniel Fountoulis, and you know it. The curse turned your wish for joy into rage. You need to fight it." She tapped her cane against the stone floor for emphasis.

Vanessa reached out with a thin probe of magic, but not enough to drain her strength. Just a sixth sense that wiggled into the man's brain. Icy dread zipped back along her connection to the butcher, so strong that it knocked her back a step. But she had to feel this curse for herself. The man swatted at his ear. Vanessa pushed harder. Primal terror arched through her as the room disappeared, replaced by night-black water, cold and heavy, her precious tentacles chopped off and floating away. Lips wired shut, black miasma coating her eyes, her shell conduit missing, magic trapped within her bursting heart as she sank into the deepest recesses of the ocean.

With a gasp, Vanessa felt her magic snap back to her, and the room as it was once again appeared before her eyes. She blinked and struggled to control her breathing. Luckily Sara's attention had been focused on the butcher, who slapped his head with an open palm.

"Are you all right, Daniel?" Sara asked, reaching a pale arm across the counter.

Like an angry bull shark, the man bared his teeth and smacked his hands down, barely missing Sara's fragile limb as she jerked back. "Get out, crippled girl!"

Sara stumbled back and red flashed across Vanessa's vision, the anger cleansing her of the revolting remnants of her fear. "I'll take care of this, Sara. Meet me outside."

The girl nodded, tears gathering in her eyes as she scrambled out to the street.

Her voice steely, Vanessa said, "I'll have those lamb chops."

With a grumble under his breath, the man went into the back and then returned with a parcel wrapped in paper and string. Vanessa stoked the anger inside her, lovingly embracing the dark emotion that fed her power. And when Daniel handed her the package, she lashed out, the spell zipping down her fingers as she clutched his hand. Exquisite onyx sparks burst through nerves and muscle.

She didn't care a whit that this man was cursed. Magic had not forced the hurtful words from his mouth. The curse only freed him to say them aloud. But she knew what resided in his deepest thoughts.

She squeezed harder. The man screeched, but she lifted her other hand, closing his lips until her work was done. Muscle shriveled before her eyes, and blood poured from the butcher's fingers. Vanessa released her grip and pulled back before it stained her skin. The butcher screamed in agony as he twisted his body to remove his flaccid arm from the counter. The limb hung lifeless at his side. Dead.

Vanessa took the parcel of meat, lifted her chin, and strode out into the street.

CHAPTER 23

VANESSA

ON THE RIDE back to the cottage, Vanessa couldn't stop thinking about the butcher and what she'd felt when she'd delved into the spell eating away at him like a parasite. She'd never encountered anything like it. The fear it had inspired had felt like something primal—alive. The curse had followed her probe and latched onto her own mind, planting a vision of her worst nightmare: maimed, powerless, and forgotten as she'd sunk into a cold, dark trench, still alive and doomed to suffer with her own thoughts for months or years or an eternity.

What could have happened if Vanessa hadn't let go when she did? She shuddered at the thought.

That sort of power fed on others, spread, and only grew when attacked. The resilience of the hex—and the power it must have taken to create it—was extraordinary. And yet, all magic, both light and dark, functioned under the same basic precepts. That meant this curse had an epicenter that it fed upon in order to stay alive. If Circe could be trusted, that source was somewhere underground. It made sense, considering how widespread the victims were up and down the coast. The possibilities were both frightening and exhilarating.

She had to find it.

But first she had to replenish her strength at the cove. The spell she'd placed on the butcher had drained her weakened body. Damn Circe and her stupid ancient library! She was still feeling the aftereffects of everything she'd done to escape the glass box.

"You're very quiet," Sara said as she led Ella down the driveway to Baros Cottage.

The steady trot of the horse was soothing, almost like being rocked to sleep amidst the waves. "I'm just tired."

CHAPTER 23

Vanessa gave a big yawn for added effect. "Could you drop me off at the cove? I'd like to sit in the sun awhile."

Sara steered the mare around the back of the house, and every cell in Vanessa's body cried out to the glittering turquoise pool. Before the horse had even come to a full stop, she slid off the side and raced to the cove, kicking off her shoes and rolling down her stockings as she went, uncaring what Sara might think.

She sank down on a sunny rock and stuck her legs into the water up to her calves. A deep sigh escaped her as the flood of the sea rushed into her pores, revitalizing her cells. She leaned back on her hands, closed her eyes, and lifted her face to the sun, drinking in the feel and scent of salt.

Vanessa opened her eyes to find Sara sitting beside her, her own small feet dangling in the water. Vanessa leaned over to see a rainbow-colored royal gramma and a brilliant flame angelfish darting just below the surface. The familiar blue-ringed octopus gripped onto the toes of her left foot.

"Look at those fish!" Sara exclaimed. "And that octopus is so cute! It has polka dots."

With a thought, she sent them all away, lest the highly venomous octopus mistake Sara's tiny toes for a snack.

"There he goes." Sara bent double to watch the little mollusk dive.

"She. There *she* goes," Vanessa corrected.

"How do you know?" Sara asked.

"Just a hunch," Vanessa responded a bit too quickly. *Stupid.* The young girl's guilelessness charmed Vanessa into letting down her defenses. She would need to guard her tongue more carefully. "All the most beautiful creatures are female, after all," Vanessa added with a grin that made Sara giggle.

The girl grew quiet, her left foot making figure eights in the water while her lame leg hung limp. When she spoke again, Vanessa had to strain to hear the words.

"Do you think—" Sara broke off, her voice strangled. "Do you think I'm disgusting?"

Vanessa met Sara's shimmering blue stare and something inside her chest fractured, a part of herself she'd buried deep emerging, blooming hard, roots reaching for this girl's sun. Understanding, silent and fathomless, passed between them in a single gaze. Two damaged creatures misunderstood, ostracized, and unique to the world.

Vanessa stiffened. Nothing good could come from this—this connection to a weak and broken human.

Yet she felt herself growing. Changing. It seemed

humanity came with vulnerabilities and sentiments she'd never experienced. As if her human heart moved to a different beat than the one she'd been born with.

"You and I, we're different, aren't we?" Pain lanced through Vanessa's throat as she saw her childhood self as the odd little Cecaelia among beautiful mermaids. "The obstacles you overcome each day, just to survive . . . Sara Baros, you are amazing. And not despite your abnormality, but because of it."

Sara nodded, tears leaking from her eyes.

Vanessa reached out and took Sara's small hand in hers. Without conscious thought, magic arched between them. Sara squeezed Vanessa's hand tight. Vanessa closed her eyes and let go, allowing the alchemy between them to flourish. Just as coral polyps spawned, died, and rebuilt, bone and sinew knit together, restoring structures. Like waves washing sand into deficiencies in a reef, magic swept over them both, healing and restoring.

Vanessa gasped and pulled back before her entire essence drained away. Eyes falling shut, she swayed. Even with her feet still in the sea, the power that had funneled through her to Sara depleted her already weakened body.

"Vanessa?" Sara whispered. "What just happened? I feel . . . odd."

"Sara? Vanessa?" Andre's voice registered in Vanessa's brain just as Sara leapt to her feet and Vanessa fell headfirst into the lagoon.

***

Vanessa dropped like a stone through the cool water, sinking until she sat among the seaweed, gripping the silken stalks, eyes closed as the sea welcomed her home. Her legs ached with a thousand needles as she fought the transformation that would fully restore her magic. It was too soon: she hadn't yet come close to accomplishing what she'd planned to do on land.

But she had a matter of moments before Andre dove in after her, so she opened her eyes and pushed off the bottom. Arms parting the water, tingling legs kicking, she swam up and broke the surface to see that Andre had already removed his boots and was shrugging out of his jacket.

"I'm fine!" Vanessa called. Even the seconds she'd spent submerged had helped improve her weakness, but she knew she needed to stay longer. "Just a moment of dizziness."

Andre stopped and shrugged his jacket back on, his gorgeous face set in hard lines.

CHAPTER 23

Vanessa's gut clenched. He'd seen something. She nearly groaned—with relief or dread, she wasn't sure—as her gaze landed on Sara. The girl stood on the outcropping, her lame leg appearing straight and strong, a look of pure wonder upon her elfin face.

Andre walked over to his sister. "Are you okay, Sara?"

"I'm . . . fantastic!" Sara ignored Andre's proffered hand and hopped off the rocks into the scrubby grass. The girl flew to her brother and wrapped her arms around his waist. "Vanessa . . . she . . . I don't know. I feel . . . new."

He put his hands on her shoulders and pulled her away from him so he could search her face. "I saw a light shining around you both, and I thought . . . I don't know what I thought. But you're certain you're all right?"

"I'm wonderful!" Sara pulled away from her brother and ran to the edge of the pool, breaking out in a pealing laugh, her cane forgotten on the rocks. "Vanessa! You have magic!"

Vanessa thought quickly. She supposed that if she really didn't have any memory of who she had been, it was possible she didn't remember her own magic. She could just go with it. Or . . . this could be her chance to come clean to Andre. To tell him at least a partial truth. Her gaze shifted up to him, his brows drawn, eyes narrowed upon her.

Silence stretched between them until Sara twirled and ran back to his side. "Andre, don't you see? She healed me!"

He didn't acknowledge what his sister said as he strode to the edge of the lagoon and barked, "Get out."

Vanessa swam to the outcropping and climbed up on the rocks, well aware that her dress clung to her every curve. She gathered the dark, ropy length of her hair, wringing out the excess water.

But besides a muscle twitching in his jaw, Andre didn't respond to her display. Instead, he picked up Sara's discarded cane and thrust it at her. "Go back to the house, Sara."

Sara took the stick and sputtered, "But she—she's amazing!"

"Now, Sara." He didn't raise his voice, but his tone brokered no argument and his sister sprinted away.

A slow smile dawned on Vanessa's face as she watched the girl run. She had done that. Healed instead of harmed. She'd healed before, of course, but never for free. Never out of compassion or empathy.

When she faced Andre, his eyes burning green fire, she knew she'd partly done it for him. To appease a bit of his guilt. Lift some of the burden he carried like shackles.

Vanessa sat on a boulder with her back to the water. “Please, let me explain.” Looking up at Andre through her lashes, she patted the flat stone next to her.

His right hand balled into a fist, and he touched the metal at his throat as if for courage or patience—she wasn’t sure which—but a moment later, he unclenched his hand and sat beside her. “You healed my sister?” he asked, staring straight ahead.

“I did, but, Andre, I didn’t know what I was doing. We were just talking. The butcher had called her a cripple, and she was so upset.” She felt Andre stiffen. “When she asked if I thought she was disgusting, I . . . I don’t know . . . I took her hand, and it was like I blacked out for a moment. I awoke in the water and saw her there . . . standing on her own.” She let emotion cut off her words.

“So you’re saying you didn’t know you had magic?” Andre asked, a dark edge to his voice.

Vanessa twisted to face him and took both of his hands. “You know I don’t remember anything about my past!”

Andre shook his head and tugged his hands from hers. “How could you not know, even with an injury? Magic is incredibly rare. It's something you can feel in—in your bones. Even if you don't remember, you should know."

It's not as rare as you think, Vanessa thought as Zika came to mind.

Andre continued. "And what I know of it has ruined this family. Devastated dozens and dozens of lives because of that cursed potion."

He shot to his feet and paced in front of her. "Yia-Yia was right about you."

Vanessa rose to her feet and bit her lip, disappointed by his reaction. Her own temper escalated. Couldn't he see that she'd tried to be good? For him? "Andre, I want to help you. For Neptune's sake, I healed your sister!"

"It always goes bad. Sara thought she was cured before, and then her leg became worse than ever." He pivoted on his heel and gripped her shoulders, staring hard into her face. "What did Weir mean when he said the archives were too dangerous for humans? What does that make you?"

"I don't know," she whispered, and for once, it was the truth. She didn't know who she was anymore. Or even what she wanted. The longer she stayed in her human form, the easier it was to picture a life here. With him.

Vanessa waited for the anger to kick in as Andre glared down at her—accusing her—but instead, every sense heightened. Andre's solid strength, the heady taste of his breath, his fingers loose cuffs around her upper arms, her stomach tightening as she raised a palm and pressed it against the muscled wall of his chest. His heart thumped hard and fast. She raised her chin, and it was like lifting her face to the sun, basking in Andre's goodness and light.

His fingers tightened on her arms, tugging her against him. Heat buzzed across her flesh as brazenness thrilled through her. He wasn't *all* principled morality. His touch burned through the wet cloth of her dress, searing her skin. But it wasn't enough. She threaded her fingers through his silken hair and gripped his neck, arching her body up against his. She felt his breath hiss out of his mouth as the very air around them went still.

Carefully, as if she were made of glass, he lifted a hand to her cheek. But she didn't want caution. She wanted passion and recklessness, a hurricane of uncontrollable desire like she felt—had felt since the first time they'd touched. Vanessa dug her nails into the muscles of his arm and pressed her lips against his, fireworks exploding behind her eyes, glorious flames shooting through her veins.

And yet she felt him holding back. Only going through the motions, mimicking a kiss. Restraining himself.

She pulled away and searched his face. Seal-black hair tumbled over his brow, lips slightly parted, the deep green of his eyes a thin rim around the swallowing black. Great Neptune, the beauty of him felt like a punch to her chest. She wanted to breathe him in, capture him, enslave him and be his slave, never let him go. But she did not want Andre Baros because of his physical perfection, but because of his perfect heart that allowed him to see past her demons. Because he made her feel beautiful and valued and good. He'd seen things in her she could only wish were real.

Was that love? Her entire being grew still. Could she *love* him?

Hot blood flooded into her neck, her face. She dropped onto the flats of her feet and bent her neck, resting her head against Andre's chest, hiding the wild current of feelings threatening to sweep her away.

"Vanessa." His voice was a rough whisper, one hand bracketing her waist and the other cupping her cheek, lifting her face. "What do you want from me?"

She met his heated stare, her eyes blazing into his. "I want you to kiss me like you mean it, Andre Baros."

CHAPTER 24

ANDRE

ANDRE GRITTED his teeth against the desire setting his body ablaze. This enchanting creature had tempted him beyond his capacity to resist. Beyond all reason. The invitation—the challenge on her lush lips—broke his self-control. He could no longer deny himself the thing he craved.

With a groan of surrender, he wrapped his arms around Vanessa's waist, pressing her full against him. His hand tangled in her hair as he captured her succulent bottom lip, nipping her flesh and eliciting a whimper from her throat before he took her mouth.

Her body burned against his, all curves and softness. He cupped her neck as he deepened the kiss. She opened her mouth to him, and he delved inside, tasting her spicy sweetness, like tea spiked with lemon. The world dissolved as he pushed his splayed hand up her back, the wet fabric like paper adhering to her steaming skin.

His breathing went ragged and he pushed her back until she hit something solid. He leaned over her, bracing his hand on rock, her body curving into his in a way that sent the earth spinning out. He kissed her like a drowning man as waves of heat washed over him.

Savagely, she tore at his shirt, buttons popping. Her hand delved beneath the fabric and met his bare skin. He bent and kissed the arch of her cheek, the column of her neck, stopping on the vein pulsing madly in her throat. She tugged at his hair, a soft growl vibrating from her chest and down his spine.

But even as he lost his head, his spirit tapped a warning on his shoulder. She hadn't answered his question. Who was she? If she wasn't human, *what* was she? A siren sent to tempt him into debauchery? The feel of her body scorching his urged him not to care. Part of him thrummed to life at her touch—her hands on his skin, fingers tangled in his hair, mouth pliant yet hungry.

But he had to protect his family. His heart.

With a ragged groan, he let her go and stumbled back.

Vanessa reclined on her elbows, chest heaving, laces undone on her bodice. Had he done that?

Saints.

Andre shoved a shaking hand through his hair and turned away from the tantalizing sight.

"Andre?"

He felt her walk up beside him, but he didn't turn. When she placed a hand on his shoulder, he stepped away and shook his head. "I need to think."

"Andre, I . . . I'm sorry I haven't told you everything." Vanessa's voice broke off. "But please don't shut me out. I need you. . . . You're the only one I feel truly knows me."

He whirled on her. "How can you possibly think that when you don't even remember your old life?"

"I don't need to remember." She shook her head as if denying her past.

And yet she knew she had magic. She had to know she wasn't fully human. He clenched his teeth, working his jaw before he demanded, "Tell me who you really are."

Vanessa blinked wide violet eyes at him. "You know I

can't do that. But I know I'm the one for you, Andre. We make the perfect team." Her beguiling lips stretched in a slight smile.

Andre searched her face for indications of deception. For those telltale signs he'd learned to recognize while dealing with his clientele year after year. But she met his gaze and didn't fidget or twitch. Her breath was steady as she walked toward him. "I did it for you, Andre. I healed Sara for you."

A long sigh escaped his chest as she reached for his hand. He couldn't deny what she'd done was miraculous. Nor could he deny their connection any more than he could stop breathing. The moment they'd just shared, the passion between them, was unlike anything he'd dreamed possible.

But he needed to know more. Much more.

After a moment, he gave a nod, squeezed her fingers, and said, "Okay, tell me how your magic works."

They strolled hand in hand, fingers laced, palms pressed together, and Andre admitted to himself that it felt right. He had to force the images of their bodies entwined out of his mind so he could focus as Vanessa began to speak.

"I felt the surge of magic once a few days after I

arrived at your cottage, but I wasn't sure what I was feeling. The power comes and goes. All I know is that it seems to strengthen when I'm touching the sea."

Sirens are witches of the sea who enchant all who hear their call. Beware, all ye who draw near. A chill tiptoed down Andre's spine as Yia-Yia's warning echoed in his mind. Hadn't he equated Vanessa's enchanting ways to a siren's more than once? He'd heard legends of sirens and mermaids his entire life. Many accepted them as fact, others as myth. The only difference between sirens and mermaids that he could recall was that sirens had magical powers to beguile and often lured sailors to their deaths.

Vanessa cast him a sideways glance. Andre gave a shallow nod for her to continue.

"Today, with my feet in the saltwater cove, my heart went out to Sara and my magic seemed to follow. I passed out for a moment and fell in. That's when you arrived."

Andre tugged her to a stop at the edge of the vegetable garden and extricated his hand from hers. "Show me."

"Promise me you won't allow it to frighten you?"

Her vulnerability tugged at his heart, and he offered a grin. "I think we've been through much more frightening experiences. Weir, for instance."

"Andre!"

"Speak of the devil and he shall appear," Andre muttered.

The savant rushed toward them across the grassy lawn.

"He isn't that bad," Vanessa chastised, and then wiggled her brows. "A bit odd, perhaps."

"What's odd?" Weir asked as he approached, grinning, the apples of his cheeks so round his eyes nearly disappeared.

Andre shoved his hands into his pockets and watched the savant as he said, "Vanessa just agreed to show me a bit of magic."

"Excellent." Weir's expression gave nothing away, but Andre could tell that Vanessa's ability was not a surprise to him. "Magic is not odd—only those who fear it are awed."

Andre checked himself just before he rolled his eyes at the strange man's penchant for poetry.

"Well, let's see it, then!" Weir bounced on the balls of his feet.

Vanessa lifted her gaze to Andre first, and he nodded. She walked a short distance to the stalks of corn swaying in the breeze, plucked a leaf, and placed it between her palms. With a whispered word, she opened her hands, and the leaf had transformed into a tiny butterfly. Andre caught his breath as the transparent green wings beat and the insect lifted into the air.

Vanessa snapped her fingers. The bug transformed back into a leaf, and she handed it to Andre.

He inspected the plant material for changes, but it appeared a normal corn leaf once again. "Incredible."

"See, Andre?" Vanessa laid a hand on his arm. "Magic isn't always a bad thing."

"Not at all, unless you suppress, and it becomes a hex," Weir confirmed in a flat singsong tone. "Defeating the triplex is cutting the curse. But worse, hunting its core would be perverse."

Vanessa whirled on the savant. "What did you just say?"

Weir shook his head as if unsure what had come out of it. Then he tapped his pointy chin. "The archival information spills out at inopportune times. Or opportune, I suppose, if the knowledge is useful." His golden eyes landed on Andre. "Was it useful?"

Tingles prickled Andre's scalp. "Archival information?"

Weir nodded. "Didn't I tell you? Every text from the ancient archives is stored in my brain."

Hope buoyed through Andre's blood even as it mingled with annoyance at Weir's having kept this nugget of information from them. "Weir, that's amazing! So you can tell us how to break the curse?"

"Er . . ." The little man scratched his head. "It doesn't work like that. I can't access the information. Like I said, it spills out when it's needed."

Vanessa stepped up to Weir. "It's all right. You said, 'Defeating the triplex is cutting the curse. But worse, hunting its core would be perverse.' That has to be a clue to how to break it."

"What is a triplex?" Andre asked.

"*Tri* would imply the number three," Weir said.

"Like a three-corded strand," Vanessa mused, eyes glinting. "Could that mean the curse comes from three sources combined?"

"If that's the case, does it mean we have to undo all three parts to reverse what's happened to the victims?" Andre asked.

Weir nodded in confirmation. "That is a likely explanation."

Andre's flicker of hope quickly changed to dismay. They had no idea where to start undoing one part of the curse, let alone three. Meanwhile, the afflicted continued to suffer terrible fates, and if what Vanessa had learned from the archives was true, their time to reverse it at all was running out.

He turned to Vanessa and grasped both her hands in his. "I never expressed my gratitude to you for healing Sara. Thank you, Vanessa." He took a breath. "Would you consider . . . perhaps it would be more efficient if you healed the cursed individuals. Could you do that?" It was much to ask of her, but he knew that if she'd done it once, surely she'd be willing to use it again and again if it meant helping the others.

Vanessa stiffened, her expression pinched. "I don't—"

"Andre, come quick." Andre spun at the frantic sound of Yia-Yia's voice. "It's Sara!"

PART 3
A VORACIOUS HEART

There is in every true woman's heart

a spark of heavenly fire,

which lies dormant in

the broad daylight of prosperity;

but which kindles up, and beams

and blazes in the dark hour of adversity.

—Washington Irving

CHAPTER 25

VANESSA

THE MOON SHONE white and clear on the deserted village square as Vanessa banged on the bloodred door of the governor's villa.

Lightless windows stared down upon her—judge and jury. A cold wind swept in from the ocean as thunder crackled through the sky. A splintered basket, paper wrappers, and dead leaves skittered across the cobblestones in an accusing whisper. *Guilty . . . guilty . . . guilty . . .*

At that moment, Sara lay near unconscious in bed, too

weak to move, the curse redoubled in her frail body, every bit of magical healing Vanessa had worked on her undone. Andre sat broken at her bedside, shoulders slumped, the hopelessness on his face unbearable to witness. When Vanessa had left, Yia-Yia was kneeling on the hardwood floor, hands folded, head bowed as she whispered in fervent prayer.

What kind of power did it take to produce a curse that could so easily override Vanessa's own magic? She'd read of black magic, dabbled in it here and there with her spells, but this hex manifested as if it lived and breathed of its own volition. As if it took on a life of its own in each host. That sort of power sped the pulse in Vanessa's veins.

Could she wield it? Given the chance, did she even want to?

She lifted her fist and banged again. "Zika, open up!"

A stern woman, dressed in a gray serge nightgown and white frilled cap, swung the door open just as Vanessa's fist lifted to deliver another round of knocks. "What is the meaning of this?" the woman sputtered.

"I need to speak to the governor." Vanessa pasted on her best wide-eyed, concerned-citizen expression. "It is urgent. A matter of life and death."

CHAPTER 25

The old woman lifted an iron candelabra high and surveyed Vanessa from head to toe, taking in her deep purple cloak fastened over a gown of sober blue. "Who are you, then?"

Vanessa lowered her hood. "Miss Vanessa of Baros Cottage. I assure you the governor will wish to see me if you tell him I am here."

The woman's eyes widened. "You know the Baroses?"

"Yes, they took me in after an accident stole my memories," Vanessa replied, and lifted her fingers to her shell conduit. This lady had approximately one minute to open the door of her own free will.

"Ah, yes, I've heard of you. The beautiful maiden in distress." Mockery laced the woman's droll tone, but she opened the door wide and stepped aside.

The housekeeper shut the door and then led the way down a dark corridor. "I'm Melody Luongo. I attended school with Esma Baros, before she married Peter, of course. Andre and Sara's parents. Such a tragedy what happened to them. The seas around here are usually calm. Fatal boating accidents are a rarity."

Something about the woman's conversational tone, as if discussing the weather, not the death of people she knew personally, raised the hackles on the back of Vanessa's neck. Or maybe it had to do with the candelabra casting shadows that appeared to dance and spin around them. And perhaps they were. The spirits of the unsettled dead roamed the earth, powerless, yet forever seeking the attention of the living.

Vanessa steeled her spine. A dour old woman and a few shadows would not deter her from her mission. Her last interaction with Zika had been playing over and over in her mind since she'd left him. She never should have doubted the darkness she'd glimpsed within him.

He knew something, and she aimed to find out what.

Mrs. Luongo led Vanessa into a dark parlor. "I will fetch the master."

The servant departed with her candelabra, leaving only dim moonlight shining through the windows. Vanessa walked over and gazed out onto the courtyard at the approaching storm, clouds moving in to conceal the stars, and the strange lion-like statue in the governor's garden again sparked a familiarity in her chest. She peered closer, remembering a human with the face of a lion emblazoned on a shield. Perhaps Weir would know more.

"Miss Vanessa, what a pleasant surprise." She whirled to find Zika wearing a scarlet dressing gown, stringy hair tied back in a tail. Deep-set eyes, ringed with shadows, were like sunken holes in his gaunt face. His dark countenance reminded her of the ghoul masks some of the older merchildren wore on All Hallows' Eve.

Thunder rumbled low and long in the distance as Vanessa said, "I was hoping you could help me, Governor Zika."

"Not sure if you've heard, but I'm not really in the business of helping."

Vanessa narrowed her gaze on him. "Like when you paid Krill to attack Andre and destroy his business? That kind of *not helping*?"

He gave a slight shake of his head, his benign expression unchanged. "No, that wasn't me."

"Why should I believe you? Who else has that kind of money lying about?"

"Who indeed?" He moved closer and raised his chin. "Now, tell me why you're really here."

Clearly, this man was accustomed to getting what he wanted. She was about to disappoint him. "Answer my question first."

"Why do you think I'd have anything against Andre Baros?"

"*Do* you?" Vanessa arched a brow.

"Not against the boy, no. But I can tell you"—Zika

gestured with a flimsy wave in the general direction of the sea—"others might have had reason to stop him."

Vanessa stilled. Zika's gesture made her think about Omis Island, and something flagged in her mind that had gone undetected before: how would Weir even have known about a mainland governor if he hadn't left the island in decades?

"Why are you really here, Miss Vanessa?" Zika's voice held a sneer, but his expression carried no emotion.

She was about to wipe the bland look off his emaciated face. Casually, tinkering with the strings tying her cloak together, she sashayed closer to the governor and cast a secretive smile. "You know more about the Grimaldi curse than you're saying, don't you, *Zika*?" She drew out his name soft and slow, deliberately dropping his title. This bottom-feeder didn't deserve her respect.

He searched her face and then, without preamble, conjured a ball of flame in his palm and threw it into the fireplace, the logs catching in a riotous blaze. "A bit chilly in here. Wouldn't you say?"

Vanessa lifted her chin and met his stare. So that was how it was going to be. No more pretense. "I see I've come to the right place." With the room suddenly stifling, she flipped back the sides of her cloak, touched the shell at her throat, and stepped closer to the governor.

Flames danced along one side of his countenance, the other half eclipsed in darkness as he asked, "What makes you think I have the information you seek?"

She smiled. "We're about to find out." Vanessa gripped her nautilus and muttered a truth-telling spell. *"Truth shall be unmoored, no lie obscured."* She crept closer, hand still clutching her conduit. "Now, tell me everything you know about the Grimaldi curse."

Zika threw back his head and laughed. Paused. Then laughed some more.

Vanessa froze, her blood running cold.

No one could resist such an enchantment. Not mermaid or human. She waved her hand to reveal his true nature. But no further layers of his being were exposed.

His laughter ceased. "How very bold you are! Casting your little spells and making demands. I must admit that I've been among these puny humans too long. No one has dared challenge me in decades."

"I am no joke, Gorgo Zika." She clenched her fists, evoking the flash of lightning that streaked across the night. "I am born of the sea and wield its might."

"No need for that." Zika snapped his fingers and the

charged heat died in her hands. "I'll tell you what I know about the curse."

Vanessa gave a sharp intake of breath as thunder cracked open the sky, releasing a deluge that raged in time with her pulse. How dare this man control *her* magic? What gave him such capability? What gave him the right?

"Before you tire yourself out," Zika said with the confidence of the most powerful being in the room, "let's have a civilized conversation and see if we can't come to a mutual agreement. Would you take a seat?" He gestured toward a grouping of chairs near the hearth.

Senses on full alert, Vanessa lowered to the edge of a settee facing the door.

Governor Zika sat across from her, crossed his legs, and steepled his long fingers in front of his chest. "Vanessa. May I drop the *Miss*? I feel we've gotten to know one another this evening."

She gave a short nod, heat rolling in her belly as she scrutinized the devil staring back at her. The breadth and depth of his power felt familiar, a tone that called to mind Triton and all his arrogant authority.

"Now, Vanessa, kindly tell me why you concern yourself with humans and this little curse," Zika began conversationally.

CHAPTER 25

She closed her mouth with a snap of teeth. He spoke her name mockingly, as if he knew her identity was a sham. But if she didn't play his game, she would learn nothing. She swallowed and then said, "Sara Baros has fallen terribly ill from the curse. I wish to stop it."

Zika swiped a hand across the scowl that had formed on his mouth. "Tell me the real reason."

"I—"

He cut her off. "You want to help little Sara and all the others, I'm sure that's part of it, but I need your *true* motivation."

It was a risk, but she'd found nothing on her own, so she admitted, "Where I come from, magic is currency, separating the weak from the strong. If you want to stay in power, you must keep up. A curse like this could be very . . . helpful."

A skeletal grin lit up his face. "Yes, that I believe." He sat back. "The Grimaldi curse, as it was named, isn't actually a curse at all, but an organic creation that grows and changes based on the infected individual's brain chemistry. It feeds on their . . . deepest fears."

Vanessa thought back to the horror she'd experienced when she'd delved into the scourge inhabiting the butcher's brain. She brushed off a shudder and leaned forward. "I'd figured that much out myself. Who created it? What sustains it? Where does it reside?" She fired out a series of rapid questions at the ghoulish man.

"Everything worthwhile comes with a price, young witch." He gave a slight shrug.

Vanessa drew back her shoulders. "I'm no witch."

"Hmm . . . I think, in time, you will see that you are."

He could call her a nymph or a dolphin if he liked; it didn't make it true. "Fine. What's your price?"

Zika spoke quickly. "A single favor, cashed in at the time of my choosing."

Vanessa rose to her feet and began to pace up and down in front of the fire. A favor could be anything. And she doubted it would be something as enjoyable as maiming a hateful man's arm. But she had to know more in order to find the source of the power. Once she had it, this devil-man couldn't touch her: his favor would mean nothing.

She spun to face Zika. "I agree to owe you a single favor. Now. Where is the organic heart of the curse?"

Zika nodded, and with a flick of his wrist, a dull tingle washed over her, magically sealing her promise, before he replied, "The nucleus is in the Hollow Sea. She furrows beneath the villages, stretching and spreading. Her roots grow stronger by the hour. By the night of the waxing moon, when it hangs fully in the sky, the curse will become so invasive the people it preys upon will be forever changed."

Vanessa could sense the lunar cycles and their link to the sea. A new moon had risen with the tide, which meant they had less than four days to break the curse before it was too late for all the people it had afflicted. Apprehension churned through her, and the memory of Sara listless and unmoving in her bed made Vanessa demand, "Where is the Hollow Sea?"

"I've answered your question. And I've already secured my favor from you. You hold nothing more for me." The governor stood and pulled a bell cord by the hearth.

"You tricked me!" Vanessa opened and closed her right hand, white flares of power flashing in her palm.

"I don't believe I did," Zika replied in a flat voice. He turned to the housekeeper as she entered the room. "Mrs. Luongo will show you out."

Vanessa nearly sputtered. But she wasn't the sputtering type. She was the vengeful type. "This is not over, Zika."

"I certainly hope not." He yawned. "Come back anytime, Miss Vanessa. This has been vastly entertaining."

Mrs. Luongo took Vanessa's arm and spun her toward the darkened corridor. Stunned, her mind twisting, Vanessa let herself be led away.

"A bit of free advice, young witch." Vanessa glanced back to see Zika's lanky silhouette framed in the doorway, the flames of the fire casting spectral shadows that danced around his head. "Humans will not accept you as you are. I speak from experience."

***

"Vanessa!" Andre bounded out the front door of the cottage as Vanessa made her way up the walk early that morning. "Where have you been?"

After leaving the governor's mansion, Vanessa had wandered along the coast all night. At one point she'd considered stripping off her cloak and boots and had begun to unlace her gown, ready to dive into the ocean and never return. Surely, these good people would be better off without a magical powder keg living among them?

Because that's what she was, now that she owed Zika a favor. He could strike the match and command her to do anything, at any time, and she would have to obey. She could hurt the ones she cared for. Or was it love, after all? For after searching her soul the night through, she'd realized what the horrid pain at the thought of leaving meant: she cared for someone other than herself.

The fact that Andre ran barefoot into the dewy grass, shirt unbuttoned, eyes haunted as he drank her in, proved he felt the same about her. *Didn't it?*

He hadn't said the words, but she'd heard it in his voice. Felt it in the way he touched her.

Could she really have this? A man who loved her? A man who inspired her to step outside herself? Was this what the merpeople talked about finding, while she'd fled from their insipid prattle?

"Andre!" She breathed his name as she threw herself into his arms. "I have so much to tell you."

He leaned back and cupped her face in his large hands, turbulent eyes searching her face. "Are you all right?"

"Yes, but no." She shook her head as he dropped his hands to her arms. "We need to leave. Get far away from here."

Andre's brow furrowed. "I don't understand. Tell me what's happened."

"I went to see Zika. He told me things about the curse." She gripped Andre's arms. "It is stronger than I realized. But if we can get away, and take Sara, maybe she'll recover."

"That's not going to work."

They both turned to find Weir framed in the doorway, hair mussed and eyes squinting as if he'd just woken, the Baroses having offered him a temporary roof until he could arrange his own lodgings.

"Why not?" Vanessa demanded. "We know the curse lives under the town, and if we can get her away from the source, then I can heal her again and it will stick this time."

"The thing lives inside her," Weir replied. "I discerned it last night while she was sleeping."

Andre jammed a hand into his hair, a look of horror on his face.

Vanessa stalked over to Weir, noting that he had bags under his eyes and lines etched around his mouth. Perhaps he hadn't slept much either. "I can do it in my true form, with the power of the sea flowing through me," she hissed under her breath.

"And how will you take Sara there without killing her?" he muttered, his eyes soft with understanding Vanessa didn't want.

She crossed her arms in front of her chest. She didn't need his pity; she needed answers. Then an idea formed that she couldn't believe she hadn't thought of before: she could transform them into merpeople, just as she'd transformed herself into a human. They could become Cecaelia and live with her in Atlantica.

Her heart soared. She could have her precious sea and Andre, too.

Weir's lips pressed together, and he narrowed his eyes. "Don't even think about it."

"Think about what?" Andre had come up behind her, his solid presence a balm to Vanessa's ragged nerves.

Weir shook his head. "I need some tea. Let's talk inside."

They gathered around the kitchen table as the morning sun rose outside the windows. Weir put a kettle on and distributed cups, setting out a bowl of sugar and a carafe of cream. Vanessa looked to Andre in question. Since when had Weir become so intimate with Yia-Yia's kitchen?

"Weir has taken over since he arrived. He's quite the domestic, though Yia-Yia doesn't much care for the help." Andre's mouth kicked up on one side.

That tiny dimpled smile sent beams of light through Vanessa's soul. He still had hope. Even if it was a small hope, the Andre she knew was peeking through the darkness of his sister's degenerating condition.

Weir poured tea into each of their cups and sat down across from them, cradling a cup in his hands. "Vanessa, I can practically see the tangle of thoughts above your head. Tell us what you learned last night."

Before Vanessa would divulge anything, she had a confession to get out of Weir. She'd been turning her conversation with Zika over and over in her mind, and believed she had solved at least one piece of this puzzle. "I was thinking, Weir," she began, her tone casual. "How exactly is it that Zika knew you were on Omis Island? And how do you know him well enough to have told us not to trust him when we first met? I thought you said you'd lived on Omis alone for decades."

Weir's gold eyes widened. "Well, I—"

"*You* ordered the attack on Andre!" Vanessa cut Weir off, louder now. "You hired Krill!"

Weir averted his gaze. "Yes."

A screech of wood preceded Andre jumping to his feet, fists clenched. "You little worm! I knew we couldn't trust you. Do you have any idea what you've done to what was left of my business?"

Weir rose to his feet and backed up from the larger, enraged man, talking fast. "I thought you would destroy me. The vision was clear. So I wanted to get to you first.

But it turned out that Circe planted the vision in my mind to try to prevent the archives from ruin, and my escape. With me gone, she has no tether to earth and has been forced to move on." His back hit the counter as Andre advanced on him.

"So it all worked out for you, is what you're saying." Andre's nostrils flared before he growled, "Get out!"

"Let's not be too hasty, Andre." Vanessa rose as she clutched her shell, ready to enchant his anger away. Weir *was* a worm for what he'd done, but he held knowledge they needed in that warped mind of his. "First let me tell you what else I learned. Zika knows much more than he's saying, but he did tell me the heart of the curse is somewhere called the Hollow Sea. Do you know it?" She decided not to mention she'd had to promise a favor to get that information.

Andre shook his head.

Weir stood, his expression vacant as he crooned, "Follow me to the Hollow Sea where unholy maidens of three guard against calamity." He blinked, eyes refocusing. "What did I just say?"

"That's the second time you've made reference to the number three," Andre said to Weir.

"The triplex!" Vanessa exclaimed. "Defeating the triplex

is cutting the curse. So hurting the unholy maidens of three—"

"Can stop the curse," Andre finished, then asked Weir, "Where is the Hollow Sea? You have to have some idea."

"I don't know. It alludes to a cave, but there are hundreds of sea caverns along this coast."

Andre pulled out his chair, spun it around, and straddled the back. "So what do we know? The curse is hidden in the Hollow Sea, it is growing, and guarded by three females . . . of some sort."

Ice dropped into Vanessa's stomach, spreading through her veins. "There was something else. He said if we don't destroy the curse by the time the waxing moon hangs fully in the sky, it will become irreversible."

"Which means we have three days," Andre said, looking sick to his stomach.

Silence sat heavy on the room like deep, cold water, dark and hopeless.

Suddenly, Weir shot to his feet and chanted, "Near them their sisters three, the Gorgons, winged. With snakes for hair—hatred of mortal man."

The savant slumped back into his chair, his face wrinkled like dull parchment.

CHAPTER 25

Vanessa reached across the table and gripped Weir's hand, bringing him back to himself. "What do the Gorgon sisters have to do with Zika?"

The savant clutched her fingers. "Yia-Yia said Zika's first name was Gorgo, and you said that your magic didn't work on him?"

"That's correct," Vanessa replied, a chill skittering across her shoulders as she followed the savant's train of thought. She'd read the name Gorgo in her studies of Greek mythology, but she hadn't made the connection. Until now.

"He's a god," he sighed in resignation, as if reading her thoughts. "Or at least a descendant, like me."

"Gorgo is a common enough name," Andre reasoned. "Surely it's a stretch to say our crusty old governor is a god. Why would he bother overseeing a string of tiny hamlets?"

"I don't know." Weir's gaze darted from side to side. "But one thing is certain: Zika isn't who he says he is."

CHAPTER 26

VANESSA

VANESSA AMBLED along the cliff path, suspended between blue sky and turquoise sea. An empty basket hung from her arm, and a list of supplies rested in her pocket. She'd offered to go into town and pick up essentials for the family, when what she'd really wanted was the time alone to think. As her body walked the rocky surface, her mind remained stuck on Weir's cryptic chant about the Gorgon sisters, and his claim that Zika wasn't who they thought.

CHAPTER 26

The Gorgons were monsters of ancient lore, born of an unholy union between marine deities. They had long faded into the mythos of Atlantica, more cautionary tale than warning. But the thought of the legendary sisters and their possible tie to the curse sent a chill down Vanessa's spine.

She breathed deep of the fresh air, her eyes continually darting to the sea far below. She'd invited Andre to leave; to escape the clutches of the curse so Sara could heal. But her dream of their becoming a family of Cecaelia had dissolved with the coming of the waxing moon, the expiration date on the curse's reversibility. It had taken her weeks to create the potion that had transformed her into a human. They didn't have that kind of time.

Her heart fractured at the choices before her. She could return to the ocean alone; answer the call that rang in her soul night and day. Or stay on land and leave behind the glory of her true self; the rush of the deep flowing through her veins, the pulse of fathoms feeding her magic.

In this human form, she would never be as powerful as she'd become beneath the sea. She would always be vulnerable to beings like Triton and Gorgo Zika.

She stopped and gazed over the precipice. One single swan dive into the waves and she could make it to her cavern by sunset—abandon all the messy ties of emotion that held her to the land.

And forsake the only love she'd ever known. Andre hadn't said the words, but she felt them in every look they exchanged, each heated touch. Their destinies were intertwined.

But he wasn't with her right now, was he? Andre couldn't leave his dying sister for even a moment. Inevitably, they were a package deal.

Vanessa kept walking. There was one other way. Only one.

If she could find the Hollow Sea and defeat the unholy maidens—which seemed more and more to be the dreaded Gorgon sisters—she could absorb the incredible power of the curse. Sara would be healed, Andre would be free of his obligation, and Vanessa would have the power of a goddess. Then she could choose how she wished to live. Below the surface or on land, she would have Andre all to herself, his sister free of her illness at last.

Vanessa climbed a flight of steep stairs and slipped through a narrow pass between whitewashed buildings, emerging in the town square. The cobblestones had been cleared of litter and the villagers appeared to be making a valiant effort at reverting to some semblance of normalcy.

CHAPTER 26

Vendors hawked their wares to the bustling crowd, and figures went about their business with their heads down and shoulders hunched. Evidence that despite the plague of the curse, life went on. It had to.

She stopped at the dairy stand and paid for a fresh pint of milk and small round of cheese. Then she ducked out of the sun and into the heavenly-smelling bakery to purchase a warm loaf of bobota bread.

Her mood lightened somewhat by the fresh delicacies in her basket, she wandered through the merchant stalls to a booth selling brightly colored textiles. A man's shirt of deep forest green caught her eye. With Andre's black hair and emerald eyes, the shirt was practically made for him. She checked the coins she had left and her remaining list of supplies and realized in order to purchase the garment, she would need to forgo the rest of the groceries on her list.

Or devise a temporary solution.

Searching the table, she spied a bucket full of loose buttons. She grinned, walked straight to the container, and dipped her hand into the wooden toggles and smooth carved-shell circles. Several seconds later, she lifted out a handful of gold pieces.

"What on earth?" a voice squeaked.

Vanessa whirled to find Maryann the schoolmistress standing right behind her. It was clear by her wide-eyed expression that the woman had witnessed Vanessa work her magic. The teacher, lovely as a sunrise in a buttery frock and dusty pink hat, backed away from Vanessa, pale beneath her freckles. "You're a witch!"

Vanessa glanced around to ensure they weren't being observed, tugged the girl behind a rack of hideous pastel dresses, and gripped her conduit, lashing out with a spell that froze Maryann in place. "You think I'm a witch, do you? That I've somehow spelled Andre to fall in love with me?" Vanessa purred into Maryann's ear. "Darling, you are sadly mistaken."

The teacher's eyes moved frantically from side to side, a muted whimper escaping her throat. Vanessa could not allow the woman to spread lies about her that might reach Andre's ears. She needed a way to get the schoolmarm out of Andre's life, and Vanessa's, without bringing suspicion on herself. She eyed a secluded stand of trees at the edge of the square. But she had no time for that. There were people everywhere.

People she could use to her advantage.

A slow smile stretched across her face as she lifted a

finger to sweet little Maryann's temple. "Hysteria rule this feeble mind until such a time that the curse is mine."

Vanessa snapped her fingers and the pretty blond woman's face crumpled as she let out a strangled cry. Then she tilted her head back and screamed, ripping dresses from the rack.

"Help!" Vanessa beseeched the nearest villagers who had turned at the young teacher's display. "I think she's been driven crazy by the curse!"

Maryann ran in a tight circle, clawing at her perfect coiffure of curls, and Vanessa worked her face into an appropriate mix of sympathy and horror.

A stout woman with steel-gray hair emerged from the crowd. "That's Miss Maryann Aprílios." She rushed over and took the manic teacher in a firm grip. "Come now, child. I will take you to your family."

Maryann screeched and whirled toward Vanessa, hands raised like claws.

Vanessa jumped back. "Oh my!"

The sturdy woman gripped Maryann around the waist and spun her back around. "Now, now . . . there's no need for such behavior. What would your mother say?"

Maryann growled and spat like a rabid animal, her

pretty pink hat hanging by a single pin off the side of her head.

"Take good care of her!" Vanessa called as the struggling pair moved away. Crocodile tears glistened in her eyes for the benefit of those watching. "Poor thing," she gushed, with a sad shake of her head.

The crowd dispersed, quite used to the spectacle of those affected by the curse, and Vanessa turned back to the merchant's stall to hide the quirk of her lips. Two problems solved with one handy hex. The prim Miss Aprílios could not spread any credible rumors of Vanessa's supposed witchery, and she was no longer competition for Andre's affections.

"Well done." The sound of hands clapping made Vanessa whirl to find Zika lurking in the shadows.

***

"Ignoring me is rather beneath you, Vanessa." Zika matched her stride as he walked at her side. After spotting Zika, Vanessa had quickly paid the seamstress for the shirt and walked away, but he had doggedly followed. "I expected more."

She kept an aloof expression as she wove through the village merchants.

CHAPTER 26

Zika tailed her like a parasitic fish, salivating to latch on to her flesh. A few residents they passed offered the governor a nod or tip of a hat. No one greeted the man with a smile. Instinct was a powerful thing. Fear might demand obedience, but it did not garner respect.

"Where is the feisty witch who visited my home?" Zika leaned in closer, lowering his voice so passersby wouldn't hear. "The one who just cursed an innocent young woman?"

"Go away, Zika." Vanessa quickened her pace, anticipating that he would cash in the favor she owed him at any moment—yet hoping against hope it had all been a bluff. What could he possibly need or want from her that he could not get himself?

At the edge of town, they passed Mrs. Luongo, the governor's housekeeper, with a basket laden with bread, meats, and cheese. The older woman flashed Vanessa a quick smile. Vanessa moved to return the gesture, and stopped, blinking to clear her vision.

The woman had multiplied into twins before Vanessa's eyes. Grins froze on their ruby lips, silver eyes rolled like pearls of white as they raised their arms in eerie unison.

Like Weir's mirror pets, the ghoulish women moved

in perfect, horrifying syncopation. Then they spoke, their joined voices a chant of despair and shattered dreams. "Make the sacrifice. Atone for your sins. Earn his favor and redemption shall win."

Vanessa's blood curdled and she gripped her conduit, heated lightning flashing over her skin. She had no interest in forgiveness or atonement. She gathered a ball of energy in her palm. Something like dread rippled in scarlet ribbons over her vision, dousing her magic. She whirled on Zika, or whoever in the seas he was. Enough was enough. Fear had never dictated what she did or did not do. She was not about to let it start ruling her life now.

But Zika was no longer there.

Vanessa's vision cleared, and she saw the housekeeper's retreating form, gray serge skirts whipping around her ankles and steely curls bobbing as she blended in with the townsfolk. Vanessa inhaled, then let out a slow breath.

"Don't you want redemption?"

Vanessa started at Zika's voice and spun to find him leaning against the corner of a building, vivid seas and the horizon splayed out behind him.

"Your little illusions don't scare me. I've seen Weir's mirror pets." Vanessa stalked past him and skipped down a cobbled staircase leading to the cliff path. "I've had enough of your games, old man."

"But you're so entertaining," Zika called after her.

"Fine." She stopped and looked up at him. "If you insist on following me, then be useful and tell me where the Hollow Sea is."

He ambled down a few steps, hands in his pockets, and stopped above her. "I'm not ready to tell you that."

Vanessa's brow furrowed. "But you will tell me, eventually? Why?"

He descended the stairs and faced her. "Answer me this: has Andre Baros fallen in love with you yet?"

"That's none of your business," she snarled.

A frightful grin split his face. "Think of it as a give-and-take of information."

Vanessa kept walking. If she told him what he wished to know, would he give her the location of the curse? Zika followed just behind her.

"I believe he has, yes," she finally muttered, when they reached the cliff path.

Zika nodded, folded his hands in front of him, and walked at her side for several silent moments. Vanessa glanced over the side of the steep cliff and calculated how she might throw him off the edge. Impaled on the rocks, even a god would need significant time to recover.

When Zika finally spoke, jarring the quiet around them, Vanessa nearly tripped over the precipice herself.

"Get Andre to ask you to marry him and I will tell you where the Hollow Sea rests."

Marriage? To Andre Baros? Why would he ask such a thing?

Nonetheless, her heart sped at the image of the two of them bound together forever, only not on land: instead, she pictured them roaming the magical world beneath the waves. Andre would make a splendid Cecaelia, powerful and sleek, and once she had the curse in her possession, she could transform him easily. Hand in hand, they would fly through the crystal-blue waters, ride the currents, swim through the rays of golden sun setting on the sea. She had so much she could show him. She would even transform Sara, too, if Andre wished.

But would they accept her in her true form? Love her as Ursula, and not Vanessa? She was the same person no matter her environment. But would Andre still think her beautiful, still flash her that mysterious, dimpled grin that she knew was just for her? As a Cecaelia, her hair flowed white as moonshine, her glorious tentacles the black and purple of midnight, her muscular curves fierce in a way her delicate human body never could be.

How could he not want her still? The thought sent her heart skipping ahead of her, ready to transform for him as soon as possible.

But perhaps she should focus on one challenge at a time. Engagement to Andre first, and then, once they were wed, they could decide where they would live. She could choose how and when to share her whole truth with him. Ease him into the idea that he'd fallen for a magical sea creature most believed nothing more than a myth.

Vanessa's feet practically floated down the path as she thought of all the delightful ways in which she could extract a proposal from the man she loved. But as she neared the turnoff to the winding driveway, a cloud drifted to block the sun, and Vanessa slowed, clutching the basket to her chest, doubt swirling in her gut.

Why would Zika bribe her into doing something that would bring her happiness? And, if she fulfilled his request, would that absolve her of the favor she owed him?

Vanessa turned to ask him all this only to find herself alone on the path. "Curse Neptune and all the saints!"

Vanessa stamped her foot. Zika had disappeared once again, and she hadn't even had the opportunity to try to pry his true identity out of his evil, corrupt soul.

But now that he'd planted the idea of marriage to Andre, Vanessa knew she would stop the world to make it happen.

CHAPTER 27

ANDRE

SOMETHING STIRRED Andre from sleep in the late hours of the night. A whispered touch on his skin. The caress of a song, a sinuous melody that wove through his dreams. Calling. Beckoning him to wake. He sat up, still half dreaming, the coverlet falling to his bare waist. Wind whistled through the open window, curtains flapping as chilled air touched his skin. The nights were becoming cooler of late. The days growing ever shorter as they neared harvest season.

Normally, autumn was Andre's favorite time of year. Fields gilded in gold and mild days ending in cozy nights. Villagers, seamen, and visitors from surrounding towns all gathered for *panigiri* festivals. Days filled with locals presenting their best produce and mouthwatering dishes, and live music, dances, and bonfires that lasted throughout the night. All Saints' Day brought a three-day carnival with a corn maze, games, costumes, and hundreds of gourds hollowed and glowing with candlelight.

But nothing could penetrate the darkness that had fallen over Andre's life. Until Sara and the others were freed from the curse, he could not rest. Perhaps that urgent thought had tugged him from his restless sleep.

He threw off the blanket, placed his feet on the floor, and crossed the room, intent upon closing the window. But a noise like a soft tinkling gave him pause. He padded to the open door and heard a clink and rustle from below the stairs. Andre knew it was likely the savant rustling around. Nonetheless, he shrugged on a shirt and tiptoed toward the stairs, searching for something he could use as a weapon. Stealthily, he lifted an iron sconce off the wall and made his way downstairs.

Light flickered from the parlor, a soft, feminine hum drifting on the dusky air. Andre lowered his makeshift weapon and paused in the doorway as he saw the only bright spot in his endless night.

Vanessa.

Dressed in a rich purple dressing gown tied around her narrow waist with silvery ribbons, she knelt before a blazing fire, laying out the makings of a picnic on a chenille blanket. Her hair cascaded in midnight waves down her back as she filled crystal goblets with jewel-bright grape juice. She sang under her breath, a hypnotic song that Andre didn't recognize but longed to know, beautiful because it came from her lips.

When he stepped forward, she lifted her head with a smile that lit her eyes like stars. "You're here," she breathed, and then patted the blanket. "Join me."

As if in a trance, he padded across the rug and lowered to his knees across from Vanessa. "Vanessa. What are you doing?"

"I made us a midnight picnic," Vanessa said as she handed him a goblet of juice. "A celebration, of sorts."

Andre glanced toward the empty sofa. "Where's Weir?"

"I gave him my bed for the night." Vanessa's brow rose. "He was more than happy to sleep on a real mattress."

"I see." Andre stared at the cup in his hand but didn't partake. "Vanessa, I don't have much festivity in me, I'm afraid. We only have two days before the curse becomes irreversible."

"I don't wish to discuss evil things tonight." She watched him beneath lowered lashes that fanned the apples of her cheeks.

"What do you wish to discuss?" he asked, his voice going rough.

"Us. The two of us together." Her lips curled with feline grace. "We make a good team, don't we, Andre?"

"Yes." He reached over and placed his hand on hers. In a short period of time, he'd come to see her as part of his life. A part he didn't want to do without. And yet, even as he watched her, flames flickering in the deep violet of her eyes, darkness rippled over her in a way he didn't understand. It drew him like the shiny edge of a blade, calling him to touch; to test and see if it would cut him.

Vanessa leaned over and picked up a slice of cake, her robe falling open to reveal a sheer nightgown. When she looked up and caught him staring, sweat broke out on his skin. Not bothering to adjust her robe, she took a nibble of cake and then began to speak in her dulcet tones. "I don't want to leave you. No matter what I might remember or where I might be from, I know I'll want you with me."

Andre gulped down his juice, then lowered the cup

and wiped his mouth on his sleeve. Vanessa had become a powerful ally, someone he could lean on and share with; she'd healed his sister and selflessly tried to help him find a cure for the curse. That part of her, he trusted with his life. Yet she'd kept her magic a secret from him, and he couldn't shake the feeling that she was hiding other parts of herself.

"Vanessa." His voice came out in a raw whisper. "In the short time we've known each other, I've come to . . . care for you. Frankly, I've dreaded the day that your memories would return and take you away from me."

She leaned forward and grasped his other hand. "They don't have to! We can stay together no matter what."

"You don't know what you're saying." Andre shook his head and pulled away from her distracting touch.

Vanessa stiffened. "I know my own mind."

He quirked a grin. "Of that, I have no doubt. All I'm saying is you don't have all the information. Making a decision before you do will only hurt us both."

"I see." She lowered her head, dark waves falling to shadow half of her face.

"Vanessa." The alchemy of their skin ignited his blood as he brushed his thumbs on both sides of her face. "You're the first thing I think of when I wake up, and the last thing

I think of when I fall asleep. Don't ever believe that I do not want you every second of every day."

"Then show me you want me forever, no matter what happens." Her urgent whisper surged through him.

He searched her face. What was she asking of him?

She leaned forward and placed a single, searing kiss on his lips. Swells of desire rolled over him, making it impossible to pull away. "I don't understand." He shook his head. But he desperately wanted to understand, to fulfill her bidding, mysterious as it was. He wanted to stop the sun from burning. Block the moon from shining—if that's what she wished. In that moment, he would do anything she asked.

A log fell in the fireplace with a snap and a hiss. "Andre, I don't want us ever to part."

Ever to part. Ever to part . . .

That's when it hit him. She wanted commitment. To bind them together legally and spiritually.

He would do anything she asked—except for that.

He sat back. "Vanessa, you don't know what you're asking. For me, the bond of marriage is sacred. An unbreakable vow before God. If I put a ring on your finger and ask you to marry me, that is forever."

"Exactly." Her smile lit the room, and she pulled a

ring from her pocket. With a pang, Andre recognized the square-cut aquamarine, the color of the clear shallow sea, bracketed by two perfect pearls on either side . . . because it had been his mother's.

Andre pulled their hands apart and reared back. "Where did you get that?"

"Don't be upset. I was searching for a pair of stockings and it just appeared. It called to me, as if it knew we were meant to be."

Andre stared at the ring his mother had worn every single day. The one thing she'd never taken off, except the day of their accident. When they were hours overdue and he'd gone into his parents' room that evening and seen the ring on top of her dresser, trepidation had swelled through him. It felt as though somehow, his mother had known, or at least had a premonition, that she would not return.

"I can't do this, Vanessa." He rose to his feet. "Someday, maybe, once we find out more about your past and ensure you aren't promised or married in your previous life."

"But I'm not!" Vanessa stood and faced him with a scowl. "I know I'm not."

Her statement was so sure and insistent that he cocked his head to one side, warning bells clanging in his heart.

"How can you know that unless you've remembered more than you've let on?"

She looked down, breaking their eye contact.

"Vanessa, if we are to have a committed relationship, we must have trust." He squeezed her hand gently. "Even if it is something hard to talk about, I need your honesty."

A soft sigh escaped her lips as she stepped closer and threaded her fingers through the back of his hair. Heat raced down his spine. "What I remember . . . what I *know*, is that you've become everything to me."

Andre's mind and body warred with each other as he stared into her mesmerizing heliotrope eyes, nearly shaking with the need to touch her. Kiss her. Worship her.

But her words didn't add up, and that sixth sense he'd always relied upon twisted his stomach. He gently unwound her arm from his neck and kept one of her hands in his. "Do you trust me, Vanessa?"

She nodded, a sort of wonder transforming her face. "I do."

"Then let's discuss this again in a few days. Once we've stopped the curse and made things right."

A smile curled her lips and darkened her eyes. "I'm afraid that's not possible, my love."

Andre opened his mouth to protest just as light flashed,

illuminating the bones of Vanessa's skull, and thunder rolled through his chest. The room tilted beneath his feet, causing him to stumble and fall.

Falling, he plunged deeper. Drowning.

He fought, but like the time he'd gone swimming after a storm and breakers took him under, rolling over his body, he was trapped beneath the waves. Blind and suffocating, he battled against the undulations taking him down . . . down . . . down. Vanessa's face appeared before him, distorted and stretched as she spoke words he couldn't hear over the roaring surf. He reached for her, but the water pounded him against the seafloor until his limbs were too weak to stand and his lungs burned like fire.

Unlike the time he'd nearly drowned, and his father's strong arms had pulled him from the undercurrents, this time, he succumbed to the smothering blackness. But it wasn't the darkness of sleep that surrounded him. The agitating surf stopped beating him down and he drifted peacefully, floating on the current. Suspended by the buoyancy of the ocean, he stared blissfully up at a lavender and cream-colored sky streaked with storm-dark clouds.

He dreamed of a joyous occasion. Smiles and kisses and a desire stronger than his own will to make Vanessa his forever. A question tore through flesh and bone, clawing up from his gut. He lowered to one knee, lifted up his mother's ring, and spoke the words he'd longed to say but hadn't dared.

"Vanessa, will you marry me?"

CHAPTER 28

VANESSA

VANESSA AWOKE with the dawn, half submerged in the gentle waves of the cove, her tentacles unfurled around her. She sat up, blinking sleep from her eyes as she searched the shore. If anyone caught her in this state, it would be over. Not even the powerful spell she'd worked on Andre to remove his doubts and enchant him into asking her to be his wife would stop the scorn that would fall upon her if he saw her true form with no preamble or warning. When she finally did show herself to him, it would be preceded by careful explanation.

She sank beneath the cool surface, the water like a caress as her dark hair floated across her vision, and she focused on returning to her human form. After she'd tucked a dazed Andre into his bed, she'd come to the cove to regenerate her magic. Overcoming his reservations had taken some creative spell work and quite a bit more power than she'd anticipated. The man's will was strong, she had to give him that.

Not that she would want anything less from her mate. A smile widened her face as she brought her right hand up and gazed at the shimmering aqua gem, its facets glinting in the crystal waters. She'd done it. They were engaged, and only days away from finding and defeating the curse. Hunger welled within her at the thought of finding such a core of power. Now, more than ever, she had need of it. She broke the surface and licked her lips. Perhaps there was a way she could have everything she wanted, after all.

"Vanessa!"

She ducked back down, heart pounding hard enough to crack her ribs. If she was caught now, it would ruin everything. She felt sea creatures hovering near. A moray eel peeked its sapphire snout between waving seagrass, a school of baby manta rays glided through the water like birds, and a playful dog-face puffer approached, drawn to her magnificence. As she sank through the clear water, she mentally shooed them away, and many legs became two once more as she pushed off the silty bottom, resurfacing with an excuse on her lips.

The wavering image of Weir solidified. He stood above her on the rocky shore. Or, rather, hunched, his shoulders rounded and back stooped. The bones of his face appeared sharp beneath thin, wrinkled skin. It looked as though he'd aged several decades overnight.

Vanessa swam to the ledge and rested her arms on the rock he stood upon. "You look worse than I feel, Weir. Bad night?"

Weir slowly lowered himself to a seated position, joints popping. He nodded toward her hand. "That's quite the sparkler you've got there," he observed, avoiding the question. "I assume your plan produced the desired result."

"Yes." Vanessa beamed. "Everything is falling into place." When she'd asked Weir to sleep in her bedroom the night before, he'd required an explanation. She'd told him everything, including Zika's request in exchange for the location of the Hollow Sea. There was something inherently freeing about Weir recognizing Vanessa's true self that allowed her to be forthcoming with him in a way she couldn't be with the other humans.

A seagull dove down, searching for a meal, and Vanessa swatted it away.

"Quite the enchantress you are. But what happens when Andre discovers the truth of your past? Do you plan to stay here, or transform him and take him under the sea?" the savant asked, head tilted in mock innocence even as Vanessa clearly heard the condemnation beneath.

"I don't see how that's any of your business."

"You wield your beauty and your scars like daggers, glittering and slicing in a single blow," Weir said softly. "If you truly loved him, you would show him who he's committed himself to."

Vanessa stared out over the glistening cove. What did this hermit know of love or devotion? He'd lived alone for the past two centuries, starved for attention and human interaction. "If you thought someone could love you, you'd do anything to keep them, and we both know it."

"Would I, though? Or would I give up everything to help those I cared about?"

Something in his voice made Vanessa turn back to him. His hand, dotted with spots and a crisscross of papery lines, rested on the rock beside her. "Weir, what's happening to you?"

His low laugh turned into a cough that sounded like his chest cracking. Once he'd recovered, he answered, "I cannot hide from my true age here. Circe's enchantment no longer protects me."

His youthful exuberance made it easy to forget the savant had lived for over two hundred years as Omis Island's guardian. Vanessa braced her hands on a flat stone and lifted herself out of the water. Weir respectfully looked away from her saturated nightgown. With a snap of her fingers, the sticky salt water whisked away from her clothes and skin, her drenched hair drying in spiral waves around her shoulders. She picked up her robe and shrugged it on before sitting beside him. "Can you go back to Omis?"

"Technically, yes, but with Circe's spirit gone, I doubt it would help me." He stared at his hands. "Nor do I want to try."

Unexpected sadness tightened Vanessa's throat. Although the man annoyed her beyond reason with his sanctimonious lectures and random spouts of knowledge, she felt a bond with him. Certainly, she didn't want to see him wither away before her eyes, not to mention he might continue to prove useful in their final efforts to dispel the curse. They needed him alive.

She reached out and took his arm, her magic surging toward him. But before her power could manifest, he yanked out of her grasp and scooted away. "No."

"I can heal you. Give you more time."

"You would heal me out of your own selfishness. You must learn to ask, and respect others' wishes, instead of acting out your mind's whims just because you can."

Vanessa bristled. "I would heal you because I . . ." She faltered. She would heal him because, beyond his knowledge of Circe's archives, she had so few friends that she didn't wish to lose him. Because she would miss him if he were gone. Her voice pitched low. "I don't want you to go."

Weir's eyes softened. "Vanessa, what you offer is a temporary reprieve. I'm not leaving yet, but when I do, it will be my time."

Chest hollow, she asked, "Your time for what?"

"Eternal life in heaven, of course." He leaned back on his arms and lifted his face to the sky. "My soul free at last."

An afterlife had never been something Vanessa gave much thought to. She lived in the moment, soaking up life like a sponge. Her legacy on this earth meant more to her than whatever came next.

They sat in silence for several long moments, the sun rising pink to light a pale-blue cloudless sky. Until Weir said, "I've done many selfish things in my life, all in the name of protecting myself and the things I thought were important. Looking back, I can see the error of my ways."

"You mean like hiring Krill to attack Andre and destroy his livelihood?"

Weir gave a mirthless chuckle. "That, among other things." He took Vanessa's hand in his, turning it side to side, the aquamarine in her new engagement ring refracting against her skin. "You don't love Andre."

She stiffened, rage clouding her vision. "I do love him."

"You're obsessed with him, Vanessa. His physical appearance. His noble goodness. Being a part of his family. The stability and acceptance he provides. You want him, and you want what he has. But that isn't the same thing as love."

"You're wrong." She shook her head.

"I don't doubt that you care for him. But real love puts others' needs before their own."

This time, Vanessa yanked her fingers from his grip. What did he know of her? "I've changed since you read my mind on the island. I chose to leave the Rhabdos behind because all I could see was Andre's face. I knew I couldn't live without feeling his touch. Without seeing him look at me with wonder in his eyes."

"Those are all good steps on the way to true devotion. But if you want real love, Vanessa, true love that lasts, it means vulnerability, letting go of control. Love means giving someone the power to hurt you." He put his hand on hers and gave it a quick squeeze. "You need to show him who you truly are, before it's too late."

Andre's words about basing their relationship on trust floated through her mind. Though she understood the concept, she didn't believe for one moment that giving someone power over her equaled love. She'd seen it for herself. Relationships were brutal and honest and gory, yes. But blind trust in another, even in someone like Andre, would make her weak. And there wasn't much she abhorred more than weakness.

She trusted herself alone.

Vanessa stood up and looked down at the withering man before her. "We have two very different ideas of love, Weir."

CHAPTER 28

***

"You're going to make it, Sara." Andre's voice sounded raw, as if he'd been crying.

Vanessa paused in surprise at the top of the stairs, where she'd been heading to her bedroom after returning from the cove. Was Sara awake at last? The girl had been unconscious since Vanessa had tried—and failed—to heal her.

Something tugged at Vanessa; she was happy the girl was awake, even . . . relieved. That day at the cove, she'd felt a connection to Sara unlike anything she'd ever experienced. Healed her without a price. Their similar experiences with rejection by those who viewed them as *less than* had brought out a softer side Vanessa hadn't been aware that she possessed.

Yet as she advanced toward Sara's room, something told her to approach quietly, so as not to be detected. She paused just outside the door in the shadows to listen.

"It's too late. The curse is burrowing into my heart," Vanessa heard Sara whisper. "I can feel it."

"Don't say that. We're not giving up!"

"But you're moving on." She hiccupped. "Building a

life . . . without . . . me. With Vanessa. You gave her mother's ring!" Accusation and hurt rang from Sara's every word.

The silence that followed buzzed with tension. Vanessa didn't move. Couldn't breathe. Would her spell hold? Did it need to? Or would Andre's true feelings for her shine through?

"I want to be with her . . . forever," Andre insisted. "I can't explain it."

Now Vanessa heard Yia-Yia's tremulous voice, apparently in the room with them. "Andre, I have to admit I've grown to like Vanessa, but we don't know anything about her past. She could be engaged to another. She could be a con artist or an escaped convict. All we know is that she has magic, and that she lied to us about it."

"None of that matters now," Andre insisted.

Vanessa pushed the anxiety from her chest in a slow breath.

"But you're my priority, Sara." Andre's voice rose with conviction. "I love you more than anything. You and Yia-Yia are my family. *Aíma tou aímatós mou.*"

Blood of my blood.

What did he mean by that? Did he love his sister and grandmother more than her?

Dread eddied in Vanessa's stomach, a rising tide of

nausea pushing up her throat. Andre had never said he loved her, even last night, when he'd been under her spell. Did he love her? Could he? Or had her enchantment been the only reason he'd said he wanted to be with her forever?

Spots flashed before Vanessa's eyes. She pivoted on her heel and ran from the urge to rip Sara's beating heart from her chest. To stop the old woman's breath in her wrinkled throat. To tear a confession of love from Andre's mouth. She'd never loved anyone until him. And he'd chosen devotion to a dying child and a decrepit old woman.

She leapt over the final two steps and pivoted toward the entranceway, her robe flying out behind her like a cape. She couldn't face Andre now. Couldn't allow him to see the darkness bubbling up from her broken soul. Sun flared through the parlor window and caught in the gem on her finger. The spell she'd woven had produced the desired result. But Andre's commitment to her was false—fake, just like her human form. She wanted to be worshiped, adored, revered. Real devotion that put her before everyone else in his life. But she'd ruined that by enchanting him, by pushing him too quickly.

Neptune doom Zika to hell! He'd forced her hand, dangled the revelation of the Hollow Sea's whereabouts over her like a prize he knew she wouldn't be able to resist. She'd questioned Zika's request for her to ensnare Andre, wondering why he'd be concerned with something that would bring her happiness—but now she understood: he'd foreseen that this chain of events would bring Vanessa only agony, and serve to weaken her as his adversary.

A knock sounded on the front door. She ignored it. Andre had been crying over his sister's pain. She'd heard it in his voice, felt his anguish radiating in her heart. No one had ever cried for her. Perhaps because of her, or what she'd done, but never over the thought of losing her. The knock sounded again, and she heard Andre's footfalls on the stairs. She straightened.

Maybe it was time that changed.

Andre rounded the corner, eyes red, mouth set. "Vanessa, why didn't you answer the door?"

He moved to stride past her, but she latched onto his arm. "Wait. I need to say something."

With a sigh, he stopped and stared down at her. The strong line of his jaw twitching.

"I'm leaving. I thought about it all night, and I—I can't accept this." She twisted the ring from her finger and held it out to him, an offering.

CHAPTER 28

"What?" Dark brows met over his eyes as he searched her face.

"You were right. It isn't fair for me to make this commitment to you when I don't have my memories."

She took a deep breath and blew it into Andre's face; the enchantment she'd so painstakingly woven dissolving in an instant.

Andre blinked in confusion, clear disorientation widening his eyes.

From outside, another knock at the door, this one even louder and more insistent. "I know you're home."

"Take it." Vanessa shoved the ring into Andre's chest. When he took the ring from her, tears stung the back of her throat. Had she hoped he'd refuse?

"Vanessa." Andre reached out and cupped her face. "Can we talk about this?"

She twisted away from his touch, shaking her head firmly. "There's nothing to discuss."

The bang sounded again, shaking the door in its frame. "Vanessa!" the voice called.

"Don't leave yet. Let me take care of this," Andre pleaded.

She gave a crisp nod. A glow heated her chest and

pinkened her cheeks. She would show him that she was first place in his heart. Blood bonds could be broken.

Andre flung open the door. "What is so blessed urgent?" he yelled before registering who was at the door.

Mrs. Luongo, the governor's housekeeper, filled the doorframe. Her odd, silvery gaze flickered past Andre's shoulder to Vanessa, and a smile slithered across her face. "Well, hello," she said pleasantly, as though she hadn't been about to beat the door down. "I have an urgent message here for Miss Vanessa."

Numbness spiraled through Vanessa's body as she moved forward to take the envelope the uppity housemaid held out to her. There was only one person whom the missive could be from. She opened the letter, and read the quick, broad strokes that sealed her fate.

Vanessa,
Bring Andre Baros to the governor's
residence at noon today.
This will dissolve the covenant
of the favor you owe me.
Sincerely,
M. Gorgo Zika

CHAPTER 28

The letter crumpled to ash in her fist, consumed by a wild surge of power and emotion. She should have known better than to believe the favor he would ask of her could be something as benign as convincing Andre to ask for her hand in marriage.

Shoulders straight, she strolled over to the crone at the door and raised a haughty brow. "Tell the governor I gladly acquiesce to his invitation."

If Zika wished for a showdown, a showdown he would have.

PART 4

THE HOLLOW SEA

For the good I desire to do,

I do not do,

but the evil I do not want

is what I do.

—Romans 7:19

CHAPTER 29

VANESSA

THE CHURCH BELL tolled six times as Vanessa rushed across the village square. A wispy aubergine cloak, the hood pulled over her head, shielded her skin from the noonday sun. On land, she'd come to appreciate the phases of the day. Midday was that hour when the azure sky burned gold, washing the land with oppressive heat that sent even the most weathered citizens indoors for a light repast or into the cool waters of the bay for a refreshing swim.

She was sure that Zika had chosen the hour of their meeting with deliberation. For Vanessa, noon was the time of day when she most longed to dive deep beneath the waves and escape the bleaching radiance of the yellow sun. She trembled at the thought of refreshing her dehydrated skin, soothing her tight pores, revitalizing her shriveled soul. It took all her focus to step nimbly across the cobbles and not allow her gaze to slide toward the cerulean sea peeking between the whitewashed buildings.

By the time she reached the governor's mansion, the church bell had reached twelve on the dot, and she'd half convinced herself what she was about to do was a sound plan. One way to break her vow to Zika was to beat him at his own game. This, she could do alone, just as she had defeated Circe. Andre need not be involved.

When she raised her hand to knock on the bloodred door, it swung open. Mrs. Luongo scowled past Vanessa's shoulder. "Governor Zika told me to set the table for three."

"Mr. Baros couldn't make it." Vanessa smiled innocently.

Mrs. Luongo tucked a few unruly strands of thick gray hair back into her bonnet and lifted her chin, inhaling so sharply her nostrils pinched. "Very well. Follow me."

Vanessa stepped into the darkened hallway and lowered her hood with a sigh. She would take the reprieve from the sun, even in exchange for the spooky old mansion. But instead of going left at the end of the corridor, toward the parlor, the housekeeper turned right and led Vanessa back outside into the courtyard. They walked over to a white-linen-covered table beneath a grove of trees heavy with ripe oranges. Fine china plates, fabric napkins twisted into the shape of swans, and crystal goblets filled with iced pink juice completed the table setting. Even the fastidious Weir would have approved.

"Have a seat," Mrs. Luongo said ungraciously. "The master will join you at his convenience."

"And when might that be?" Vanessa's brows rose as she met the woman's gaze. Did she imagine the swirl of night dancing like black holes in her smoky pupils?

Defenses raised, Vanessa stepped closer, but the housekeeper pivoted and stomped back into the house. Vanessa stared after her and let out a low sigh. She'd been out of the sea too long if she perceived an old servant as a threat.

Shrugging off her paranoia, she walked to the immaculately set table and downed a glass of juice. Where was the old turtle, anyway? He'd called her here, and she didn't appreciate being kept waiting. She refilled her cup from a sweating glass pitcher and drained the juice again. Somewhat refreshed at last, she shrugged off her cape to reveal a midnight-blue gown she'd magicked up at a hair's notice. The dress was more formal than the occasion called for, with a crystal-studded underskirt and sheer satin overlay embroidered with lavender shells and swirls. But the sharp vee of the waist and golden laces tying together the off-the-shoulder bodice made her feel fierce and powerful. Just as she'd intended.

Vanessa wandered over to the fountain. The lion statue gushed into an enormous pool the approximate circumference of the Baros family's parlor, and almost as deep as Sara was tall. An appealing tang in the air made her nose twitch, and she reached into the water, bringing her wet finger to her mouth.

"It's the salt you're drawn to. Purifies the water."

Vanessa whirled to find Zika in a pale linen suit and cream top hat. He smiled wide. "Feel free to take a dip if you like."

The man didn't seem the least bit disconcerted that Vanessa had come alone. Hackles rose on her neck. No one liked to be considered predictable, least of all her. With as much grace as she could muster, she returned his mild expression. "Perhaps later."

"Then, please, take a seat." Zika gestured toward the

garden table. "What of you and Andre? No engagement yet, I see." His glance darted pointedly toward her bare hand.

With no intention of playing his game, Vanessa wandered around the edge of the pool and fingered the golden shell at her throat.

"Actually, Andre did ask me to marry him. He's completely besotted with me, as you can imagine." Vanessa glanced over her shoulder at Zika and then trailed her fingers through the spray of the fountain, the briny water sparking in her soul. "But alas, I gave the ring back first thing this morning."

"I imagine the boy is quite heartbroken," he said contemplatively, and perhaps a bit too eagerly.

"Quite," Vanessa confirmed, and continued her stroll around the pool. Sweltering sun beat hard on her bare shoulders, the lure of the cool, salty water a siren's call. She rounded the far edge of the fountain, one hand still immersed.

"And what of you? Do you even have a heart to break?" Gorgo asked.

She whirled on the frail-looking man, magic fluttering over her fingertips. "I need to know where to find the Hollow Sea, and I have no intention of doing you any favors to obtain the information."

His gaze flashed to something behind her and he arched a thin brow. "Are you so sure about that?"

The squeal of hinges sounded as Vanessa turned to find Andre opening the iron gate to the courtyard, a frantic expression on his face. "Vanessa!" he called out as he approached.

Vanessa rushed toward the boy she loved. "Andre, you need to get out of here. This instant!" she hissed at him when she was close enough.

"I'm not leaving. I read the letter." Andre cut a look to Zika, and then back to her as he whispered, "If the favor you owe him has to do with me, then I should be here."

"This has nothing to do with you," Vanessa insisted, the lie tripping easily off her tongue.

"You don't have to do everything on your own!"

"Mr. Baros, I've been expecting you. Come in, come in!" Zika called in a jovial tone that put Vanessa's teeth on edge.

In her distraction, Andre pushed past her and strode into the courtyard, the gate banging shut behind him. "I'm not here for a social call, Governor. What do you want with me?"

The edge of Zika's eye ticked, his smile turning vicious.

CHAPTER 29

Vanessa followed Andre, but when she reached the edge of the fountain, her feet seemed to trudge through invisible mire. Andre pulled ahead of her, and the harder she pushed her legs to move, the slower her steps became. She watched Andre approach the ancient being and dread gripped her heart—a terror like she'd never felt. Zika intended to hurt Andre. She could read it on his face as he glanced at her to make sure she watched from her near-frozen position—he wanted her to witness what he was about to do.

To Andre.

"When I told you about Omis Island, Vanessa, I thought Circe might take you out of the picture," Zika said as oily streams of magic burst from his hands and latched onto Andre's ankles. "But when I realized all you wanted was the power the curse held, I knew your lies and your greed would ultimately hurt our little local boy more than I ever could." The ebony ropes latched onto Andre's legs, then his arms, locking him in place. "All I had to do was wait for him to fall for you."

Andre struggled, wide eyes seeking out Vanessa as he cried, "Run!"

But she couldn't run. She couldn't even move as Zika's immobilization spell held her in thrall. She strained to lift her arm, reach her conduit, but her limbs refused to obey her command.

A gurgled scream escaped Andre's throat as unctuous torrents slithered into his mouth. He gagged, his face turning purple.

Vanessa's thoughts raced through her mind even as her body held still. Zika was trying to kill him.

Andre choked and threw his head back, inky stains garroting his neck, strangling tight.

Rage and panic pounded in Vanessa's brain. She wasn't strong enough to break Zika's hold over her. Her body felt liquid, the hex stealing even her will to fight. She squeezed her eyes closed, searching internally for some spark of power that he hadn't reached.

Instead, advice her father had given her on his deathbed rang like a battle call through her petrified mind. It was one of the only things he'd ever said to her. Advice that her young heart had turned into a life's mantra.

You're the predator or the prey in this life, darling, and the predators survive.

Vanessa's eyes snapped open as Andre began to convulse. Pain threatened to splinter her heart as she looked away. She didn't think she could exist on this earth without him. No matter what their future held.

CHAPTER 29

Fury boiled within her, trapped and useless.

Predator. You are the predator.

She sent out her senses, searching for a weapon. For a way out. She had a matter of seconds before Andre suffocated like a fish out of water.

Or a human *in the sea*.

The soft tinkling of the fountain met her ears, so close that she could almost touch it. *Salt water.* She dug deep within, and like plucking the strings of a harp, awoke her voracious soul. She moved her lips, the words silent.

Lift me up and bring me home, this command I own.

Wings of water flashed out and carried Vanessa off her feet, plunging her into the pool with a splash. Still immobile, she dropped beneath the surface and floated to the bottom, flat as a board. The salinity filled her pores and she opened her eyes. A wavering image of Andre as he struggled above the surface sent her pulse echoing like a drum in her ears.

If that puny being thought he could take Andre away from her, he had another thing coming.

A roar bubbled out of her mouth as the transformation took her, legs dividing and growing, power surging like a hurricane through her veins. She rose on six powerful tentacles.

Grasping her conduit, she burst through the surface, lightning crackling across her skin. "Release him, now!"

Gorgo turned to her, eyes sunken in an ancient face, and smiled. He'd allowed the disguise of the governor to fade, revealing his true self, hideous and gleeful, blood dripping from his gums, teeth stained red.

"Look at your true love, Andre Baros!" he mocked. "How *beautiful* is she now?" The cords wrapped around Andre forced his head toward her.

Vanessa had no time to consider her love's thoughts as her power slashed across the courtyard, black as night and just as deadly. Zika might be immune to spells of persuasion, but she'd like to see how he handled a zap of lightning. He opened his arms wide, as if accepting the power into himself, convulsed once, and then toppled to the ground.

Vanessa clenched her fists on the second blast, the magic sizzling back into her cells and crackling across the surface of the fount. Andre slumped over and struggled for breath, no sign of Zika's inky spell on his skin. She breathed a sigh of relief. "Andre, are you okay? Are you hurt anywhere?"

Tentacles propelling her, she glided through the water

to the stone edge of the wading pool and reached for him.

He jerked away from her touch and fell, stumbling to his knees. Eyes wide with horror, his gaze raking over her body. "God in heaven, *what* . . . are you?"

She was still human, still Vanessa from the waist up, but her transformation had ripped her gown, the silk floating like seaweed wrapped around her tentacles. "I am—"

Before she could answer, Andre bent and retched on the cobblestones.

She reached out again. "Let me heal you."

"No!" Andre inched away from her. "Don't touch me."

He was trembling, shaking so hard that when he tried to stand, he lurched to the side and fell against a table. In her desperation to save his life, she hadn't thought of the shock he would feel at seeing her aquatic form—even from the waist down. She had to show him that he had nothing to fear from her. Zika still lay motionless on the ground, so Vanessa dove under the surface and allowed her human form to return. She had to get Andre out of there before the monster woke angrier than before. But as her human legs returned and she mended her dress, her chest had never felt emptier.

Fully human once again, she climbed over the edge

of the fountain to where Andre stood. Shoulders rigid, he backed away from her, his eyes darting to Zika and then back to her as if contemplating the worse of two evils.

"I have no idea who or what you are," Andre said, voice raw, "but I'm getting out of here."

"Andre, I'm still the same person," she called as he jogged toward the gate.

She looked at his retreating form, incredulous. She'd saved Andre's life, and this is what she got in return? Revulsion and scorn? Ungrateful, selfish little—

And yet. It had been a shock to Andre, certainly. She'd said herself she wanted to prepare him to face what she truly was.

She decided to turn her focus to Zika, who still owed her a bit of information about the Hollow Sea. Vanessa stalked toward his prone form, knowing that if she could find the Hollow Sea and break the curse, Andre would forgive her for her deception. And surely, apologize for his brief lapse in respect and decorum.

The door to the house banged open and the housekeeper appeared, eyes flying to Zika. "Master!" She ran to his side and fell to her knees, shaking his shoulders. At her touch, Zika stirred, but as he rose, his form blurred. The harder Vanessa focused on him as he stood, the more the image of him slipped away.

Vanessa backed up a step, the old man's wrinkled face transforming into fierce feminine lines as flesh melded and re-formed. In the blink of an eye, the monstrous change was complete.

Zika was a woman.

But not just any woman. Her limbs flowed in a sinuous dance as she glided forward, eyes blazing fire in a terrifyingly beautiful face. Eels burst outward from her scalp, slithering and hissing as her mouth split in a ravenous smile full of fangs.

Vanessa could not tear her gaze away.

Because she'd just looked into the eyes of Medusa.

CHAPTER 30

VANESSA

AT FIRST, SHE couldn't feel the pain.

The rock beneath Vanessa's feet began to creep up her legs, solidifying skin, muscle, and bone, turning her to stone. Shock kept the solidification of her flesh from registering with her nervous system. Then, the agony hit, like the poison of a thousand jellyfish stings burning through skin. Like shark teeth tearing muscle and bone. An endless scream tore from her lungs as she tried to clutch her nautilus, but her arms wouldn't move. A quick glance confirmed gloves of stone creeping up over her elbows.

"Vanessa!" Andre's anguished cry registered, and Vanessa felt a sharp pang of relief that he'd stayed, then concern that he'd stayed, and then pain. Only a deep, unending pain.

Her mind still raced, even as her body froze in place and time. Zika had been Medusa, all along. Legend had it that Medusa had been killed by Perseus, her head chopped off and placed in a bag to use as a weapon. Clearly, someone had put her back together. But what was she doing here, in this small seaside town? Vanessa swallowed her cries and focused on her enemy. She'd be damned if she gave that hideous being the satisfaction.

Just then, Mrs. Luongo blurred before Vanessa's eyes and split into two—just as she'd done that day in the village. The figures wavered, flashing scales and diamond eyes, then returned to their dowdy housekeeper disguise. But there were still two of them.

Zika-turned-Medusa stalked toward Vanessa, the transformed Mrs. Luongo–monsters on either side, and even through her agony, recognition sparked. With their polished silver eyes, steel hair wriggling for escape from their prim white bonnets, they could be nothing else.

The Gorgon sisters, complete with their leader, Medusa.

Medusa came close and cocked her head, snakes arching toward Vanessa, tongues flicking. "What a lovely addition to my collection you will make, little witch. Although I would have preferred you in your natural form. Perhaps we can rectify that later."

As the stone reached Vanessa's chest, her heart sped as if fleeing death. Would she become trapped in her body, still alive? Would she see without being able to feel? Hear but be unable to respond? Desperation and pain sparked a last surge of magic from within her, cracking the stone encasing her chest. But Medusa stepped closer, her serpents whispering against Vanessa's face.

Eyes closed tight, Vanessa felt the resurgence of Medusa's spell encapsulating her heart. The beat slowed, her mind sluggish. And then she heard a new voice.

"Step back from her, Gorgon!"

Weir.

A flash of light penetrated Vanessa's closed eyelids, but she didn't dare look as a screech sounded from the monster-woman. Hissing filled the air. Another flash made her squeeze her eyes tighter. A sibilant shriek rang out, shooting daggerlike pain into her ears, growing in volume.

CHAPTER 30

Tears gathered in Vanessa's eyes, all of her senses under assault.

Then it stopped.

"Flee this place, you disgusting excuse for a god, or feel my wrath," Weir cried. "And take your sisters with you!"

What was he doing? He didn't have magic off Omis Island. At least that's what he'd told her.

A door slammed and a strike of heat hit her chest, melting back the stone. But she didn't dare open her eyes as she drew in the most delicious gulp of air she'd ever breathed. Fire brushed her limbs to her fingers and toes, but her muscles gave out and she collapsed into strong arms. Andre's scent of clean woodland herbs surrounded her, and her lips lifted in response.

"They're gone. You can open your eyes now, Vanessa," Weir instructed.

She blinked, her eyes slow to respond, but when her vision cleared, Andre stared down at her, fear distorting his features.

And she knew not all was lost.

***

Weir had brought Andre's horse and wagon with him to the governor's mansion. Weak as she was, Vanessa curled up and napped all the way back to the cottage. They pulled to a stop at the edge of the cove and without a word, Andre picked her up and carried her to the water. She didn't know what to say to him as he lowered her gently to the edge.

Then he walked away.

As Vanessa sank to the bottom of the pool and sat among the swaying forest of seaweed, she wasn't sure if the ache in her chest was a physical remnant from her solidified arteries or the agony of Andre's rejection. Heartbreak was a new feeling for her.

She ran her fingers through the slick kelp leaves and wondered if Weir had been right. Perhaps love did mean giving another the power to hurt you. Because her pain in that moment rivaled the agony inflicted by Medusa's spell.

But it was warped with anger. No one bested her and got away with it. Medusa or not. Man or woman. It didn't matter. The monster Gorgo had manipulated her for the last time. Before the transformation, Zika had admitted his motivation had been to hurt Andre, and as far as she could tell, he'd succeeded in thoroughly devastating him.

Heat flared in her veins. The question was—what would she do about it? With Medusa revealed, there wasn't much she *could* do. Especially in human form. But if she could absorb the power of the curse . . . She sighed out a stream of bubbles. The Gorgon sisters protected the curse.

Weir had said, *Follow me to the Hollow Sea where unholy maidens of three guard against calamity.*

The triplex.

She huffed with frustration. What did it matter that she'd figured out Weir's riddle? She still had no idea where to find the Hollow Sea.

A juvenile puffer fish bobbed toward her, and she beckoned it closer, flicking its nose just to watch it inflate like a ball full of spikes. Carried by the current, the animal listed to the side and floated away, tiny fins helpless in its bloated state.

Alone. Drifting. Mind spinning.

Just like her.

Vanessa pushed off the bottom and swam up toward the light. She loathed asking for help, but the archives buried in Weir's mind could have the answers she needed. She surfaced and spat out a mouthful of water.

That was the easy part.

On the bank, she perched on the rocks, dread curdling in her gut. She had no idea what to say to Andre. Or how to mend what she'd broken. The look on his face when he'd seen her aquatic form . . . She swallowed hard. And that wasn't even the half of it. She had no idea how to tell him the whole truth about who she was and where she came from.

"Ugh," she groaned and glared up at the sky. Weir would probably know how to fix that, too.

***

Vanessa entered the cottage by the kitchen door. She smoothed the silk of her gown and gathered the dark waves of her hair over one shoulder, dried and perfectly coiffed with magic. Her decorum teacher had always said a lovely, well-groomed appearance would go a long way to persuade others to your side. As a child, she'd rejected most of what the old mermaid had said, but now, as she understood men's reactions to her, she could no longer discount it.

Besides, she needed every advantage she could get when facing Andre, even as the memory of his rejection of her tentacled form still stung.

Raised voices echoed down the hallway. Vanessa paused to listen.

Had Andre told Sara—and, Neptune forbid, Yia-Yia—her secret? How would they react? Sara would have a thousand questions and demand to see her Cecaelia form immediately. The old grandmother would most likely cross herself and chase Vanessa out of the house with a broom.

She stepped into the doorway of the parlor to find that Sara sat curled in a chair under a pile of blankets, shivering despite the warmth of the late afternoon. Weir lay prone on the sofa, his normally dark curls a startling white, his face withered like that of a human who had been immersed in water too long. She held back her gasp. The savant now appeared to have aged sixty years in a single day. Andre stood facing Weir, his back to the empty hearth, arms crossed over his chest. Yia-Yia was nowhere to be seen.

"That's exactly what I'm saying," Andre insisted. "Zika's housekeeper *was* Mrs. Nasside, the old woman who led me to the Grimaldi treasure . . . or curse . . . or whatever."

"I've never known Medusa to have the power to shape-shift," Weir spoke low. "Then again, I also believed her dead, as did the rest of the world."

"Or a myth made up to scare little children," Sara added.

"Medusa is, unfortunately, very real . . . and part of the triplex . . . guarding the curse," Weir said, his words drawn out and breathy.

"But why? And why here? She's after something. . . ."

"What could our little coast possibly have to offer?" Andre pressed.

"It must have nearly killed her to hide her true nature all this time," Weir mused.

"Meaning what?"

Weir's eyes stark, he said, "The Gorgon sisters were made out of the terror, not the terror out of the Gorgons. Terror is what feeds them, keeps them in existence. They incite fear, breed it, then feed off it like a source of nourishment."

Vanessa moved into the room. "So they created the curse."

Weir's head snapped up. "Yes. The fear the governor incited among the citizens with his tyranny was no longer enough to satiate their ravenous hunger."

"But why involve Andre?" Sara asked.

Weir shrugged and attempted an answer but was seized by a coughing fit so profound she thought his chest might crack open. Vanessa watched him and knew he wasn't long for this world.

Vanessa took a surreptitious step closer to Andre, but he shot her a dark look that caused her instead to divert to the chair opposite Sara, her heart sinking. Fathomless silence descended on the room, broken only by the sound of Weir's struggle. Vanessa laced her fingers together in her lap, waiting for someone to speak. Andre shifted his weight and leaned a shoulder against the stones of the hearth.

When Weir's breathing finally calmed, Vanessa cleared her throat and faced him. "How did you do it, Weir?"

"What? Save you from . . . that demon woman?" Weir pushed himself up on the pillows at his back. "That is my—"

His words dissolved in another hacking fit. Vanessa changed tack, feeling the urgency of their limited time with this strange, magical, kind man. "Weir, what should we do now? The triplex guarding the curse is led by Medusa, but it's all irrelevant if we don't know where to find it."

They were at a dead end.

Vanessa might have been the only one capable of stopping the curse and absorbing its power, but without its location, Medusa and her sisters would win, and the curse would take the lives of those infected. Including little Sara. Vanessa couldn't even look at the girl, knowing she'd failed her. She needed to plan for what came after, and that meant speaking to Andre to try to explain. If she hoped to salvage anything she'd created since coming to land, she would have to face her mistakes.

"Andre." She stood. "May we speak in private?"

"You can talk to me here," he responded without looking at her.

She glanced at Sara, her blue eyes wide. If Andre didn't mind that his sister knew the truth—that there had been a villain in their midst—then she didn't mind either. "Fine." Vanessa lifted her chin. "I am what is known as a Cecaelia—daughter of the sea and earth. I do have tentacles when I'm in the ocean, and some traits of an octopus, but I'm mostly mer. I live with full-blood mermaids and mermen in a kingdom under the sea called Atlantica. As far as I know, I am the only one of my kind."

Sara gasped in wonder. "Does everyone in . . . Atlantica . . . have magic?"

"No, the king and I are the only ones. It's a power I've always possessed, but do not know why. I am unique, even in my own realm." Inexplicably, her voice broke.

Andre straightened, his eyes softening for a moment before he clenched his hands into fists and shoved them into his trouser pockets.

Vanessa continued. "I found a spell that could turn me human and decided to start over and live on land, at least for a while. The idea of a clean slate was too tempting to resist. And I longed to experience more of the world . . .

see, smell, and taste everything the land had to offer." She decided to leave out the part about wanting to come to land to try and find the sort of power that would make her unstoppable in the water.

She folded her hands and stared at her fingers, choosing her next words carefully. "The day I washed up on the beach, I overheard Sara calling out to the Sea King for help with the curse. I knew he wouldn't lift a finger to help a human child. Contact between our worlds is forbidden, so I thought . . ." She'd thought she could possess more power and return to Atlantica triumphant. But that was before. Before her soft human heart had sucked her into a cyclone of emotions. Her eyes latched onto Andre's, refusing to let him go. "I thought I could help. Though, when you took me in, I fell in love . . . with your family." She swallowed. "Once I'd earned your trust, I couldn't reveal my deception, knowing how it would hurt you."

"And you think it hurts less now?" Andre barked. "I fell for you! I asked you to marry me!" He stalked toward her. "You lied about everything. Including your *species*! How many legs do you have? Eight? Ten?" His face took on a horrified visage. "I fell for a *fish*!"

"Andre!" Weir snapped, anger making him forget his

weakened state as he raised his hoarse voice. "That's enough."

Andre swallowed and took a step back. "When were you going to tell me the truth? After our wedding? After I'd committed to spending my life with you?"

"I gave you your ring back!" Vanessa spat.

"Oh, how magnanimous of you." Andre cocked his head to the side. "Couldn't handle the guilt?"

Guilt was not an emotion she gave any power to, but perhaps she could achieve what she'd set out to accomplish when she'd returned his ring, to force his hand into finally admitting to her—and to himself—that he loved her. She stepped close to him and stared up beneath her lashes. "Andre, my feelings for you are real. This human form is real. The woman you developed feelings for is right here in front of you. But if you can't accept that, if you don't love me, then I'll go, and you never have to see me again."

She reached out and entwined their fingers.

For one elastic moment, he didn't speak. His face was a granite mask as he pulled away from her touch, and he replied without emotion. "I never said I loved you."

"Andre, no!" Sara cried.

But he couldn't take the words back as they ground

against her soul, burrowing into her mind. Andre had never loved her.

Love means giving someone the power to hurt you.

She remembered Weir's words as, eyes burning, something hot tickled her cheeks, and Vanessa reached up to swipe it away. Tears. A foreign feeling, her throat burned as heat built in her chest. She swallowed down the pain. "I was just trying to help," she said.

Andre glared at her. "Look at us! Weir is dying because you forced him off his island. Your presence has pushed Yia-Yia closer to the edge of senility. And you've given Sara false hope and then smashed it over and over."

"That's not fair." Regret thudded within Vanessa's heart. He was partly right.

"You know what's not fair?" Andre pounded his chest, eyes blazing like a forest at sunset. "That the Gorgons used me to spread the curse. But you've made it so much worse by twisting their anger into a scourge that can't be stopped. Now, dozens of innocents will pay the price tonight when the moon rises."

"You don't know if that's my fault."

Andre stepped forward and stared down into her face, and ground out, "You don't know it isn't."

Blankets fell heedless to the floor as Sara struggled to

her feet. "Andre, stop this! Vanessa is incredible. Like a mermaid but with magic. All she's ever done is try to save us!" She looked at Vanessa with all the admiration and softness she'd held for her before she knew the truth.

Andre's frown wobbled as he looked down at his sister. "But she's been lying to us, imp."

"Can you blame her? Look how you're reacting."

Sara's thin arms wrapped around Vanessa's waist, and she thought, perhaps, her heart might shatter as she wound an arm around the girl's back and pulled her closer. No one had *ever* defended her like that.

The first sign of hurt showed in the crinkles around Andre's eyes. He swallowed hard, his voice raw. "Have you really been trying to save us, Vanessa? Or have you lied about everything?"

Suddenly, her jealousy of Sara earlier that day, of her place of prominence in Andre's heart, seemed petty. She gave the girl a squeeze and locked her gaze on Andre's as she whispered, "I didn't lie about the love I feel for all of you."

Andre searched her face for a prolonged moment, then exhaled toward the ceiling. "Fine. Let's focus on finding the Hollow Sea before the moon rises."

A tinkle of clinking glassware preceded Yia-Yia as she

brought in a tray with fresh lemonade and orange cakes. "I'd stay far away from the Hollow Sea." Yia-Yia shook her gray curls as she set the tray down. "The ancients buried their dead there for centuries. It's where murdered spirits play."

Vanessa, Andre, Sara, and Weir turned simultaneously to stare at the old woman. Speechless. Had she known the location this entire time? Vanessa thought back. Yia-Yia had never once been in the room when they'd discussed it. Until now.

"Where is the Hollow Sea, Yia-Yia?" Weir croaked from the couch.

"Not far." She sliced the cake as she spoke. "There's a great hole in Zakyntho Cliff just outside of Pilos that leads there." The old woman smiled. "Cake, anyone?"

CHAPTER 31

VANESSA

"ZAKYNTHO CLIFF?" ANDRE gasped. "That's where I tossed the box containing the cursed potions."

"Perhaps not by coincidence," Weir said from the sofa just before another coughing fit took him.

Vanessa watched wide-eyed as he doubled over, hacking up blood. Yia-Yia rushed to his side with a fresh cloth to wipe his face and placed the back of her hand against his forehead. "You're burning up. Has the curse infected you as well?"

"No . . . ma'am," Weir choked out.

"Then we can fix it." Yia-Yia stood and marched over to Andre, speaking in low tones. "It's the putrid throat. We'll need a concoction of eucalyptus, cinnamon, and rosemary."

"Yes, and cypress as well," Andre confirmed. Then, without a glance in Vanessa's direction, he strode away.

Had he forgiven her? Could he ever? He didn't understand now, but once he saw her power, he would. He would love her more. There had been a moment when Sara had defended her, when she'd confessed her love, that she thought he might accept her for who she was and put away his anger. But then Yia-Yia had appeared.

Vanessa faced the old woman, watching her for signs of delusion as she fussed over Weir, clearly troubled by his condition. "Why is the Hollow Sea important?" Yia-Yia asked.

"It could be the key to . . . stopping the curse," Weir replied.

Yia-Yia mopped his forehead and then lifted a glass to his lips. "How can it be stopped?"

Weir's eyes shifted to Vanessa. "It will take great strength and sacrifice."

"I'm sure my Andre has what it takes to stop this nightmare," Yia-Yia said with confidence.

Vanessa walked over to join them. "Yes, he does." *But he won't have to,* she thought as she took the rag from Yia-Yia's hand. "I'll take care of Weir, Yia-Yia. I believe Sara needs a rest."

The girl had slumped back into the chair half asleep, but the position couldn't be good for her already damaged muscles. Yia-Yia gathered Sara up and helped her up the stairs.

Vanessa pulled a chair close to Weir, dipped the rag in cold water as Yia-Yia had done, and placed it on his heated forehead. "The old woman seems lucid enough," she murmured to him. "Do you think she really knows the location of the Hollow Sea?"

"I do. As soon as she said it . . . I remembered the history books . . . speaking of the sinister place. A perfect spot for a curse . . . based in fear," he croaked before another coughing fit shook him.

After he calmed, she lifted the glass to his lips, and he took a slow sip.

"If the three maidens guarding the curse are led by

Medusa, I can't defeat them. Not in this form." The words tasted sour in her mouth.

"Ahh . . . but you can." Weir swallowed hard and focused on his next words. "When Perseus cut off Medusa's head, he stole her immortality. And even when her sisters brought her back, they could not restore her eternal nature. She can be destroyed."

Hope glimmered in Vanessa's chest. And then fizzled. Immortal or not, Medusa's powers were formidable.

"I need to ask you a question." Weir closed his eyes, throat convulsing as he fought off another coughing fit. "What do you plan to do when you find the curse?"

"Stop it, of course." And she fully intended to. She would save Sara and the others. But she didn't say she would destroy it.

Weir nodded weakly. "Bag . . . get my—"

The savant's words cut off and he sat straight up, his eyes transforming into a galaxy full of stars as he spoke loud and strong. *"Relinquish that which you fear, sacrifice what you most revere, and the curse will disappear."*

Blood roared in Vanessa's ears as Weir slumped back on the pillows. A prophecy from the ancient texts. But what did it mean?

"What did I say?" Weir asked feverishly.

Vanessa repeated the odd rhyming divination. "Do you think it means I will need to face my fears?" It seemed too obvious. She didn't fear much, but even she had to admit that Medusa scared her.

"Perhaps you'll be required to let go of your fears in some way, rise above them. But it tells us one important thing."

"What's that?"

Fresh wrinkles formed across his pasty cheeks, his neck folded upon itself like an ancient turtle's as he breathed, "The curse can be defeated. Now, my bag, please . . ."

Weir's eyes cut to a crumpled leather sack at the end of the sofa.

Vanessa snatched up the bag and placed it into his hands.

Weir gazed out the window, where the late afternoon sun tipped the trees coral and soft yellow. A dreamy smile spread across his face, as if he could see something that she could not.

"Weir, did you want to show me something?" Vanessa asked.

Slowly, the savant turned back to her. "Something I wish to give you." He lifted open the sack and rummaged inside for what felt like an eternity.

CHAPTER 31

A smirk floated around his lips that recalled the mischievous man she'd met on the island as finally he pulled a narrow glass box from the sack and handed it to her. "This is how I saved you from Medusa, and this is how you will defeat her and her Gorgon sisters."

Vanessa gaped at the intricately carved stick mounted inside the case as shock waves flashed over her skin.

The Rhabdos.

"What? How?" Vanessa shot to her feet, trembling. She dropped back into the chair, unable to tear her gaze away from Circe's legendary conduit.

Weir's wrinkled hand grasped hers. "You have a chance to have it all, my girl. Save the town, rescue those you love, and earn the trust of the boy you've chosen." His voice pitched low. "For most of my supernaturally long life, I put Omis Island above everything, even my own happiness. These last days, spent among other people who have quickly become friends, showed me how much I'd missed. I now regret so many of the choices I thought were noble, but it's too late to change what I've done. That's why I'm gifting you this wand. It gives you the power to choose your destiny."

Weir's eyes darkened with a mix of sorrow and hope. "Don't be like me and settle for what comes easily, when you have the means to fight for a happy ending."

"I'm not sure I want *happy*." She spat out the word like a sickly sweet bonbon. It seemed so mundane. She'd never wished for a peaceful, repetitive, predictable life. Each day just like the one before it. The thought made her skin crawl.

"Darling Vanessa, happy can mean anything you want it to mean." Weir coughed but cut it off with sheer willpower to finish what he wanted to say. "Most people give up when things get hard. They take the path of least resistance and think that will satisfy them. But some things—those worthwhile, unique, precious things—are worth the cost that it takes to achieve them."

Vanessa tugged her gaze away from Weir and stared down at the box in her grip. The staff pulsed within, an otherworldly glow calling to her as if longing to connect with her flesh. She could leave right then, Circe's conduit in hand, and return to Atlantica with more power than King Triton could dream.

"Vanessa." Weir's voice took on a warning note, as though he could read her mutinous thoughts. "If you keep doing the things you've always done, you'll get the results you've always had. Would you call that happiness? The curse does not attach value to . . . honorable emotions such as love. If you choose its power, you could become someone incapable of . . ." Weir gasped, his last words strangled. "Think before you . . . act."

Vanessa listened to Weir's counsel, but knew he was wrong. She was strong enough to command the curse while holding on to who she had become as a human and all the glorious emotions this heart held. She could be whoever she wished to be, and no one could tell her different.

Vanessa stared down at the glass case and trembled. With need or confusion, she didn't know, but her fingers gripped the box, and it shattered into stinging shards. Blood dripped from her fingers, but Vanessa only felt elation as she took Circe's precious wand in her hand and lifted it up. Magic tingled on her tongue like champagne. Scarlet rays of sun caressed her skin, fire melding the wand to blood and flesh.

A smile, slow and sure, split her face. She might not know what she wanted, or what her *happy* looked like, but with this gift—she couldn't lose.

***

Time spun out and Vanessa wasn't sure if seconds or minutes had passed, but when she came to herself, Weir's stare traveled out the window as if the direction of his gaze joined him with the newborn stars.

She wiped off her hands, stowed the staff in her pocket, and leaned over Weir's body. "Weir?" She shook his shoulders, but his fixed gaze didn't waver. His chest didn't move.

"No . . ." Vanessa moaned as she searched his throat for the telltale beat of a pulse. His flesh felt still and cold. Frantic, she leaned in and placed her ear against his chest. Silence.

Panicked, she gripped her conduit and placed her hands on his chest. She wasn't ready to lose him. A shock of power could restart his heart. Bring him back to her. Give him more time.

But in that moment, Weir's own words came back to her.

You must learn to ask.

I'm not leaving yet, but when I do, it will be my time.

My soul free at last.

She sat back and wrapped her arms around her waist.

He had given without taking. Laughed in the face of danger. Saved others without saving himself.

And look where it had gotten him. Vanessa's arms shook as anger coursed through her veins. How could he leave her when she needed him most? When she'd finally found another magical being who understood her? It was incredibly selfish.

Throat burning, she reached out, closed his eyes, and spoke the only benediction she knew. "Depths be gentle and take this mighty soul into your bosom as he rests cradled in your waves. Forever."

She positioned his arms across his chest as naturally as she could and straightened the blankets around him. Kneeling at his side, she swiped the hot tears from her eyes, salt water mixing with blood on her fingers. The second time she'd ever cried, all in a single day. If love meant giving someone the power to hurt you, then the bitter ache in her chest proved she was capable of more emotion than she'd ever imagined.

She leaned closer, kissed his weathered cheek, and whispered, "Thank you, Weir Adamos, for sharing a bit of your life with me."

CHAPTER 32

ANDRE

ANDRE'S LUNGS ached with unshed tears as he pushed Ella faster, her hooves thundering toward Zakyntho Cliff. He'd known it was coming, but the loss of Weir, whom Andre had come to value as a trusted friend despite their admittedly odd start, tore through the jagged pieces of his already shattered heart. The girl responsible for his pain clung to his back, uncharacteristically silent.

Yia-Yia had given them directions to the Hollow Sea

through her tears as they'd gathered around Weir's body. Vanessa had said little. Something in her demeanor felt different, as if those precious last moments with the savant had changed her somehow. Her pleading for his understanding was at an end. Focused and determined, she'd galvanized him with a single statement: *We can still save Sara.* Then she'd pushed him out the door, reminding him they had mere hours before they ran out of time.

The sun slipped toward the surface of the ocean as they traveled, streaking the horizon with its dying fire. Vanessa wrapped her arms tighter around his chest and his traitorous heart longed for her despite her lies. The weight of her deception still stung, but her body pressed against him reminded him of their connection and how she'd revitalized his life. How many times had he thought about how she'd lifted his burdens and quickly become a partner and his closest friend?

Part of him couldn't blame her for her deceit. Mermaid lore had romanticized the idea of such beings for the ears and eyes of human children, but Andre had never believed them to be real, complex creatures with thoughts and dreams, families, and communities of their own. Vanessa had said she was unique in her world, but he'd read between the lines—she'd been an outcast, even among mythical beings. She'd longed to start fresh while experiencing more of the world. As someone who had lived in the same town, meeting the same people and visiting the same string of villages his entire life, he could relate to the need to escape and explore on a soul-deep level, even as he hated that such a need had led her to deceive them.

"Are we getting close?" Vanessa asked softly, voice vibrating in his ear.

"Zakyntho is just ahead, but we need to travel inland," he said back over Ella's pounding hooves. As he spoke, a split in the cliffside appeared, just as Yia-Yia had described. He pulled on Ella's reins, slowing her gait as he steered her through the narrow gap in the rocks. The tight passage grew more narrow overhead, deep shadows clutching like inky fingers. As they traveled deeper, a vacuum of sound cut off the rhythmic crash of waves, encapsulating them. A fleeting stench of decay pushed against the mineral scents of rock and the salt of the sea.

Chills crawled down Andre's neck beneath his jacket. He inhaled sharply and fought a shudder as he ran a hand over the hilts of the daggers tucked into his belt. Their solid presence was reassuring.

This place felt . . . off. As if the very air shouted a warning to turn back. Ella's trot slowed, but when Andre prodded her with a light squeeze of his knees, she stopped completely. He clicked his tongue and commanded, “Ella, walk.”

But the loyal horse didn’t move. A stiff breeze, laced with rot, pushed through the fissure, lifting her mane and ruffling Andre’s hair. The horse backed up several paces and neighed, shaking her head in agitation. “Easy, girl,” he soothed, patting her flank. He couldn’t blame her reluctance. This place could scare away the devil himself.

“Let’s continue on foot,” Vanessa suggested.

Andre gave a nod before swinging off the horse and helping Vanessa down. She wouldn’t meet his gaze and stepped away from him as soon as her feet hit the dirt. He tied Ella’s lead to a scrubby branch, double-checked that his daggers were secure on his belt, and then faced Vanessa. Her violet eyes shone like jewels in the near darkness, her countenance radiating hurt and something that might have been resolve.

Or secrets.

If Weir had given her information, he needed to know what she knew. He stepped closer, but what came out of his mouth surprised him. “I’m sorry for the things I said tonight,” he murmured.

A sigh. “I never meant to hurt you, Andre.”

He reached for her, but the image of her shimmering ebony tentacles with their violet suction cups clinging to the stone fountain pushed across his mind, and he closed his fist, pulling back. With an exhale, he shoved his fingers through his hair. Vanessa's face shuddered, loose waves of hair blowing into the night, her lush mouth set in a line of pain, eyes sparkling defiantly as though she saw his inner thoughts and dared Andre to voice them. And suddenly the two sides of her became clear to him: the fierce and powerful Cecaelia reconciled with the brave, vivacious human woman.

He'd always longed to experience the unique and exotic. In his wildest dreams he couldn't have conceived of such a remarkable person. His beatific woman with the wicked smile.

Urgently, he clasped her shoulders, desperate to make her understand. "Vanessa, I—"

His words were cut off by a streak of lightning. In the bleached aftermath, they both stared, transfixed. The flash had come from the narrow opening at the end of the tunnel.

Thunderous silence followed. The moment was lost in the stark reminder of what lay ahead.

Andre turned. "We should go."

CHAPTER 32

Vanessa grasped his hand, and she blinked up at him fervently. "Despite all our obstacles, I foolishly believed you could be the one to love me for who I am inside . . . the dark and light . . . the vainglorious, giving, selfish, passionate, ambitious whole of me. But even if you don't, I would never want to leave you with regrets. Because I can tell you this, Andre Baros: when I'm with you, I'm a better person than I ever thought I could be."

His brain zeroed in on what she had said. Leave him? The very thought of her leaving pulled the words he should have said long ago from his soul. He cupped her face in his hands. "I love you, Vanessa."

His lips crashed against hers, hands tangling in her hair. She moaned against his mouth and he nearly forgot where he was and what lay before them. But another flash of light forced them apart.

Her lips curled up. "And I love you . . . more than I ever thought possible."

Urgency tightened Andre's chest as he said, "No matter what happens now, I don't want you to leave. We can make this work."

Vanessa took his hands and moved them from her face to clasp them in front of her chest. "I have to tell you something. I'm not quite sure what it means, but before

Weir died, we were talking about stopping the curse, and he spoke in his strange rhyming voice." A tremulous smile shook her lips. "He said, 'Relinquish that which you fear, sacrifice what you most revere, and the curse will disappear.'"

Andre's brow furrowed as he tried to process the riddle. "Saints! What does it mean? Why couldn't he ever speak plain?"

"I think the first part means I have to face my greatest fear. Weir said the Gorgons were made from terror, so that part makes sense."

"But what do you have to sacrifice—"

Lightning struck, cutting off his question. Another bolt crashed quickly on its tail.

Danger flashed in Vanessa's eyes "We're out of time."

CHAPTER 33

VANESSA

HAND IN HAND they ran, another bolt striking so close that Vanessa stumbled, blinded by the flash. Andre yanked her to her feet with brute strength as they raced forward. The ground beneath their feet disappeared, pebbles rolling under Vanessa's slippers as Andre tugged her back. A gaping hole yawned before them. Her stomach bottomed out as she stared at the great void in the earth. Or, more precisely, a crater carved into solid rock. She leaned forward and peered over the edge, twilight skies reflecting in a pool far below. The near-perfect oval cavern had been formed by the power of the ocean rushing and receding, its vaulted walls etched like a cathedral.

The Hollow Sea.

She kicked a rock and counted to thirty before she heard its splash as it met the waters. A greenish-yellow glow caught her eye from the far corner of the cavern below. Medusa and her sisters were down there somewhere, guarding the core of the curse.

She fingered the Rhabdos in her pocket and craned her neck to get a better look, but Andre yanked her back.

"I can't allow you to sacrifice yourself to rectify my mistake."

She met his frantic emerald eyes and arched an imperious brow. "You can't *allow* me?"

Lightning flashed and she whirled in time to see the source; the bolts were traveling up from the far corner of the cavern, its aqueous glow growing brighter by the moment. Motion caught her eye, and Vanessa could just make out the writhing movements and sinuous locks of the Gorgon twins. Medusa's immortal watchdogs.

"Vanessa, let me do this!" Andre pleaded.

CHAPTER 33

"How, Andre? With a couple of knives and your righteous anger? I have to absorb the curse. It's the only way to stop it." She yanked the staff out of her pocket. When it touched her skin, it flared to glimmering life—one with the magic flooding her veins. "Stay here so you don't get hurt."

Andre's eyes widened as he took in the staff. "What is *that*?"

"A little gift from Weir." She grinned and jumped off the ledge into the abyss.

As Vanessa fell, dread closed her throat, the air heavy and humid. She let her momentum carry her down and reached out her senses to the pool, but could discern no bottom, just the bones of the dead snagged on the rocks and tangled upon jagged ledges. The reek of moist rock, mold, and minerals only found far underground mixed with the acrid scents of blood and rot. How many more bodies had sunk fathoms below? Yia-Yia had been right: this place was a tomb.

Something caught her eye near the rocky outcrop, and she used a bit of magic to guide her fall toward the peridot glow of the curse. A flash sparked and she veered out of the lightning's path, crashing clumsily into a rock wall, her feet landing on a narrow ledge.

Vanessa shook off the jarring of her bones and

straightened. That's when she heard the whispers, babbling and surging in her ears. Murmurs just outside her hearing, like gibberish. Or incantations. A few words surfaced from the feverish chant.

Stheno, feast. Euryale, on flesh. Eat prey.

Stheno and Euryale, names of the Gorgons.

Medusa's sisters had the same ability to turn flesh to stone, and if Vanessa understood their mutterings correctly, these monsters would proceed to consume their statuary.

Heat flamed inside Vanessa's chest, the thump of her pulse drowning out the hissing cacophony as she crept along the shadowed wall. As Weir had instructed, she needed to take the sisters out first. She ducked behind a boulder and peeked over the edge. A chromatic ball hovered inside a stone archway, beating with blood and bile and brilliant black alchemy. Sorcery of such power she had never witnessed. The heart of the curse.

Need rose inside her chest, a hunger that washed away all caution. Vanessa burst from her hiding place. The Gorgon sisters swung toward her, clawlike hands raised, hair flying and hissing like a hundred serpents. Vanessa kept her eyes on the undulating orb and swept the staff wide, coaxing waves from the pool of the dead.

She had no intention of becoming anyone's dinner.

CHAPTER 33

With a mighty heave, she swept the water up and slammed its mass into the sisters. They screeched and fell backward. Vanessa sidled forward, pushing the water into open mouths, driving it down their throats. The creatures arched back, swatting at the water, fighting for breath.

A drone sounded inside her head, rising in volume. The heart of the curse crackled, forks of light spewing into the night. She was running out of time. Blinded, she stepped closer to the sisters, their outlines flopping like guppies. Why weren't they drowning?

As her vision returned, movement caught her attention from the right and left. A slide and slither followed by a banshee roar could only mean the arrival of Medusa.

With a single command, Vanessa stilled the waves and changed the staff into a sword. The hilt tight in her hand, she sliced down, enchanting the blade so it wouldn't miss.

The first head rolled, snakes dying on a sibilant exhale. Vanessa didn't hesitate before swinging again, steel slicing flesh and bone with a wet slush. She dared to glance down, and two sets of eyes stared back at her, swirling like dying supernovas.

"What have you done?" Medusa cried, her voice a susurrated screech.

Vanessa reached down and snatched one sister by

the dead snakes of her hair, lifting the head like a trophy. "What does it look like, old hag?" she taunted as she spun and kicked the other head into the fathomless pit.

Medusa screamed and slithered forward on a giant serpent tail. Vanessa spun toward the monster, keeping her gaze aimed at her talon-like fingers. She raised her sword, but before she could attack, her gaze caught on stones smashing to the ground.

Andre raced toward her down a flight of stairs etched into the cavern wall.

CHAPTER 34

VANESSA

A SMACK SENT VANESSA REELING.

Reflexively, she turned toward what had hit her. But before she could get her bearings and hex the monster, Medusa's enormous tail struck her behind the knees, dumping her onto the hard stone floor. The staff-sword flew out of her hand and skittered over the rock, teetering on the ledge, over the pool.

Vanessa gripped her shell conduit and reached for the staff with her magic. Power surged through her fingertips as Andre leapt down the last of the stairs, a dagger in each hand. "Face me, beast!"

Lightning, brighter and greater than before, bolted from the pulsating curse as it wound tighter, ready to fragment. They had little time. White spots danced before her eyes. The staff flew to her and she caught it in midair, then pointed it at Medusa's undulating body, a curse on her lips.

Before her hex could land, however, the monster jerked back. Her vicious roar shook the ceiling, bits of rock raining down. A silver-hilted dagger quivered in Medusa's biceps. Andre's arm arched back to throw another as Medusa lashed out wildly with her tail, knocking the knife from his hand. Vanessa raced back to the fight, avoiding the monster's slithering head. She clutched the staff and pointed, power streaming outward like glittering beams of light, but her aim was off, and her hex flew wide.

Andre struck again, this time landing a blade in the creature's throat. She gurgled, black blood pouring down her neck. Again, Vanessa called on her magic, summoning the sea, ready to finish this monster off as she'd done with her sisters. But only cold fire filled her veins, her human body too weak to produce more than a spark of magic.

Medusa surged forward, wide mouth full of wicked

teeth, serpent-hair flying toward Andre. Vanessa screamed a warning as Andre squeezed his eyes shut and threw his last dagger. His aim was true, the blade slicing into Medusa's chest. The monster froze, eyes wide, and dropped to the stone floor.

"Don't look!" Vanessa screamed. "The snakes are still moving."

Andre rotated toward Vanessa, shoulders curled, broad hand pressed against his gut as if he might vomit. "I . . . I . . ."

Vanessa understood, even as words failed him. He'd never killed before.

She rushed toward him, tucked the staff in her pocket, and took his hand. "You had to stop her."

He nodded silently, his eyes darting to the glowing curse. "Don't do this, Vanessa." His voice a raw whisper, he took both her shoulders and turned her to face him. "This curse . . . I can feel its evil, even if I can't understand it. If you take it inside of yourself, it will taint your soul."

If Andre only knew that her soul was already tainted beyond deliverance. Vanessa stared over her shoulder at the undulating ball. Arches of light flashed around it, building in power. Soon it would divide and fly into each of its victims. Like a second beating heart, they wouldn't be able to survive without it, yet it would slowly kill them. If that happened, it would be too late to stop it. Too late for her to ingest its dark power.

She looked at him, pleading with her eyes. "Don't you see? This is the answer. With the curse's power, I can transform you into the most stunning mer-creature Atlantica has ever seen. We can live under the sea and turn back into humans whenever we like to spend a few months on earth. We can travel, see new lands. We could have the best of both worlds."

Those verdant eyes that she loved so much searched her face. He looked tempted, but shook his head. "I can't leave Sara and Yia-Yia."

Vanessa had expected him to say as much—he wouldn't be the Andre she loved if he hadn't. "They can come with us." The old woman would never survive the transformation, but he didn't need to know that. She grinned hopefully. "How much would Sara love to be a mermaid?"

Andre gripped her hands to the point of pain, his eyes wet with emotion. "This isn't the way. Please, Vanessa. We'll figure everything out. Just destroy it. I love you. Isn't that enough?"

Forks of light hurtled into cavern walls, rocks crashing

into the stone floor and splashing into the pool. They ducked, still holding hands. Even as her hunger for the curse clawed in her chest, she gave him one last reassuring smile before she released his hands and took Circe's wand from her pocket.

She stood. "I have to stop it. Now." She looked down at the beautiful man with the noble soul. For an ordinary person, Andre Baros's affection would be more than enough. But in this moment, faced with the actual choice between the two, Vanessa knew her path; she had bigger dreams, magnificent plans. Legacies to create. She hoped he could be a part of it all, but the key, pulsing over her shoulder, waited to meld with her blood.

Vanessa swung toward the enchanted orb. As if summoned, her steps were sure and urgent, heart pounding with desire. Her destiny within reach. She neared the ball of green fire and lifted the staff.

"Well done, my dear." A voice boomed from the shadows as the wand flew from her grip.

Vanessa whirled to find Medusa, slithering forward as snakes danced around her head and indigo swirled in her wide eyes. Vanessa jerked her gaze down as Medusa plucked Andre's daggers from her throat and chest like pesky sea urchin needles. If the devil woman wasn't immortal, as Weir had said, she was remarkably impervious to injury.

Medusa held Andre in thrall, his eyes rolled to white as he hunched at the monster's side. Medusa grinned to reveal wicked teeth and twirled the Rhabdos lazily in excessively long fingers.

Vanessa gripped her conduit and stalked toward the monster, fixing her gaze on Medusa's angular lips.

Medusa grasped the staff and pointed it at Andre's throat, causing him to gasp for air.

Vanessa froze.

"When I lured you here onto land with the curse, I knew that ultimately, in the end, you would bring me this treasure." Medusa nodded toward the wand.

"Lured me?" Vanessa asked. "I came here of my own free will!"

"Of course, transforming into this glorious human form was your idea." Medusa waved the staff toward her. "But why come to this particular coast? This quaint little village? It was the terror, my dear. The call of all that boiling terror drew you right to us."

The blood seemed to drain from Vanessa's head as the cavern spun. The monstrous woman had manipulated her entire journey. The destiny she'd believed she'd created for herself had been a setup.

Rage boiled to overflowing. She would kill Medusa just like her coven-sisters. Vanessa pulled power from her core. But the monster's rambling caught her attention.

"I've pined for the staff for centuries—it is the key to my immortality, you see. My eternal domination. But my sisters and I could not set foot on Omis Island; Circe would have destroyed us instantly. The closest I could get was this godforsaken village, where I watched and waited, the staff just beyond reach. I needed someone powerful enough and selfish enough to free Circe once and for all so we could finally get to the island and secure the staff." Her voice slipped in and out of sibilant hisses. "I brought you to this village, then sent you to Omis Island, not to find a cure for the curse, but to bring down the island's enchantments. I anticipated your confrontation with Circe's spirit but couldn't be sure which one of you would prevail." Medusa's face reflected a grotesque approximation of a smile. "You, Ursula of Atlantica, exceeded my expectations! Ending the witch goddess and her little guard in the process." Medusa cackled with glee as she poked the staff into Andre's neck. "It was more than I could have hoped that you would bring me the staff as well."

Vanessa's mind churned as she tried to absorb Medusa's words. She had to stop Medusa before she killed Andre and stole the staff. But she was weakened from her fight with the Gorgon twins. No doubt just as Medusa had planned.

A dazzling flare of energy danced to her left. The curse. If she could absorb the curse's power, she could replenish her strength. She sidestepped toward it, fingering the golden shell at her throat. Perhaps in glorying over how she'd manipulated Vanessa from the start, Medusa wouldn't take notice.

But Vanessa wasn't so lucky.

Medusa pushed Andre in front of her like a shield as soon as she started advancing, stopping Vanessa's magic cold. The monster lifted her chin with such imperiousness, Vanessa longed for the moment when she would wipe the earth of this creature's overblown superiority—snake-hair and all.

But then she spoke.

"Go ahead and take my beautiful curse if you must. All you have to do to possess its power is kill that which you love the most."

CHAPTER 35

VANESSA

VANESSA'S CHEST heaved, her heartbeat crashing in her ears.

Medusa breathed deep, watching the horror play across Vanessa's face at the revelation she'd just unleased. The impossible choice.

Vanessa averted her gaze just as indigo eyes sparked and Medusa's scaled body slid forward. The monster's nostrils flared wide as she grew larger, feeding on Vanessa's fear.

Yes, she could admit this time to the abhorrent feeling of dread that pulsed and churned in her gut. Fear and love were both new emotions for her. But love's indomitable power was undeniable. And its sacrifice—the alchemy of love's forfeiture—was the heart of dark magic.

For this reason alone, she believed Medusa told the truth about the condition for absorbing her magnificent curse. If anyone would know how to possess dark magic, it would be Medusa. But that didn't mean Vanessa had to play by the crone's rules.

She gripped her conduit, digging deep for reserves of power. "What is this, old witch?"

Medusa shoved Andre toward Vanessa and he stumbled to her side, blinking and disoriented.

"Va . . . nessa?" Andre muttered.

Medusa's spell still clouding his brain, he listed to the side like a sinking vessel. She rushed over and led him to a flat rock where he collapsed back on his elbows. The beautiful sacrificial lamb. *Neptune, no!* She shook the thought from her mind, brushed the silken hair out of his eyes. "Stay here and don't look at her. I'll protect you." Her voice broke as she whirled away.

Even as she spoke the words, though, Vanessa doubted herself. At that moment, a creature clawed and bit inside of her, fighting for release. The monster she'd let go of in order to curate a life on land—to create this fabulous human being that personified all her most secret aspirations. As a human, she had admiration, desire, freedom, respect mixed with a bit of awe. She'd even found things she had never dreamed of . . . friendship, belonging, love, even sadness. Vanessa had brought all of that to her.

But Ursula *needed* the magic of that curse, demanded that she use it to show this perpetrator of fear what terror felt like.

Hair flying around her face, dress ripped and streaked with Gorgon blood, Vanessa sprang toward Medusa. Fury energized every part of her, but Medusa raised the staff and Vanessa slammed into a wall of air. "You're almost out of time, sea creature. The curse will become irreversible in . . ." Medusa trailed off and gazed up through the enormous hole in the earth at the sliver of moon that hovered in the lightening stars. "Three minutes' time."

The curse pulsated in the corner of Vanessa's vision, wrapped in a halo of illumination that grew larger with every rotation. Vines of lightning spiked out, cutting into rock like the branches of an enormous tree. Unable to resist its magnetism, she stepped closer. Grudgingly, she acknowledged the perfection of the hex's sorcery. She took another step. The power, tangible and warm, carved a hollow out of her chest. A void that only it could fill.

But the price . . .

Andre. Broad shoulders, seal-black hair falling over the most compassionate eyes she'd ever encountered below the sea or above. The strong line of his jaw clenched as he tried to shake off the muddle of Medusa's ensorcellment. She longed for his strength, his touch, the dimpled smile that had an enchantment all its own. The thought of losing him wrenched her heart with physical pain. Her hand rose to her chest, pressed against the ache.

But could he fill the gaping hole inside her spirit?

The promise of the curse called like a siren song over her shoulder. Endless power would make her a queen.

"Two minutes, sea witch," Medusa called.

She bristled at the name. Perhaps at its accuracy, as she considered sacrificing what she loved most in the world to gain power. She'd fooled herself thinking she was doing this to absolve Andre of his guilt over the curse and ensure their happy future. Those were fortunate by-products, for certain; but her true motivation had never changed. To show those hagfish in Atlantica, including their pompous king, that she was better than them. That even though they treated her like the silt stuck to their fins, she would wield more power than they could ever dream in their fish-brained lives.

She spun toward Andre and clutched her nautilus. His death would be painless. He wouldn't even know she'd done it. Just drift off and never wake up. She stepped toward him, and her throat locked.

Choosing magic over love would have grave consequences. Yet this power was her destiny. The reason she'd been drawn to this land, to the Baros family.

She took a step closer to Andre.

And Weir's voice echoed in her mind.

Think before you act. Fight for a happy ending.

The core of the curse spun faster and faster, gaining energy. If she did become the vessel for it, she would have to change back into her true form. No way could a human body contain that kind of power. Tears sprang to her eyes, clouding her vision, her heart hammering in her ears. Vanessa had become her identity. Her ideal version of herself. The woman everyone wanted to be or wanted to be with. The thought of giving up this body, her time on earth, nearly brought her to her knees.

That's when she realized the truth of Medusa's statement. In order to transfer the curse, she needed to give up what she loved most. As the core spun and flashed, nearing its zenith, she realized what she loved more than anything else. What she needed to give up—at least, for now.

Vanessa.

Before she could second-guess her decision, she took hold of her conduit and lifted it to her mouth, speaking the words that would begin the permanent transformation.

Immediately, the bones of her legs weakened as they worked to dissolve into cartilage. Flesh and muscle sliced open to form gills on either side of her neck. The vines of light extending from the curse's core broke and slithered inside her. Her hunger insatiable, she grasped the sphere with both hands and, as cries of protest rang in her ears, slammed it into her chest.

A high-pitched keen escaped her throat as the curse devoured her from the inside like a living being too large for its host. Terrible pressure spiked through her core. Pain like she'd never known possible. It would rip her apart. Fear sparked in her veins and she reeled on her feet.

With her remaining strength, she hurtled herself toward the pool and dove deep. She inhaled sharply, her burdened and battered body welcoming the precious salt water flooding her cells, healing her wounds, and saturating her body with renewed strength. Her legs unraveled into beautiful tentacles, and as she breathed deep, immense power sizzled through her blood—the curse's magic hers and hers alone, at last.

Ursula once more, lips stretched in a full smile, she pushed up and flew onto the edge of the pool. With little more than a thought, she curled her finger, and the staff flew toward her. She reached out, ready to grasp it, fingers tingling with anticipation, but Medusa yanked it back.

"That's mine, crone!" Ursula lashed out with a rope of magic and lassoed the top of the staff in midair.

Medusa's inky tendrils wrapped around it from the other end. Ursula added another rope, strengthening her pull. But the creature doubled her efforts as well.

Tiring of their tug-of-war, Ursula conjured a bolt of power and cast it at Medusa's hand. Instead of simply cutting the ties of the monster's hold on the staff, Ursula's newly enhanced magic incinerated the serpent's flesh. The creature screamed as her fingers, then her hand, flaked away into ash. The spell traveled down her black magic tendrils, lighting the staff on fire.

"No!" Ursula yanked the staff toward her even as she sank back into the water. But it dissolved into ash in midair, destroying the Rhabdos and all its glorious power.

Fury pulsed through Ursula's fingers, and she flung out

her arm, green bolts of lightning rushing from her fingertips. Fire splintered across Medusa's flesh. Ursula tilted her head and watched, fascinated as the snake-woman's arms and tail convulsed. Black blood poured out of the serpent's ears, eyes, and mouth. But Ursula didn't stop.

Heat and light forked from her hands into Medusa's seizing body. The power of the curse beyond her wildest imaginings, a hurricane swirled through her veins, filling her with elation as she attacked.

Bolts of energy splintered Medusa's chest, and the monster of centuries-old legend stiffened, lifeless eyes wide, as she fell silent forever.

Ursula ducked down and inhaled the sea. She could exist outside the water longer than the average fish, but she still needed to breathe from the ocean. She reemerged, water sluicing down the strands of her pearl-white hair, relieved but unsurprised to see Andre stirring. "The curse is no longer attached to others. I can feel it swirling inside me," she said, unable to keep a note of pride out of her voice.

Andre stilled but didn't turn around when he whispered, "You even sound different."

She didn't know how to respond. She *was* different. Her human thoughts and emotions were quickly fading.

CHAPTER 35

The tides tugged at her, summoning her back to the currents of her former life. She sank lower in the water, half submerged, her arms resting on the rock ledge.

"Thank you." Andre had turned toward her voice now, his head bowed.

She still felt the draw of him, a seed of light like a fledgling star in her heart, reminding her of the love they'd shared. But from where she sat, he seemed small. Insignificant in her world. Just an ordinary, beautiful man.

"Andre," she called in a perfect imitation of Vanessa's higher voice. "I must go."

His shoulders stiffened. But he rose, then walked toward her, not meeting her eyes. She ducked down for a quick breath, and then patted the ledge. "Please come and sit."

He lowered on one knee and faced her, his expression like stone.

"Hold on for one moment," she said, then leaned around him and, with the whip of a single tentacle and a slice of magic, took off Medusa's head.

"There, that's better. Can't have her coming back to life, now can we?" She smirked, but he still wouldn't look at her face.

She was larger and more muscular as a Cecaelia,

nearly double in size. The bones of her face were more prominent, her eyes a glowing purple instead of Vanessa's jeweled lavender. But his rejection hit harder than she would've expected. "Andre. Do I look that different?"

He finally turned and let his eyes sweep over her face, her hair, even her tentacles. When he met her gaze, his expression softened. "No, just more . . . fierce."

Ursula smiled. The response was so *Andre*.

The spark in her heart gave a little pinch. She had loved this human. And he had loved her. But she had a king to overthrow, worlds to rule, lives to puppeteer. Anticipation and her newly found dark power coursed in her veins, begging for release. With one final look at him, she smiled.

"Goodbye, Andre Baros."

Then she swam down and away, toward a tunnel to the sea.

But the reverberation of something large entering the water made her stop and whirl around.

Andre swam toward her in his clothes. Bubbles streamed from his lips as he mouthed the word *wait*.

She swam back and tugged him to the surface, their heads even at the waterline.

He sucked in a breath, then cupped the side of her face and kissed her mouth, soft and slow. She closed her eyes as the world stopped spinning around them with the slide of their wet lips. The Hollow Sea, the dead body of an ancient monster, the cursed power vibrating inside her, all were insignificant in the heat and light pulsing between them.

She reached out and brushed his tears away, wondering why it had seemed so important, just a few short hours ago, that he cry over her. She'd never wanted to fall in love. And yet having someone's full devotion and feeling desired was an addictive rush.

A feeling she didn't necessarily need to give up.

With this newfound power, she could transform him right now into the handsomest Cecaelia Atlantica had ever seen. Her face warmed as she visualized the color of his tentacles. Perhaps a marine blue banded with green stripes to match his eyes. He could be her plaything. Her trophy from her time spent on land. A prize to keep on her arm and flaunt in those superficial mermaids' faces. Imagining their jealousy made her shiver with anticipation.

"Come with me, Andre," she commanded. "I can transform you to be my perfect mate. Our future would be unlimited. The entire world ours to discover. We can become human whenever we like and explore every continent, then return to our kingdom under the sea."

And rule, she thought with a sidelong grin.

Stark longing crossed his face as he searched her eyes. Then his brow wrinkled. "What about Sara and Yia-Yia?"

"I'll take care of them. Sara could come with us. And Yia-Yia." She grimaced, knowing the improbability of the old woman surviving such a transition. "Or they could both stay on land. But I would provide for their needs. They would want for nothing."

He stared past her. "Except for me. If I left, it would break both their hearts." His gaze returned to hers, selfish desire and duty warring in his eyes.

Aíma tou aímatós mou.

Hadn't he said he loved Sara and Yia-Yia more than anything? She was asking him to choose passion and adventure over family.

"Yes," he said, shocking her. "If you'll provide for my family, and we can visit them, I'll go with you."

His smile was like a tsunami washing memories through her brain. How he'd carried her in his strong arms when she could've walked. Overcoming his fears as they'd faced Omis Island side by side. His noble spirit as he tried everything to rectify the curse he'd unleashed. Their lips and hands and bodies sparking fire every time they touched.

But even as he longed to go with her, she felt fear in his pulse, the stiffness of his limbs. Annoyed at his weakness, she realized he would be a liability, not an asset. He would ultimately weaken her, even without meaning to. A true queen needed to be feared, not loved.

She no longer needed this attractive young man's affection. But there were those who did. If for no other reason than that, she would let him go. Allow him to return to Yia-Yia and Sara and create a life for himself.

She tucked all their memories away in a dark corner of her heart so no one would ever know she'd once carried such a vulnerability for a human man. Then, one hand to his cheek, the other on her conduit, she wiped the last two minutes from his memory—revoking her invitation. Rewriting their goodbye.

Without so much as a blink of confusion, he asked, "Will I ever see you again?"

"The ocean is vast. Our paths will likely never cross," she replied, allowing the coldness in her blood to enter her voice.

Treading water, he lifted his father's medal over his head and handed it to her. "Part of me will always love you."

"And I you," she whispered, realizing that it was true. "But we were never meant to be."

For one last precious second, she memorized the strong

lines of his face and slipped the cord holding his medal over her head, tucking it underneath the golden shell her father had given her. "Thank you, Andre. For everything."

Then, with a splash of tentacles, she dove down deep. Each stroke of her powerful body reunited her with the sea. She was weightless as she flew out of the tunnel and into the magnificent ocean, her larger destiny overtaking her heart and mind. Manta rays, a sea turtle, and a school of yellowfins glided in her wake as fresh power and resolve flowed in her veins like the tides of the moon. The memory of the boy with the fathomless eyes was already fading away.

EPILOGUE

15 YEARS LATER

THE GIRL WITH a fall of seal-black hair and eyes green as the forest at dawn clutched the hand of her young cousin as they tiptoed across the rotting boards of the old dock.

"Why do you think Uncle Andre tells us never to come down here?" the little blond boy asked after taking his thumb out of his mouth for a moment before promptly returning it to its rightful place.

Older and far wiser by several years, the seven-year-old

girl thought for a moment before she replied, "Papa says dark memories and wicked intentions lurk here."

With a soft pop, the boy took his thumb out again. "Mama says if you face your fears, they can't scare you."

Aqua water like glass gave way to deeper layers of turquoise as the pair passed the cove and stopped at the end of the dock to stare at the sea.

"Aunt Sara is very brave," the girl whispered, a blast of wind catching in the banner of her dark hair. It was hard to believe her wild and wonderful Aunt Sara had been deathly ill as a child. Now, Aunt Sara was a picture of health and not only helped Papa run the Wagon of Wonders, but also served as the newly elected governor for all the villages along the coast.

The boy leaned over and stared into the water, clutching Nessa's hand tight. "What are we looking for?"

"The sea witch lives down there," the girl whispered as if the name itself might summon the creature.

The boy shuddered but didn't look away. "Is she good or evil?"

"Father says perhaps a little of both. She saved our family and the entire hamlet from a horrid curse, but she's terribly powerful. Sometimes he sees her here by the light of the waxing moon."

EPILOGUE

"Why does she come here?"

"Aunt Sara says it's because she's watching out for us, making sure fear never takes hold of this town again."

The boy nodded, eyes growing heavy, ready for his bed.

Nessa continued. "Papa says one should never call on the powers of a witch unless they are prepared to pay the price."

"That's nice," the boy murmured and tugged on his cousin's hand. "Come on, Nessa. It's getting dark."

The boy pivoted away from the water and wandered back up the dock. But Nessa stayed, staring out into the sea until a glint caught her eye. She leaned over the edge of the boards, and that's when she saw it just beneath the surface: a pair of glittering amethyst eyes staring back at her from the depths.

Their gazes locked, and Nessa's heart froze in her chest. A smile full of teeth flashed just before the creature dove back under in a swirl of black and purple.

Nessa watched until the dark tentacles disappeared, recalling the bedtime story her papa would tell her about a magnificent sea creature who had lived on land for a fortnight and changed the lives of everyone who knew her forever. Her papa didn't have to explain that the enchantress of whom he spoke, his eyes faraway and glowing, and the sea witch were one and the same.

In that magical moment between twilight and starshine, the sea still rippling in wide circles, Nessa saw a glint of gold floating at the surface. With a glance over her shoulder, she saw her cousin making his way toward Baros Cottage. She lowered to her knees and reached out, knowing that if the sea witch had set a trap, she could disappear without a trace. Pulse clamoring, she reached down, scooped up the shiny object before it could sink, and yanked her arm back.

Her breath caught. Could it be the Saint Raphael medal from the story? The one the hero had given to the sea creature before she disappeared from his life? She'd always suspected the tale held an element of truth for her father in the way he told it. But the last line of the story haunted her. Probably because she didn't quite understand it.

Nessa stared down at the shiny metal in her palm, the shadows that sometimes haunted her father's gaze finally making sense as she leaned over the water and whispered the ending of the fairy tale into the night. "Happily ever after means giving someone the power to break your heart."

POSTSCRIPT

REPORTS OF THE creature swirled around Agios Limani and the surrounding islands for decades after the curse was broken. Some said she was a beautiful sorceress with hair made of pearls and curves of starlight, though you dared not gaze directly at her face lest you be drawn into the depths, enslaved for eternity.

While others claimed that to glimpse the turn of a

midnight tentacle brought blessings upon your house, and if you were fortunate, a single wish.

What they never shared, those who took the sea witch up on her offer . . . was the price.